Praise for Jodi Thomas's novels . . .

TWILIGHT IN TEXAS

"Tender and emotional . . . [A] sweet tale."
—*Old Book Barn Gazette*

TO WED IN TEXAS

"Entertaining."
—*Publishers Weekly*

"Tender, sweet, funny and touching."
—*The Romance Reader*

TO KISS A TEXAN

"Compelling . . . fans will appreciate Thomas's subtle humor and her deft handling of sensitive topics."
—*Booklist*

"[A] poignant, exciting, emotional story . . . Jodi Thomas understands the workings of a woman's heart and a man's mind."
—*Romantic Times*

continued on next page . . .

THE TEXAN'S TOUCH

"Delightful and memorable characters and a roller-coaster pace . . . Another wonderful read from a true shining star."
—*Romantic Times*

TWO TEXAS HEARTS

"Jodi Thomas is at her remarkable best in *Two Texas Hearts*."
—Debbie Macomber

TEXAS LOVE SONG

"A warm and touching read full of intrigue and suspense that will keep the reader on the edge of her seat."
—*Rendezvous*

FOREVER IN TEXAS

"A great western romance filled with suspense and plenty of action."
—*Affaire de Coeur*

TO TAME A TEXAN'S HEART

*Winner of the Romance Writers of America
Best Historical Series Romance Award*

"Earthy, vibrant, funny, and poignant . . . a wonderful, colorful love story."
—*Romantic Times*

THE TEXAN AND THE LADY

"Jodi Thomas shows us hard-living men with grit and guts, and the determined young women who soften their hearts."
—Pamela Morsi, bestselling author of
Something Shady and *Wild Oats*

PRAIRIE SONG

"Thoroughly entertaining romance." —*Gothic Journal*

THE TENDER TEXAN

*Winner of the Romance Writers of America
Best Historical Series Romance Award*

"[A] marvelous, sensitive, emotional romance . . . spellbinding."
—*Romantic Times*

THE TEXAN'S DREAM

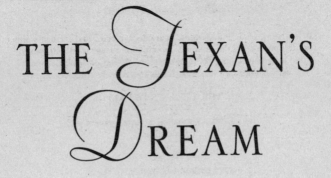

JODI THOMAS

JOVE BOOKS, NEW YORK

THE TEXAN'S DREAM

A Jove Book / published by arrangement with
the author

PRINTING HISTORY
Jove edition / November 2001

All rights reserved.
Copyright © 2001 by Jodi Koumalats.
Cover photo by Wendi Schneider.
Cover design by George Long.
This book, or parts thereof, may not be reproduced in any form
without permission.
For information address: The Berkley Publishing Group,
a division of Penguin Putnam Inc.,
375 Hudson Street, New York, New York 10014.

Visit our website at
www.penguinputnam.com

ISBN: 0-515-13176-8

A JOVE BOOK®
Jove Books are published by The Berkley Publishing Group,
a division of Penguin Putnam Inc.,
375 Hudson Street, New York, New York 10014.
JOVE and the "J" design
are trademarks belonging to Penguin Putnam Inc.

PRINTED IN THE UNITED STATES OF AMERICA

10 9 8 7 6 5 4 3 2 1

PROLOGUE

Pittsburgh, Pennsylvania
August 11, 1875

CHARLIE O'RILEY GRIPPED HIS DAUGHTER'S ARM with bruising force. His dirt-covered fingers dug deeply into her flesh. "Remember, not a word for one year. If you get in touch with me, you'll be the cause of both our deaths."

Karina Paige O'Riley fought back tears. On the way to the station, she'd seen two houses on fire. A man in the street told them the O'Conner men had been killed and Mrs. O'Conner badly burned. He didn't know the name of the other family, but bodies covered with blankets lay in the street. When Karina asked, no one seemed to know the whereabouts of the O'Conner children.

"Don't do this, Papa," Karina whispered. "There must be another way. Let me stay and fight. I have to know what is happening."

"No!" Charlie insisted, his voice so near panic even

his whisper crystallized in the air. "I'll not have my daughter dying. You're to disappear so deeply into the west not even a McWimberly can find you." He handed her a train ticket and a few bills. "I booked passage all the way to California, but get off at any stop along the line where no one will notice you've left the train. Keep on the move. Never stay too long in one place."

He cupped his hands around his only child's face. "Lose the accent as fast as you can."

"I have to know," Karina cried. "I'll die waiting a year."

O'Riley's face softened. She was all he had left of his dear wife. "All right. In three months, you can send word to Father James. He'll get it to me and, if I'm still alive, I'll let you know. But I'll not come for you for a year . . . I swear."

"But . . ."

He glanced behind him, then turned back to his daughter. "Now, don't go arguing with me this time."

"But Papa . . ." Karina decided it wasn't right leaving the man she planned to marry without at least saying good-bye. "What about Devin?"

"He knows," her father answered. "He told me to tell you he'd see you in a year."

"Anything else?"

Charlie grew impatient. "No. He's got more important matters to attend to now, Karina O'Riley, and so do you." Shoving his daughter on the train, Charles O'Riley handed her a small suitcase filled with all she'd had time to pack. "Keep looking over your shoulder and be very careful whom you trust. There's a packet in your case that I want you opening only if something happens to me. Otherwise I expect you to return in a year with the seal still intact."

Karina tried one last time to argue. "But, Papa, I need to stay here and help you if trouble is coming."

"Go!" He sounded angry, his voice carrying above the noise of the train. "Disappear! It may be your only chance at staying alive."

Kansas City, Missouri
October 10, 1875

Karina O'Riley straightened her worn traveling jacket and smoothed the pleats of her faded plaid skirt. "May the saints and angels watch over me double-time this hour," she prayed as she lifted the wooden door knocker. The money her father had given her was gone, and her brilliant idea to hide out in school for six weeks had kept her dangerously long in one town. "I've got to get this job."

All the news she'd heard from home was a small article in the paper about union problems in the Pittsburgh mills. No names were given, only that there had been some violence.

She had no money for food, much less a train ticket back home, and she could feel the McWimberlys coming nearer every day. What if the violence was spreading? One mile closer to her. One step closer to killing her.

She imagined herself lying in a snowy gutter, her face pale and thin with hunger. One of the McWimberly clan stood above her, his gun pointed at her heart. As she looked at him, she knew he wouldn't even waste a bullet to kill her. A fight that had started in the mills of Pittsburgh between two Irish groups would not end until all of one clan were dead.

Karina locked her icy fingers together as she waited for someone to answer her summons. Without this job, she might have to contact her father or starve.

Her father had worked in the steel mills since he came to America at sixteen. He'd moved up to foreman before Karina had been born. Since she was old enough to remember, there had always been meetings at her house. Secret meetings. Closed meetings. None of the men talked about what went on in front of her, but she knew her father was a powerful man. Powerful enough to have enemies.

Karina glanced over her shoulder at strangers passing on the street, then she knocked again. This job would be perfect. If they'd only hire her, she'd be leaving town tomorrow. Surely, no one would find her in Texas.

The placement agent had handed her the address with a shake of his head. "You're the last one I'm sending for this position as bookkeeper for a Texas rancher. Even though jobs are scarce, the few people I've talked into applying haven't been interested past the interview."

He grinned at Karina. "If you don't get this position, you might consider another line of work, Miss O'Riley, or perhaps get married."

Karina shuddered. Another line of work seemed unlikely when she couldn't find a position in the one she'd spent all her money being trained for. And marriage? She'd considered that only a few months ago, but apparently Devin hadn't. The fact that he'd sent word with her father rather than coming to say good-bye himself nagged at the back of her mind.

Wind whirled snow flurries from the street as a carriage passed. Karina huddled closer to the door, wishing she had a real coat and gloves. But when she'd left Pittsburgh, the air was warm and she'd had no time to pack extra clothes.

She prayed what her father called his Irish prayer. "Lord, don't let today be as bad as yesterday, nor tomorrow as gloomy as I fear."

She knew the problem with her employment wasn't her marital status or the location of the position. The trouble lay in the fact that people wanted bookkeepers to be accurate and truthful. Not exactly her strong points. No experience and poor marks in school weren't powerful recommendations. When faced with logging in numbers, she had to concentrate to keep from daydreaming. She'd barely made it through the school. Everything on her employment record was a lie except her name. She'd shortened it to simply Kara O'Riley. No one would probably bother to follow her this far west, and she had to keep something of her family with her. O'Riley was a common name. And Kara sounded very American.

Kara removed her glasses and folded them into a case she always kept in her handbag. Maybe these Texans wouldn't be so picky about honesty and accuracy. In the two weeks since finishing school, she'd knocked on the door of what seemed like every business in Kansas. She was too young, too inexperienced. One man had said he would have hired her if she'd been married, but a single girl wasn't likely to stay long.

But with forty-three cents in her bag, she'd better acquire a position before dinnertime or start getting used to not eating. The last job in the file was about to meet the runt of the litter from Miss Abigail's Business School. Kara could only pray they'd somehow be a match. No matter what the working conditions, she'd remind herself of her father's words and of the forty-three cents.

There. She lifted her chin. She could be *very* accurate when necessity demanded. Truthfulness might prove a wee bit more difficult.

ONE

From the second-floor landing Jonathan Catlin watched a slender young woman wrapped in plaid walk into his lawyer's office. She looked as out of place as mesquite among all the layers of mahogany furniture.

He was an expert on being out of place, he thought. Jonathan closed his eyes and leaned into the shadows of the second-floor hallway. He knew, if she noticed him, all she'd see was a man who, from polished shoes to white collar, looked every inch the gentleman.

But it was a facade. A mask as meticulously applied as war paint.

In the past few years he'd roamed the world exploring, trying on cultures as easily as one might clothes. But none fit. He no more belonged in New York, or London, or Africa than he did at home among his kin. But with his grandmother's death, his travels were at an end. At least for a while.

He was about to be anchored to thousands of acres of land in Texas. All he wanted to do was help a friend in trouble at Fort Elliot, get the ranch in running order, sell it, and then continue his drifting.

But tomorrow morning, he not only had to return to the ranch, now, his lawyer, Clark, was insisting he take someone with him to help straighten out the books. His grandmother's will had given Jonathan twelve months to make the Catlin Ranch a success, or all the land would go to the state of Texas. Except, she'd insisted, for small portions allotted to longtime employees.

Jonathan didn't care about the land. But, if he wanted to travel, he'd have to make the ranch run, at least until he could inherit and sell the place.

He couldn't help but wonder how resolute this woman in plaid would be if she knew the danger she was about to step into. Besides living on a ranch bordering the frontier with the Indian Wars in full fury, she would be walking into a long-running feud that left no wounded, only casualties.

Jonathan slipped through the side door of Clark's office as the applicant reached the top of the stairs and greeted Clark. The slight hint of an Irish accent flavored her soft voice.

Jonathan listened through a connecting door as Clark offered her a seat in the other office. The lawyer explained how his client needed a bookkeeper for only a year and was having trouble finding someone willing to travel so far for a temporary position. Clark didn't add that he'd searched a week for a man to fill the job. Nothing. Considering a woman was a compromise Jonathan had reluctantly agreed to.

He had to leave at dawn, with or without a bookkeeper. If this woman didn't fit the requirements, he

would look in Dallas and trust his luck to hire someone
not already working for Horris Wells. Wells was a
greedy man who'd hated his neighbors for years. Now,
with the passing of Catlin land from one generation to
another, he saw his chance to gain.

"Your papers are in order."

Clark's voice drifted through the open doorway between the offices, drawing Jonathan away from thoughts
of the ranch.

"You understand the job is only for one year. At the
end of that time the books should be in order and hope-
fully in the black."

"Aye, I mean, yes, I understand."

"It's Miss Kara O'Riley, correct?" Clark bellowed as
he waddled around a massive oak desk. "You're not
married."

"Yes, it is Miss O'Riley," the woman answered directly as she pulled glasses from a small bag. "At least
for a year. I'm to be married then to Devin O'Toole. As
soon as I return from Texas, if I get the job, of course."

Jonathan twisted so that he could study her face
through the slight opening. The uneasy feeling that she
was lying washed over him. He would've guessed her
unclaimed. She had that "never been kissed" look about
her. If she lied about a fiancé, he wouldn't blame her.
In this world a woman was safer if all thought a man,
even an absent one, was in her life.

He looked closer.

Her glasses were too large for her tiny nose and dis-
torted her face slightly. Even in a town like Kansas City,
where men outnumbered women by double, she'd not
be among the first to be asked to dance. Yet she seemed

so sure of this Devin O'Toole. Maybe the Irishman did exist.

"You also understand, Miss O'Riley, that you must be able to leave tomorrow." Clark glanced toward the open side door and caught Jonathan's stare. The attorney waited for permission to continue.

When Jonathan made no move, Clark turned back to Kara O'Riley.

She nodded.

Clark played with his watch chain when he felt uncomfortable; Jonathan watched the lawyer imprison his fingers in the gold braid. From his hiding place, he couldn't help but wonder if Clark worried about the woman being able to handle the job, or if Clark feared she was stepping into a lion's cage, tempted by the job as bait.

"You're so young," the lawyer mumbled. "Are you sure your father and husband-to-be will allow you to travel so far?"

"They've both more important matters to attend to." The woman turned her face to the side and removed her glasses.

Jonathan caught the sadness in her eyes and guessed she was just repeating words she'd heard. She was not a woman treasured by anyone. It wouldn't have been so bad if she hadn't known . . . but she did.

She glanced at the side door but showed no sign of noticing him poorly hidden in the shadows.

In the few seconds her reply took, Jonathan saw the determination of someone preparing for battle, not simply an interview. Her eyes drew him even from six feet away. She had warrior eyes, he decided, doing what she had to do. Fire smoldered in the green depths, hinting she might fight even when she knew the cause was lost.

Clark changed the subject as he took his place behind the desk. "I understand. You come highly recommended. The agency said we must take you. If it's travel you want, we have the job for you."

Kara O'Riley nodded. "Aye, I am ready to leave today. My lease is up on my room, and I saw no need to renew until we talked. As we speak, my landlady is probably placing my bag on the porch."

Clark smiled, apparently surprised by such eagerness. "You understand that the position is in Texas, and we are prepared to pay your traveling expenses?"

Jonathan watched the woman nod. Clark drew an envelope from his desk as he ran through a list of things she might need.

Jonathan moved away from the doorway while she listened to the job's description. This one just might make it through the interview, he thought.

Then she'd be his problem.

Kara hurried into the hallway and closed the door to Mr. Clark's office behind her. She leaned against the wall and tried to slow her breathing as she whispered thanks to the saints and guardian angels. She had the job! By dawn tomorrow, she'd be safely out of Kansas City.

Clutching the envelope tighter, she laughed softly. Fifty dollars! Proof they wanted her. Clark said she could take the money and buy whatever she thought she might need for the year in Texas. He emphasized the money was part of her traveling expenses, not her salary.

Before dawn tomorrow she would buy luggage, clothes

and a hundred other things. She held the money against her chest and twirled. In all her life, she'd never been able to buy more than a few things brand-new. Now everything would be store-bought. Fifty dollars. A fortune.

A shadow moved at the end of the hallway. Kara froze. The thought crossed her mind that someone had lain in wait to steal the envelope.

She quickly shoved the money into a pocket hidden in the lining of her jacket. Reminding herself she was an O'Riley, she prepared to fight. No one would take anything from her easily.

The shadow formed into a tall man wearing a great coat that made him look more like he floated than walked toward her.

"You got the position," he grumbled.

Kara blinked at him, hoping to lose some of her fear. As he came into focus, he looked even more menacing. He was tall and powerful, with movements as silent as a cougar hunting its prey.

"I'm s-sorry," she stammered. "I don't see well from a distance. I didn't notice you standing there."

"A blind bookkeeper?"

He didn't smile and, now that she could see his face clearly, she guessed he'd never be the kind of man who'd be a thief. More likely a killer. His hair was dark and too long to be stylish. His blue-gray stare went right through her. His face could've been carved from granite. If there had been an ounce of softness, he would have been handsome. But no ounce was there.

A vision of herself lying in this hall, her neck snapped

by this murderer, her eyes wide open in death, flashed across Kara's mind.

"I'm not blind." She pushed the image away. If he meant to kill her, he'd hardly stop to talk. "Only a little nearsighted."

"That could prove deadly in Texas." He moved suddenly, silently, to her side. "How will you see a rattler before he strikes? When they bite, you've only time to write your will before the poison moves through your body and into your heart. They say you paralyze an inch at a time until you can't even close your eyes but are forced to watch the faces of those watching you die."

His eyebrows drew together as he added, "Or will you see a raging buffalo or longhorn charging you so fast his hooves sound like thunder? The horns will lift you off the ground before you have time to scream."

Kara held her head high. She wouldn't allow this man to intimidate her. She wouldn't. From the cut of his fine coat, she'd guess he'd never had to work all day for wages that wouldn't buy enough to satisfy hunger. He'd never been all alone with no one to trust.

The stranger moved directly in front of her. "How does a nearsighted person tell direction when the plains are so flat there are no landmarks? In winter, the snow blinds a man so easily that he can take a wrong step between the house and the barn and freeze to death before finding his way back. If sighted folks have problems, you wouldn't have a chance."

"I am not afraid," Kara lied. She was no pampered lady. She'd grown up on the hard, working-class streets of Pittsburgh.

The man laughed seemingly more at himself than at

her. "Clark's a fool to think you'll survive the trip out. He should've warned you. You're not prepared."

Kara was starting to wish the man *were* a thief. He would be far less frightening. "Mr. Clark gave me money to buy a coat and boots. By dawn, I'll be prepared. He didn't say it would be easy."

"Did he explain you'll have to shake the coat out each morning before you put it on so that the scorpions that nested there during the night won't bite you? And your boots will always have to be checked for tarantulas at dawn. They can be far deadlier than snakes."

Kara pictured herself lying dead as wagons passed along a rutted road a few feet away. In her vision, a snake had bitten through perfectly good stockings to her leg. A family of scorpions crawled across her hand. And a tarantula hung from her throat like a hairy brooch. With her last heartbeat, she could hear the thunder of buffalo heading toward her.

"Maybe I should reconsider." She tried to hold her imagination at bay. It couldn't be as bad as this stranger painted.

The man's low voice chilled the air.

"Some say the creatures are the least of a newcomer's worries. They say the wind will drive you mad. Out of loneliness, you'll hear voices in the breeze and screams in the storms."

Kara backed toward the door of Mr. Clark's office. "I have to . . . I have to . . ."

The dark stranger stepped away. "I just wanted to warn you." He almost sounded apologetic, making his stories all the more real. "Texas is no place for cowards."

Kara hurried into Clark's study, the envelope in her hand.

Clark was gone. Only one of the secretaries stood beside the desk.

"I must see Mr. Clark." Kara tried not to sound hysterical. Starving to death suddenly sounded like the lesser of two evils.

"He's already gone," the secretary answered. "I told him you were talking with Mr. Catlin in the hallway. He took a deep breath and left down the back stairs, saying something about beating the snow home."

"Mr. Catlin?" Kara remembered Clark mentioning that name.

The secretary smiled. "Yes, your new employer. He's the man you'll be working for. I believe the orders on the envelope say you're to meet him at the Mayflower Arms Hotel at dawn."

Kara stared in disbelief. The shadowy figure in the hallway with those dark eyes and horrible stories was her employer!

The woman must have seen her fear. "Oh, don't worry about him. I'm sure most of the things folks say about Jonathan Catlin aren't true."

"What things?"

The woman hesitated. Her need to gossip quickly won out over common sense. "They say he was raised with savages and, despite his dress and polished manners, a wild animal lurks just beneath the surface."

"You can't mean that!" Kara didn't want to believe her one chance to get out of town was with a madman.

"I don't know. I've been told that he's one of the richest men from Kansas City to Galveston, yet women at social functions avoid him as if he were a diseased beggar." She nodded slowly as if swearing her words were true. "He moves silently, like he's been trained to hunt. And his eyes. There's no kindness in his eyes." The secretary leaned closer. "They're the eyes of a killer."

The secretary wasn't helping. "I have to see Mr. Clark," Kara mumbled, remembering she'd thought almost the same thing about the man.

"I'm afraid it will have to wait until tomorrow." The secretary moved to the door. "But you're welcome to leave him a note." She smiled sadly back at Kara. "I'm sure Mr. Catlin is still downstairs if you have any questions."

Unable to move, Kara watched the woman hurry away. The last person she ever in her life wanted to talk to was Jonathan Catlin. He'd planted enough horror stories in her imagination to provide months of sleepless nights. She might have thought the secretary only gossiping if she hadn't met him . . . hadn't heard his voice . . . hadn't seen his haunting eyes.

Kara placed the envelope filled with money on Clark's desk and reached for a pen. She'd leave the money and a note explaining how she'd changed her mind.

She'd leave here just as she came—with no job.

Kara's fingers gripped the envelope. "And no money," she whispered. "And no warm coat. And no food tonight. And no place to stay."

Lifting the pack of bills, she reconsidered. Maybe she could take a few dollars just to see her through the night.

No. If she took money and resigned, that would be stealing. But if she took all the money she could say she changed her mind later, after she'd had a meal and paid for a night's lodging.

She stuck the envelope back in her pocket thinking this way would be far more honest. She'd return tomorrow, tell Mr. Clark her decision and offer to work off the missing balance in his office. Who knows, maybe he'd even keep her on here.

She took two steps toward the door before she remembered the secretary saying Jonathan Catlin was still downstairs. Kara never wanted to run into him again.

With only a moment's hesitation, she moved to the windows. She'd exited through second-floor windows more than once these past weeks when the rent was due. It should be no problem now.

Only this second-floor window seemed higher than any she'd tried before. She lowered herself over the sill until she hung by her fingers, said a quick prayer to the saints and guardian angels, then dropped.

Any vision of being crippled when she hit the ground vanished a moment later when someone walking below broke her fall.

TWO

Jonathan looked up and saw plaid a moment before pain shattered his world. A wool-wrapped sledge-hammer plowed into the side of his face. He tumbled to the ground, the airborne weight now resting on his chest.

With one hand covering his eye, he shoved at the body on top of him and fought his way out from under yards of material. He rolled, then stopped as the cold, solid earth grounded him.

"I'm sorry!" came an Irish voice. "I didn't see you."

Jonathan opened one eye, the only eye he could, and stared at the bookkeeper. Fighting to control his rage, he brought her features into focus. She lay in the frozen dirt of the narrow backstreet, as close to him as a wife might sleep beside her mate.

Swirling snow drifted across their bodies, trying to brush them away as easily as it did bits of paper and leaves. Jonathan didn't move. He didn't feel the cold or the wind. He just stared at the strange woman beside him and attempted to control his anger enough to breathe.

Kara O'Riley slowly sat up, testing each joint for damage. Her wool cap had tumbled and a long strand of midnight hair wiped across her face.

To his amazement, Jonathan saw anger in her eyes. She seemed to think he'd bothered her terribly by being in her way.

"Madam, I was wrong." Jonathan's blood seeped between the fingers he held over the cut just above his throbbing left eye. "Your nearsightedness won't get you killed, but it will me! What were you doing?" he shouted, blowing a frosty breath into the air. Had he lost all survival skills in the week he'd been surrounded by buildings?

"Oh, it wasn't me sight," she defended herself, her accent thickening as her anger climbed. "I always close me eyes when I drop." She leaned closer, touching him on the arm. "Speaking of eyes, one of yours is looking poorly. I think it has the imprint of me heel against it."

Jonathan shook free of her touch, wondering how many of his brains were scrambled into the dirt. It took him a moment before he reasoned out the impossible and glanced up at the window above.

"I took a shortcut," she said as if her exiting from the window made sense. She retrieved her cap and stuffed the wayward strand beneath it.

He stood without offering her a hand. Any woman who jumped out of windows was perfectly capable of taking care of herself, or else was completely insane. He had no idea which and he wasn't sure he wanted to find out.

But as he smeared blood off his cheek, she was beside him once more, blotting his wound with her handkerchief and pushing his hand away so that she could see the cut.

Jonathan tried to gently shove her aside, but the woman had the persistence of a starving horsefly.

"You really should have that cut seen about, Mr. Catlin." She patted at the blood with her small hankie.

He fought the urge to swat her away. "I'm fine."

She didn't relent. "Oh, no. You never know. You could get an infection that would blind you and make the whole side of your face shrivel up. A wee cut can fester and grow."

Jonathan stared at her with his good eye. He'd been wrong about her. He should have warned the scorpions and snakes. "My lodgings are only a block away. I think there's a doctor who offices nearby. I'll have him take a look at it." He had suffered enough black eyes in his time to feel a doozy of one coming on now.

"I'll guide you." She hooked her arm in his as if she now considered him not only wounded but senile.

Jonathan fought the urge to comment about the outrageousness of her suggestion since she was not wearing her glasses, but decided for once in his life to give in. Since she had no idea where they were going, he led her toward his hotel.

Within a few steps, her limp made him stop. "Are you injured, miss?"

"No," she answered without letting go of his arm. "Your face broke the heel of my shoe."

"Sorry," he caught himself saying before he thought.

With him bleeding and her limping, they moved down the street to the doctor's office in silence. As he remembered, the office was next door to the hotel. The same aging doctor who took his meals in the hotel greeted them wearing a white laboratory coat stained with tobacco drippings.

Jonathan couldn't help but be thankful it was early. He'd seen the doctor take enough liquor at dinner to be able to operate on himself without chloroform, provided he could hold the knife.

The old man wasted no time asking questions; while Jonathan removed his coat, the doctor got out the tools of his trade. He cleaned the small cut on Jonathan's forehead and applied crushed yarrow leaves to stop the bleeding. "You've got the worst black eye I've seen, son. Bar fight?"

Glancing at Kara, who was patting his arm like he was a house cat, Jonathan offered, "No, she gave it to me."

The old man shook his head. A few drops of brown dribbled from the corner of his mouth and fell unhampered to his lab coat. "Is that true, miss?" he mumbled.

"Aye," she answered. "He got in my way."

Jonathan watched her carefully. She was little more than a ragamuffin, but she held her head high. As she shifted, she kept changing height because of her uneven heels. But she was adventurous, he'd give her that. No woman he knew would jump from a window. And she was mothering. She'd pestered him to death trying to keep him from bleeding on the way over.

An idea sloshed across his throbbing brain. A mothering woman might be just the answer for helping out his friend. He glanced up at her hair once more. Black, all right. Perfect. She could be the key he needed. If she didn't drive him mad first, Jonathan thought, she might be of some use during a stop he must make before reaching the ranch.

The doctor left the room to prepare a cloth soaked in leaves and bark. The office grew suddenly confining with neither of them talking to one another nor looking directly at the other.

Jonathan's thoughts were filled with plans. A black-haired woman would walk in and out, past the guards without problems. But was she adventurous enough? If she could jump from a window, she might be.

She broke the silence. "If you are waiting for me to apologize, Mr. Catlin, you'll be growing older before me eyes."

"I wasn't expecting an apology." Jonathan used two fingers to carefully touch the swelling on his face. It felt like warm oatmeal covered with a thin layer of skin.

"Then you'll be firing me, and I won't be waiting for you at dawn outside that big fancy hotel of yours."

Jonathan opened his mouth to answer, "hell yes," but reconsidered. She shifted slightly, and he noticed the dirt and rips in her thin jacket. Even with one eye, he could see no one would wear such a light jacket on a day like this unless it was the only coat she owned. And while he was guessing, he'd wager the shoes with one heel were her only pair.

He looked at her face carefully. Without the glasses she was pretty enough. But the feeling that no one treasured her, no one cared about her, haunted him once more. Maybe that's why she tried so hard with the mothering. She wanted someone, anyone, to care just a little that she was there.

Jonathan frowned. He had no time or desire to get involved. Miss O'Riley would have to take care of herself.

"Did Clark give you money for expenses?"

She lifted her chin and stared out the window. "He did, and I'll be returning it to him, if 'tis fired I am."

"It's fired you're not," he mocked, remembering her telling Clark that her things were probably on her landlady's porch. "But, I'd like you to stop wasting time here and get the supplies you need. Give the doorman at the Mayflower Arms your former address, and I'll have your things picked up and brought to the hotel. Which, by the way, isn't fancy or big. There should be no problem booking you a room for the night, so you'll be sure to be ready at dawn."

She didn't move.

Jonathan lifted his coat as he stood. "It's starting to snow. Take my coat."

"Oh, no." She backed away. "I couldn't."

He held the coat for her. "Nonsense. I've only got to walk a few feet to the hotel entrance. All I want to do for the next few hours is put the poultice the doc is making on my eye and drink my pain away. You can't be hurrying about the streets in a torn jacket."

She turned away from him and allowed him to place the coat over her shoulders. "I've heard herbal tea is good. You might want to drink that with a touch of whiskey blended in."

Jonathan let his hands rest on her shoulders for a moment. It had been a long time since he'd been so near a woman. He slowly breathed in her scent. He wanted no one in his life, but now and again the nearness of a woman stirred his senses with a longing for something he'd never known.

"Thank you." She moved a step away, hugging the coat to her. "I'll be back as soon as I can, Mr. Catlin."

He dropped his hands, feeling foolish for touching the shoulders of his own coat so lightly. "Buy warm clothes for the remainder of winter and have them delivered to the hotel. I'll see you at dinner to check that you haven't forgotten anything. Where we're going, there will be little chance to buy more."

When the doctor returned with a pack for Jonathan's eye, she slipped out the door without a word. Jonathan couldn't help but wonder if he'd ever see his coat, or her, again.

"Lie down for a few hours with this on your eye, and it'll cut the swelling." The old man folded the cotton square into an oilcloth. "Nothing will help the color. It'll be black and blue for days."

Jonathan took the cloth package and paid.

"A bit of free advice," the doctor offered as he opened the door for Jonathan. "Stay away from that Irish lass."

"Thanks." Jonathan turned up the collar of his jacket. "But your advice is a little late."

The old doctor shook his head. "Already terminal. I was afraid of that."

Jonathan rushed into the wind. The icy air felt good on his wounded face. He smiled thinking of what the doctor hinted. Let the doctor think what he liked. Jonathan wasn't in the habit of explaining anything to anyone. It didn't matter anyway. The old man had no way of knowing that no woman would ever mean anything to him. He might not be out of his twenties, but he'd already watched one too many people he loved die. No one would ever again get close enough to matter.

At the hotel, Jonathan made Miss O'Riley's reservations and ordered a bottle of whiskey and hot herbal tea sent to his room. The Mayflower Arms was an old hotel that specialized in pampering guests. All the rooms had sitting areas and fireplaces. By the time Jonathan built up the fire and relaxed into one of the overstuffed wing-backed chairs, the whiskey and tea awaited.

He poured himself whiskey and downed it, leaving the tea untouched. While the liquid warmed his body, he unwrapped the cotton eye cloth the doctor had made. It smelled of elderberry and tobacco.

He smiled, then winced at the pain. Kara O'Riley had done the impossible. She'd surprised him. Blindsided him completely.

Jonathan swore he'd never let it happen again. From now on, he'd watch her every move. A wee little Irish girl would have no chance of getting the better of him again.

THREE

SNOW FELL LIGHT AND COTTONY AS KARA LIMPED down the street. She wrapped Jonathan Catlin's warm coat around her and grinned. The saints were certainly good to her today. First a job, then money, and now a fine wool coat to walk the streets in. She wouldn't have to run from place to place, she could just walk along as warm as can be.

Boots, she thought, boots would be her first purchase. Warren's Boot and Shoe Store closed before the mercantile. From the darkening sky, she guessed there was little time left. Boots had to come first. Mr. Warren had his name printed on heavy brown bags so everyone would know she'd bought something there.

Kansas City was a menagerie of stores strung together by uneven boardwalks. Banks, saloons and hotels lined the main street, but the side streets held the more interesting shops where Kara could find what she needed. There, ladies and prostitutes brushed shoulders as they selected material and hats. Farmers' wives made wide circles around the unwashed. Chuck wagon cooks in the mercantile ogled the women, and cowhands wandering the backstreets looked for pleasures to relieve them of their money.

Kara knew the shops well, though most she'd only peered inside through the windows. On days she didn't have work, she'd still leave the boardinghouse early, so no one would talk. Then she'd walk the streets, waiting for a reasonable time to return.

She'd memorized the names of the store owners. Though she didn't know them, she pretended she did, calling each by name as she passed their businesses. No one knew her, for she was rarely a paying customer. But that didn't matter. As long as she knew them, she didn't feel so alone.

The cobbler, Mr. Abraham Warren, made fine shoes for ladies who arrived in carriages. Once, his assistant had patched Kara's shoes. She'd stood in the store and waited while the young man worked. She watched ladies dressed in finery come in to try on shoes, then complain about how they fit. Mr. Warren waited on them. He smiled when he passed Kara, but he never spoke to her. A cobbler must surely know when someone has to wait for a repair, they owned only one set of shoes.

When Kara entered his shop, Mr. Warren motioned for her to see the assistant. With her limp, there could be no question what was wrong.

But Kara passed right by the assistant and sat in the chair at the front of the store. "I would like to buy a pair of shoes and a pair of boots, Mr. Warren."

The old man's eyebrows disappeared into his bushy gray hair. "Two pair?"

Kara nodded. "If you have what I need on hand. I've no time to have them made."

"You'll be paying for them and taking them with you today, miss?"

"Miss O'Riley." Kara offered her hand. "And I will."

Warren touched her hand lightly. "Very fine, Miss O'Riley. I'm sure we'll be able to fit you properly."

Suddenly boxes appeared around her. Kara straightened with pride. "Now, I'll be buying no fancy shoes. Come dawn, I'm going to Texas and I'll need boots and shoes to last a year."

Warren nodded as he sorted through the boxes. In less time than she thought possible, she walked out of the store wearing new shoes and carrying a bag with boots inside. She buttoned her warm coat and carefully turned the bag so that the shop's name showed. If she were staying in Kansas City, she'd use the bag to carry everything just to let folks know that once she'd been able to buy new shoes from a fine shop where they called her by name.

To her astonishment, she'd already spent six of her dollars. Six whole dollars. Four for the boots and two for the shoes. She always thought new shoes would feel grand, but after a few minutes they felt too narrow, pinched her toes, and the heel slipped when she walked.

Kara laughed. She was rich indeed if she could complain about her new shoes.

At Bayley's Mercantile she began her shopping in the stationery department. She'd need a ledger book, pens, extra paper and a leather writing case to carry everything in. For the first time since she'd graduated from Miss

Abigail's school, Kara would look like a real book-keeper.

The next aisle held store-made skirts and blouses with lace at the collars. Since she saw no place to try on the clothes, Kara guessed at her sizes. Three white blouses, two dark skirts, undergarments, stockings, a shawl, two nightgowns that cost all of eighty-five cents each and a short traveling coat of wool. As she rounded the aisle, she selected a brown raincoat that she thought reasonable, at four dollars, and necessary.

The store grew dark. Kara carried her bundle to the front. In a few minutes, someone would light all the lamps so that late shoppers could continue. She needed a total before picking out a hat, gloves and luggage. What she had selected must cost twenty dollars. At least a few coins had to be set aside to pay a boy to help her carry everything and for the night's lodging, in case Mr. Jonathan Catlin didn't pay for her hotel room. He might not, she reasoned, since her employment didn't officially start until dawn.

Her fortune was dwindling fast. She wanted to add a five-dollar watch to her stash, provided there was enough left over. After all, a bookkeeper should know the time.

As she waited, half-hidden behind her bundle, the clerk talked with a tiny woman wrapped in a huge black shawl that was large enough to hide two small children in its folds. The woman slowly counted out her pennies from a small change purse.

"I'm sorry, ma'am, but I can't let you have any more on account," the clerk whispered as the customer ahead of Kara kept counting.

The woman held out her handful of pennies. "But I have almost enough for the milk and bread."

The clerk looked like she might cry. "I'm sorry, ma'am, but Mr. Bayley said I'm to let you have nothing until you've paid at least a portion of your bill. He's already let you go months more than he normally would, what with your husband dying and all."

"But if I pay any on the account, I won't have money for the milk or bread." The woman sounded logical, but her voice shook slightly. Her white, thin fingers held to her shawl as though the whole world had grown suddenly cold.

The clerk pulled two quarters from her pocket. "I could let you have this. With your pennies, you could buy something from the market tomorrow."

The tiny woman coughed, shrinking into the huge shawl as she did. "My children haven't eaten for two days as it is. I can't put them to bed another night with empty bellies. If you could give me just a little for them. I'm not all that hungry myself."

Kara's gaze met the clerk's over the pile of new store-bought clothes. I'll have no use for a watch, Kara thought. Probably no one in Texas cares what time it is anyway.

"Excuse me." Kara moved around the clothes. "I hate to interrupt, but I just came into a little money, and I have to spend it before dawn. I wonder if you'd allow me to pay for . . ."

"Oh, no, no." The little woman backed away.

"Please." Kara offered her hand. "I'm leaving for Texas where I'm sure I'll have no use for money. You'd be doing me a favor."

Kara laid ten dollars on the counter.

"All of it?" the clerk asked. She stared at the money as though it were a fortune.

"Every dime," Kara answered. "And make sure there's ten pounds of potatoes."

The little woman started to protest as the clerk quickly filled boxes with supplies. Flour, sugar, coffee, bacon, tins of peaches and green beans and a wool blanket on top of each box.

"No argument, please," Kara said. "You'd be doing the same thing for me if I were in your place. This way we're both doing each other a favor. I won't have to worry about the outlaws robbing me on the road."

Tears rolled down the clerk's face as she slid two boxes of supplies across the counter. Salt, soda, tea, milk and two loaves of bread. "I put in a bottle of medicine that will soothe that cough, Mrs. Adams, and the candy for the children comes free with this large an order."

Kara pulled out another ten. She could do without the raincoat and the third blouse, and her luggage could be carpet, not leather. "Put ten dollars against her bill so Mr. Bayley will let her buy here again."

The clerk nodded while the woman stared in disbelief.

"I really appreciate this," Kara said. "You don't know what a worry I was having thinking I'd be carrying all this money."

A boy who had just finished lighting the lamps offered to help Kara and Mrs. Adams cart the boxes. Kara promised to be right back for her clothes and entrusted the clerk with her bag of boots until she returned. With the tiny woman leading the way, they marched down the street while people stared.

The night grew darker with fewer and fewer street lamps. The path turned from board walkways to worn ruts between the buildings. Kara's new shoes made a squeaking sound after she stepped in a puddle, and she had to walk on her tiptoes to keep from drawing attention.

The widow's house was little more than a shack, but Kara noticed it was neat. While the boy built up a fire in the grate, the widow snuggled her two children into the new blankets, and Kara stacked the food along the bare shelves.

"Thank you," Widow Adams whispered. "If you're ever back from Texas, stop by. I promise I'll find a way to repay you. I'll never forget you."

"It's not necessary to repay anything." Kara smiled, feeling warmer inside than any new coat could ever make her. "It's enough to know that I have a friend if I return. There's something terribly lonely about leaving a place with no one to notice you're gone. I think it would be like walking in the sand and not leaving a footprint."

"You now have a friend," the widow promised. "I'm Mary Ann Adams and I'll give you my address. You can write me when you're settled. Just use this address with an 'in the back' note on the envelope. The postman will bring it around."

Kara felt herself about to cry as she accepted the scrap of paper. "You've already paid me back." She thought of how she'd write when she got to Texas. Everyone there would know that she had a friend and wasn't all alone.

"I promise I'll write and if I send a letter along to my father, will you post it from here?"

"Of course." Mary Ann looked like she might question the strange request, but didn't.

Kara added, "I don't want anyone back home to know where I am, unless, of course, my fiancé, Devin O'Toole, shows up." She wondered what would be the odds on that. A man who couldn't make it to the train station probably wasn't going to come this far for her.

Mary Ann nodded. "Any favor I can do, I'll do gladly."

A few moments later, they hugged and Kara walked out with the boy from the mercantile. While she tried to figure out how she was going to make her remaining money stretch to buy what she needed, the boy whispered as he walked beside her, "That was mighty nice, what you did back there, miss, buying all that food and saying you'd write."

"Thanks," she answered, only half-listening.

"But, how do you figure that little woman is going to cook all that food, being I used the last of her coal to stir up the fire?"

Kara forced herself to keep walking as his words sank in. She could do without new undergarments. After all, no one saw them. They'd probably be no more comfortable than her noisy new shoes. If they squeaked any louder, she'd have to take up whistling to block the sound.

She stopped walking. "Can you buy coal this late?"

"Yes," the boy answered. "But two buckets will cost you a quarter." When she hesitated, he added, "I'll deliver it free every week for a few months if you'll trust me with the money ahead of time."

"We'll both deliver a few loads. Then with your weekly deliveries they'll have enough to last the winter." The ledger book would fit in her suitcase now that she'd decided to leave out the raincoat and the needless new undergarments. And the book didn't need a leather pouch just so she could look professional. Who would be looking at her anyway? Extra paper was a waste. It would probably only ruin on the trip.

An hour later, her new shoes hurt so much she no longer cared that they made noise. Kara and the boy found a place to buy coal and hauled it for blocks in tin buckets. Her plaid skirt was more gray than plaid, and the fine wool coat Jonathan Catlin had loaned her looked like it had been dyed to match.

The widow thanked them several times and wanted them to join her for supper, but Kara had to get back to the mercantile. She must buy what she could and return to the hotel. Jonathan Catlin had asked her to join him for dinner. It was already long past time. Surely he'd understand that she'd been shopping.

As they rounded the alley to the street, a huge woman leaned out her first-story window. "That was mighty nice of you folks to buy the widow all that food and coal, but who's going to haul it out of here when I kick her out? She ain't paid a month's rent since her husband died. He was a good man. But all men are the same. Once they're dead, they're worthless. She can't stay any longer."

"But you can't do that." Kara stormed toward the landlady. Kara had seen her type before in almost every place her family had lived. They were always sweet and promising all kinds of things when you first rent, but when you fall a few weeks late they turn sour.

"Look, deary. I don't want to, but I got people waiting who'll pay good money. I ain't no charity ward. She'll find somewhere else."

"How much does she owe?" Kara figured she could do with one new blouse, after all she'd have a new jacket to wear over it most of the time. And who needs a shawl when one has a jacket? The shawl would have to go.

"Three dollars a month." The woman grinned, showing bits of her dinner between her teeth. "She's five months behind."

Kara counted out twenty dollars and used all her change to make one more. "Well now she's two months ahead."

The fat woman stuffed the bills in her bustline. "Fair enough. I don't mean to be hard, you understand. It's just business."

"I understand." Kara walked away with two dollars left in her envelope. Two dollars left of the fortune she'd had only a few hours ago.

I can buy a nightgown and the ledger, she thought. I didn't really need all the other things.

The boy walked beside her. "You wish you hadn't given all your money away, miss?"

"No." Kara laughed. "I only wish I had a wee bit more."

When they reached the mercantile, the lights were out. Kara stared into the window at the shadow of her pile of clothes.

"I'm sorry, miss," the boy said. "We'll be open to-morrow at nine."

"I'm leaving at dawn." She added, "I couldn't have bought much anyway." She handed the boy one of her last two dollars.

"Oh, no, miss," he protested. "My tip's only a dime, no more."

"You earned it tonight, but I need you to do some-thing for me tomorrow."

"Name it." The boy stuffed the bill into his pocket.

"I left a pair of boots in the store. You can't miss them, they're in a fine Warren paper bag. Could you take them back to Mr. Warren, get the money, then take it to the widow?"

"I could, but won't you be needing the boots or the cash?"

"No. I'll be miles away by the time the store opens, and I'll have no use for money where I'm going. I'm off for the wilds of Texas. No doubt the buffalo and scorpions will kill me just as quickly in old clothes and noisy shoes."

She turned and squeaked away, thinking about how, without boots, she'd be an easy target for the rattlers as well. That is, if Jonathan Catlin didn't kill her first for buying nothing with his money and ruining his fine wool coat.

This fine day had become exhausting. And she had a feeling the worst was yet to come. Dinner with Mr. Cat-lin.

FOUR

A LOG TUMBLED INTO THE DYING FIRE, SHAKING Jonathan from his nightmare. The same nightmare he'd had since he was five. He was running. Running with terror so thick in his throat no breath could pass. Screams filled the air behind him. Savage yells, death cries. He fought his way over the newly plowed earth, afraid to look back.

The smell of burning flesh lingered as he pulled himself from the past. Jonathan downed the last of his glass of whiskey and stretched his legs toward the fire, trying to forget his dream. A dream that waited just beyond consciousness, always coming to life at night, shadowing his days.

Most people wanted to remember what they dreamed and used those memories for amusing parlor conversation. Jonathan only wanted to forget. But even when he managed to push this one aside, another waited to take its place.

He'd been five the first time his world shattered, fourteen the second time. But never again. No person, no place, no possession would ever matter to him again. They couldn't. He'd never survive a third time.

He pulled an old watch from his vest pocket. Eight forty-five. Kara O'Riley should've been back from the shops an hour or more ago. Most of them closed at dark or soon after.

Swinging from his chair with practiced ease, Jonathan froze before he took a step. The pain along his cheek returned. The mirror above the mantel reflected the source of his discomfort. He was relieved to see that most of the swelling had gone down, and he could open his left eye slightly. The skin around the cut and along his cheekbone flared in varying shades of black and purple, but it would heal.

He ran his fingers through his hair as he moved across the room and into the hallway. There was no time to wait. The dining room closed in a few minutes, and he hadn't eaten all day. He'd be willing to bet the bookkeeper hadn't either.

Jonathan pounded on her door. "Miss O'Riley!" he shouted as if there were no other guests on the floor. He'd feed her, then give her the details of her employment. She had a right to know just what she was getting into, or at least as close as he could explain. How did one explain the Catlin Ranch?

The door opened an inch. "Yes?"

He couldn't see her clearly. "I believe we're having dinner together."

"I'm not hungry," she answered. "But thank you for the invitation. I'll see you at dawn, Mr. Catlin."

He pushed the door open wider. Cold air rushed from

her room into the hallway "Nonsense . . ." Any words he'd been about to say vanished when he saw her. She was almost covered in dirt and looked exhausted. Her proper bun had fallen on one side, and her face was smeared with coal dust.

"What happened to you?" he asked in a harsher tone than he'd intended.

"Nothing," she lied as one tear cleared a path down her cheek.

"Get undressed." He thought he saw panic blink in her eyes a second before he continued, "I'll order you a bath delivered at once. Then, I'll have dinner served in my room in one hour. Don't be late."

He didn't give her time to argue. Backing out of her doorway, he walked several feet down the hall before she closed the door.

Jonathan couldn't stop the grin that spread across his lips. He could be making wrong assumptions from her state. Maybe his "wee" bookkeeper made a habit of jumping out of windows. No telling how many others she'd damaged since he'd given her his coat. Kansas City wasn't a town with a great many buildings over one story, but he felt sure there were enough to keep her busy.

After he ordered the bath and dinner, Jonathan returned to his room and waited. As he poured himself another drink, he listened to the maids deliver the tub and hot water. He'd paid them double for speed and also to attend to whatever Miss O'Riley needed. Though why he bothered astonished him. If he had any sense, he'd fire the little lady. She didn't seem to be able to walk the streets of town without looking like she'd been run over by a wagon carrying coal. How could she ever survive in Texas?

Food was delivered and set before the fire with the two huge chairs turned to the table. It looked cozy, Jonathan thought. A word he never recalled using before.

The waiter smiled, fussing over the table as if he thought it "cozy" also, a rendezvous between lovers.

Jonathan didn't explain. When the waiter left, Kara appeared in the doorway. Her hair was parted in the middle and hung down her back in damp strands. The skirt and jacket she wore were the same ones he'd seen earlier. The maids must have brushed the wool skirt and mended the jacket. She wore what appeared to be a clean white blouse, but it had a frayed collar. It couldn't be one she'd just bought. She'd forgotten her glasses, and he wondered how she found his room without them.

Her beauty was an unexpected blow to his gut. Without her glasses and wearing her hair long, she was one-hundred-percent trouble wrapped up in perfection. Even though he'd only seen her in a shadowy hallway, then later after she landed on him, he couldn't believe he hadn't noticed her.

Most of the women he'd talked to in his life had been weathered ranch wives with skin of leather, or painted, powdered girls at the saloons. Even in rags, Kara O'Riley outshone them all, and Jonathan knew he'd be facing problems if he took her into a country with few women and thousands of lonely men.

"Where are your glasses?" he asked without moving from the doorway.

"I must have forgotten them," she answered, sounding puzzled. "My father said I should only wear them when

I have to, lest I become dependent on them."

"I expect you to wear them from now on, Miss O'Riley. I'll not have an employee running into things." Or men falling over her, he almost added.

"All right." She frowned.

Jonathan remembered his manners and motioned her in. "I thought you'd also be wearing your traveling clothes."

"I am." She hesitantly stepped into the room. "I only came to tell you that I don't think I should be in a gentleman's room. So, I won't be having dinner with you tonight."

Jonathan raised an eyebrow and stared at her closely. "You wouldn't be here, Miss O'Riley, if you had arrived when the hotel dining room was still open. Besides, you're not a lady in a man's room. You're my bookkeeper."

He wanted everything clear between them from the beginning. No misunderstandings. "In the next year we'll be spending a great deal of time alone together and, I assure you, you'll be perfectly safe from any advances you fear I might make."

She glanced at the food but didn't move when Jonathan motioned for her to take a seat.

He opened a lid, revealing a baked chicken. "As far as I'm concerned, Miss O'Riley, you are not a woman at all. When I look at you I see nothing but someone to keep my accounts."

He'd give truth to his words, he told himself, even if he had to blacken both his eyes on a regular basis. "Now, let's eat before this meal gets cold."

She took a step closer, staring at the food instead of him.

Jonathan continued as he sliced a piece of meat for each plate. "I don't know if Mr. Clark explained everything in enough detail." He added a portion of potatoes. "I've inherited a ranch. I need someone I can trust. I'll pay all expenses, and a good wage, but I expect loyalty."

"You can trust me." She glanced up at him as she took her place at the table.

"Can I?" he wondered aloud. How could he possibly trust a woman he'd known only hours? "If I do, I expect you to be on my side and not sell out, no matter what you're offered. If you hire on to work for me, you work for *me*." He'd be willing to bet she'd be offered double the salary in less than a month to spy on him.

" 'Tis a fair request." She watched him break open a loaf of bread.

Jonathan handed her a piece. "But a warning. If you cross me, there'll be hell to pay."

Fear danced in her eyes a moment before the stubbornness he'd seen earlier replaced alarm.

"I'll be on your side as long as you treat me with the same respect you would a man doing your books. I want no restrictions because I am a woman. I expect no special consideration. I'll live up to my part of the bargain if you'll live up to yours."

"Fair enough," he agreed. As Jonathan watched her, his respect for her grew. She'd asked for a chance, the same chance he would give a man. He wanted to ask when she'd been made to feel so inferior, but he did not pry into her past. Neither would he allow her to look into his.

If she knew him better, she might not volunteer her
trust so quickly. In a matter of days, she'd hear the rumors about men he'd killed. About how he'd lived as a
savage. About the way he kept people at a distance.
She'd hear soon enough that he cared for nothing and
for no one.

He had no doubt she'd be told how cold and heartless
he could be. Would she be loyal to him then? Would
she stand at his side, maybe even fight beside him?
Would anyone—man or woman?

Jonathan watched her eat and knew he'd guessed right
about one thing. She hadn't had a meal today. He liked
that she didn't try to fill the air with chatter. He needed
the time to think everything out, to plan. When he asked
her a few questions, she appeared to be honest in her
answers, even telling him about the widow and the boy
and how the store closed before she could return. She
made no apology for her actions, but simply said she'd
make do with what she had.

Jonathan frowned. He'd be willing to bet she'd been
tricked. The boy had probably seen her at the shoe store
and knew she had money. He'd had plenty of time to
arrange everything with the widow. The clerk was likely
in on the scam also. They were, no doubt, having a great
laugh on how they tricked the young woman out of her
advance money.

And this was the person he was going to have to trust
with his wealth? A person who couldn't hang on to fifty
dollars for an afternoon? When Jonathan realized he
hadn't said anything for several minutes, he looked
across the table.

She still held her fork, but she'd leaned her head

against the wing of the chair and was fast asleep.

Jonathan lost interest in the meal. He shoved the table away and leaned back in his chair, watching her sleep. There was something peaceful about sitting across from someone with only the crackle of the fire to break the silence. She was easy on the eyes. Like watching a slow sunset on the plains.

I'm a fool, he thought. She's little more than a girl. He couldn't take her on the journey to Texas, much less plant her out on his ranch. It hadn't been an hour since he'd told her she was not a woman, but a bookkeeper. And here he sat, watching her sleep, like he had nothing better to do with his time.

Lighting a thin cigar, he exhaled the smoke slowly and stretched his long legs toward the fire. If he had any sense he'd give her three months' pay and thank her for applying. He and Newton, his foreman, could manage as they had for a month. Never mind that they both hated the hours it took to balance the ranch books. Better that than place some innocent woman in danger.

The idea that he might somehow be putting himself in danger also gnawed at him. This plaid-covered nymph could do nothing to him, Jonathan told himself as he watched her. Nothing.

He closed his eyes and thought of all the problems awaiting him. He'd need all his skill to protect himself. He couldn't be watching out for her. If she wanted him to treat her as he would a man, then so be it. No more. No less.

When the cigar was only ashes in the tray, Jonathan stood. "Miss O'Riley," he said, not wanting to startle her. "O'Riley?"

He touched her hand, lifting it in his. "It's time we turned in."

Her fingers were warm, soft to his touch. He could hear the steady slow rhythm of her breathing and wondered what her day must have been like to exhaust her so completely.

"Kara," he tried her name. No, that wouldn't do, too personal. "O'Riley."

He couldn't bring himself to yell and startle her awake. The only other choice was to carry her to her room.

Pulling one of her arms up and over his shoulder, he knelt and lifted her. She felt so light.

To his amazement, she leaned her head against his shoulder and moaned softly.

Jonathan didn't move. He didn't even breathe. What if she awoke and found him holding her like this? He'd probably frighten a year off her life. But he couldn't set her back down. He'd chosen his plan of action.

Carefully, he carried her across the room. By the time they reached the hallway, the warmth of her sleeping body penetrated through his clothing to his chest. He moved slowly to her door, allowing his chin to brush slightly against her hair.

Amused at himself, he decided this certainly wasn't the way he'd treat a male bookkeeper. But then she'd never know he carried her. It didn't matter.

As he would have guessed, she hadn't bothered to lock her door. He stepped inside her room, now warm from a glowing fire. For a while, he just stood there, listening to her breathe, feeling her against him. She was a strange creature, unlike any he'd ever encountered.

Something inside her wouldn't allow her to fear, not the unknown, not him.

He placed her gently atop the covers, lifted her hair, and spread it across the pillows. When he circled the quilts to cocoon her, she snuggled into the warmth like a child. He reached to remove her shoes and noticed she'd come to dinner in her stockings.

Pulling his gaze from her, Jonathan looked around the room. The remains of her bath still sat by the fireplace. One suitcase, hardly big enough to hold his great coat, lay opened on the floor. The clothes within were little more than carefully mended rags. Lifting his coat, he reached in the pocket. He discovered a bill of sale for a pair of shoes and a pair of boots, one dollar stuffed into a crumpled envelope and an address scribbled on a scrap of paper.

A muddy pair of shoes warmed in front of the fireplace, but no boots. The bill had been from Warren's Boot and Shoe Store. Jonathan had seen the bags with the name on them, but no boots were in Kara's room. Somehow she managed to spend forty-nine dollars in an afternoon and had nothing to show for it but one pair of shoes that looked like they wouldn't hold up many more days.

The realization that she'd been tricked angered him.

Jonathan picked up his coat and the address scribbled on the paper. He'd find out who'd swindled her if he had to walk the streets until dawn.

Ten minutes later, Jonathan asked the hack to wait while he tapped on the door of Mary Ann Adams. The lighting was poor and numbers were scarce in this part of town. The note had added "in the back" to the address, and this shack was the only one he saw that looked like it might be livable.

He'd almost decided the house was unoccupied when a woman opened the door. "I'm sorry, sir," she whispered. "You must have the wrong address."

"Are you Mrs. Adams?" Jonathan glanced at the note. "Mrs. Mary Ann Adams?" He saw worry and fear blend in the woman's eyes. "Do you know Kara O'Riley?" Jonathan quickly added, wondering why the woman seemed to still be playing a role of poverty. "I found your address in her pocket."

The door opened wider. "Yes. I'm her friend. Is she hurt? Oh, please, tell me there hasn't been an accident. She told me the saints would watch over her all the way to Texas."

"No," Jonathan answered. "She's fine." He wasn't sure how much he wanted to tell this woman. "She just lost a bag, and I said I'd go look for it."

A child cried in the background. The woman left the door open as she disappeared into the darkness. "Come in by the fire. I'm not awake enough to think clearly."

Jonathan let his eyes adjust as Mrs. Adams comforted the child. He noticed the stack of food on the table and the coal bin running over.

The woman lifted a child from a bed, wrapping them both in a shawl before turning to face Jonathan. "You must also be her friend," the woman said. "She was wearing your coat earlier tonight. I must say, it fits you better than it did her."

"The bag." Jonathan didn't want to waste time talking. "It contained boots she'll need."

The woman shook her head. "I remember no bag. She

carried only these groceries when we left the store. I'm sure if she'd had a pair of boots, she'd have switched them for the shoes she wore."

"New shoes?"

"Yes. She said they hurt her feet. She may have left the boots at Bayley's Mercantile. I know she had several things accumulated on the counter when we met."

Jonathan thanked her and started to leave.

"I hope she didn't spend too much on us." The woman halted him with her words. "I tried to stop her."

Jonathan touched his swollen eye. "So did I. Once."

He left, stopping next at the mercantile. Even in the poor light, he saw the pile of things on the counter with a Warren bag sitting next to them.

He'd been wrong about Kara being gullible. She'd told him the truth. Much as he hated to admit it, he needed someone he could trust. He could do without foolish games of love and the burden of family and friends. In his world, all he needed was honesty.

Within an hour he'd awakened the boy sleeping in the storage room. The boy knew where the clerk lived, who finally agreed to take Jonathan to Mr. Bayley. Jonathan managed to buy Kara's selections amid a chorus of grumbling from everyone but Mr. Bayley. With the promise of huge orders to follow, Bayley agreed to let the widow work part-time in the back, filling orders. There, she could let her children play amid the boxes, as long as they stayed out of the way. Jonathan knew he could get merchandise shipped far cheaper closer to home, but he felt it was a fair bargain. Bayley seemed a good man who'd carried Mrs. Adams for longer than most would have.

When he returned to the hotel, Jonathan moved silently into Kara's room and placed the boxes around. In the morning he'd tell her they had been delivered, nothing more.

Before leaving, he smiled down at her, realizing anyone who'd just given away so much money just might go along with his plan when they reached Fort Elliot. A dark-haired woman who could lie easily, who loved adventure and who had a big heart. Kara O'Riley just might be perfect for his plan.

FIVE

RAIN TAPPED ON THE HOTEL WINDOWS ANNOUNC-
ing a watery dawn. Kara stretched and shoved the covers
aside. Memories of yesterday sliced like a floating ribbon through her thoughts. She'd been so tired last night,
she couldn't remember coming back to her room after
dinner with Mr. Catlin.

She yawned and looked around. The tub was still
there, along with her muddy shoes. Her bag from Warren's containing her boots rested on a chair by the fire.
A stack of boxes filled the other wing-back. Kara tiptoed
to the fireplace. Cautiously, she lifted the lid of the first
box, then the next and the next. All the things she'd
selected at the mercantile were there. And more, far
more. Another pair of shoes, a warm robe, a hat with
gloves to match.

Kara jumped as someone tapped on her door. "Miss?"
a woman's voice asked. "Miss, you up yet?"

"Come in," Kara said, putting the lid back on a box
containing two blouses.

A maid opened the door. "Good to see you awake. Mr. Catlin sends you coffee and a message that he will be leaving in less than an hour."

Kara simply stood in the middle of the room staring while the maid built up the fire and began the packing. The woman laid out Kara's new jacket, blouse and skirt along with new undergarments and finally, the raincoat.

As the maid kept up a pace of running in and out of the room, coffee warmed Kara enough that she finally dressed. Boxes disappeared. A leather suitcase arrived, seemingly from nowhere. The cold bath was removed. A breakfast of fruit and steaming biscuits waited by the fire.

Just when Kara sat down, someone pounded on her door loud enough to wake anyone still sleeping.

"Miss O'Riley?" Catlin shouted from the other side.

Kara took a deep breath, deciding once and for all to stop being afraid of the man. She was going to be working for him for a year. Without knowing it, he might have saved her life by offering this job. The least she could do was stop jumping every time he appeared.

She slowly opened the door and faced him. "Yes?"

The westerner who stood before her was completely different than the gentleman she'd met yesterday. Gone were the polished black shoes, the tailored suit, the white undershirt with its stiff collar attached. Before her stood a man in leather, from his dark brown jacket to the moccasins that laced almost to his knee. His shirt was a deep blue, open at the top, and his pants a heavy cotton twill with copper rivets along the seams.

"Mr. Catlin." Her gaze fell to the gun belt strapped

around his waist. The Colt looked like it had been molded to perfectly conform to his leg.

He pulled on leather gauntlets unlike any she'd ever seen. They had fringe on the cuffs along with a beaded circle design. The gloves would have appeared military except for the design of tiny beads.

"We leave in ten minutes," he said when her eyes finally raised to meet his.

"All right," she answered, realizing he was wearing what her father would have called his "ever'day clothes." Somehow the leather and weapon fit Jonathan Catlin just as her father's heavy overalls had been made for his barrel-chested, strong-armed body. In a strange way, though Catlin and her father were nothing alike, she felt safer than she had since the night her father shoved her on the train.

Her calmness took Jonathan off guard. He stumbled over a few words before finally saying, "Send your bags down as soon as you can. I'll be waiting in the lobby."

"Aye, I will," she answered. "And as your book-keeper, I must ask you for the receipt from Bayley's Mercantile. I'll be repaying you out of my salary each month for these clothes you somehow purchased in the middle of the night."

"That won't be necessary."

She held out her hand and waited.

Catlin looked like he might bolt and run. For the first time she realized how young he was. She'd just turned twenty, and guessed him not five years her senior. Some-how, when he'd been trying to frighten her, he'd seemed so much older. But now, as she confronted him, he looked like he was unsure how to react.

"I don't have it with me." His fists tightened the leather of the gloves as he spoke.

His lie was transparent, but she could hardly search him, so she said simply, "I'll wait."

Ten minutes later when she joined him in the lobby, she reminded him that she was still waiting. Jonathan didn't say a word, only motioned it was time to leave.

As the doorman pulled back the huge oak door, Kara saw that the gentle rain that awakened her had turned into an icy downpour. A river of mud, halfway up to the hotel steps, flowed through the street. The hack that awaited them was repeatedly splattered by passing wagons in the gray predawn light.

Lightning flashed, and the wind shoved the storm into the lobby. Kara pulled her raincoat tightly around her and headed toward the opening.

The wind took the challenge, whipping around her skirts. She fought for footing, a cry for help escaping before Kara could stop it.

An arm, solid and strong, moved around her shoulder.

"Are you all right?" Jonathan Catlin's mouth was an inch from her ear.

Instinctively, Kara rolled toward him. His arm steadied her and they moved outside. She could feel the warmth of his body. They reached the end of the walk and his grip tightened slightly.

"Allow me," he whispered and swung her off the ground.

Her cry of surprise was lost in the leather of his coat as he carried her the few feet to the coach and sat her safe and dry inside.

"Thank you," she managed to say.

Jonathan didn't reply. He seemed to be concentrating on making sure all their luggage was aboard. When he was finally satisfied, he opened the door once more to join her. The damp wind tugged at his coat, and he hesitated a moment before stepping in.

Kara glanced up and caught the flicker of lamplight off metal several yards behind Catlin. She heard the report of a rifle a second before Jonathan lunged forward. A bullet shattered the wood of the hack's window, missing Jonathan only by inches.

Kara screamed. Jonathan's Colt materialized in his hand. They both watched the shooter disappear between two buildings.

"Drive!" Jonathan shouted, rolling into the seat beside her. "We have to make it to the train before someone takes another shot at us."

The coach rocked and tossed on the muddy road. Catlin checked his guns. Visions of her own death flashed through her mind.

"How did they find me?" she whispered. "How did they find me?" Her entire body began to shake with a chill colder than she'd ever known.

Jonathan's warm arm encircled her, pulling her close against him. "Are you all right, Miss O'Riley?"

Kara looked up at her employer's frowning face. He'd asked about her, but he wasn't even looking at her. He watched the window as if expecting more trouble.

She should tell him she couldn't go with him. She had no right to put his life in danger. But if she didn't go, she'd surely die. Whoever had followed her would find her again. And this time, there would be no Jonathan Catlin between her and the rifle.

"The man . . ." She tried to slow her breathing. "The gunman was trying to kill *me*."

Jonathan looked at her with smoky blue eyes. Eyes with a depth a hundred years older than the man. "No," he said calmly. A slight smile brushed his lips as if he thought her suggestion childish. "The bullet was meant for me. Though I would have thought my enemies would have tried a few other ways before murder became their choice."

If he thought his words would reassure her, he was mistaken. Kara found little comfort in the fact that she was racing across Kansas City with a man who might have at least as many gunmen after him as she did.

"If you want to reconsider the job, I understand. I didn't think even my neighbor, Wells, would go to such extreme measures." When she didn't answer, Jonathan continued, "Once we're on my land, you'll be safe enough. I'll stand between you and harm's way until then."

Kara looked at the madman sitting beside her. Not only did he think the bullet had been meant for him, he thought he could somehow protect her. He had no way of knowing that if McWimberly sent one man, he'd send another and another until all the O'Rileys were dead. She'd been a fool to think she'd traveled far enough to be safe.

"I want to go on with you," she whispered, suddenly far more afraid than she'd been since the day her father ordered her to disappear. Until now, she thought her father had overreacted, wanting her gone because he thought she'd be more in the way than in danger. She told herself no one would follow her. But now she knew. No matter what Catlin believed about some man named Wells, Kara knew the bullet was meant for her.

SIX

❦

KARA WATCHED THE SUNRISE THROUGH THE WIN-
dow of the motionless train. True to his word, Jonathan
Catlin had protected her. He'd been watchful, efficient,
silent ever since they'd climbed into compartment B-3
on the southbound train out of Kansas City.

Closing her eyes, she wished she were home. Was this
how it would be for the next year? Always afraid, worried, looking over her shoulder, working for a man who
never said more than was necessary.

She glanced at the caged animal who masqueraded as
her employer. He'd paced the small compartment for
over an hour. The porter told him three times that the
train would be delayed until the rain slowed and a low
place in the track line could be checked. But Jonathan
Catlin was not a man who took bad news gracefully.

"I'll be fine," she said for the fourth time. "If you'd
like to walk down to the smoking car, there may be more
news." She knew he wanted to leave her, but he'd promised.

"No, I'll stay." He sat across from her as if he'd ordered himself to do so.

Kara waited several minutes. Finally, she could endure the silence no longer. "Mr. Catlin, perhaps you'd tell me why you believe your neighbor, Mr. Wells, was shooting at us?"

Jonathan turned from the window and looked at her as if he'd forgotten she was there. "Until this morning, I didn't think his hatred had gone far enough to kill me in cold blood. The Wellses and the Catlins haven't gotten along for thirty years. Around that time, Wells's son used to sneak over to Catlin land to visit a young daughter of a man who worked for my grandmother."

He leaned back on the seat as he continued, "The boy wasn't more than seventeen, the girl sixteen. Both parents told them to stay apart, but they were in love and must have decided to run away together. There had been trouble with rustlers that fall, and one night a Catlin guard shot at a shadow running. Young Wells died, the girl prematurely delivered a baby she carried, then also died before sunup. At least that is the way I've heard the story told."

"But why should that be trouble for you if it happened thirty years ago?" Kara needed to talk. She knew the man who shot at them hadn't been from the Wells Ranch, but if Catlin thought so, her secret would be safe for a while longer. Maybe long enough to get away from the McWimberly who had followed her.

Jonathan shook his head. "Wells blamed the Catlins for his son's death. He swore he'd see them all dead and the ranch abandoned. Every year he gets older and more determined. We've been missing cattle and men over the years, but since my grandmother died, I understand it's gotten worse."

Kara knew she should tell him the truth about the man in the rain who shot at them. But if she did, he might not take her with him. "Maybe the man wasn't shooting at us. Maybe he was shooting at someone else and we just got in the way. The man who hired me, Mr. Clark, must've not thought the threat all that bad. After all, he didn't tell me about it."

"You'll be safe when we're on Catlin land." Jonathan reached for her hand resting only inches away from his own. Just before he touched her, he pulled away. "We've got our own set of guardian angels."

"I hope so," she whispered, wishing he could truly promise such a thing.

Before he could explain, the door to the compartment rattled open. Jonathan's Colt cleared leather at his side, but he kept the barrel even with his leg.

A huge, bearded man pushed his way into the tiny space. As if his size wouldn't frighten the average person to death, he wore more weapons than Kara had ever seen on one man. Long Colts strapped to each leg and a rifle carried so easily in his left hand it looked like an extension. A long knife hung from his gun belt and another's handle poked out of his boot.

To Kara's amazement, Jonathan holstered his only weapon.

"What are you doing here?" Jonathan almost spit the words at the giant.

Kara panicked. Jonathan must surely have lost his mind. Of course the man was there to kill them. She could imagine him killing them both, twisting their limbs apart, tossing them out the window as the train rushed through this open country. No one would ever find her body, or at least not all of it. Her new clothes she'd just bought, her father's packet he'd given her when she'd left home, even her new hat would forever ride the train. And maybe, once in a while, someone might wonder whatever happened to the people in compartment B-3.

The giant growled like a bear, then lifted both his shoulders in a shrug. "Hell if I know why I bother, Kid. The McLains thought you might be needing some help getting out of Fort Elliot. Lucky your train is delayed or I would have missed you."

The hairy giant glanced at Kara as if just noticing she was in the room. "Begging your pardon, ma'am. I didn't mean to scare you. I'm a friend of Johnny Boy here. Name's Wolf Hayward."

There was no humor in Jonathan's sudden laugh. "Warden is more like it than friend. He's part of the McLain clan my sister married into by accident. I feel sure if she'd known what a pestering brood they are, she'd have reconsidered." Jonathan stood to face the man called Wolf. "And stop calling me kid or Johnny Boy before I whittle you down a few feet and see if there is any blood beneath all that hair and muscle."

Wolf laughed without backing down an inch. "You've been threatening to kill me in more than one language for better than ten years. Many's the time I thought of letting you try, but my sister and your sister are both married to McLains and I don't want that whole family mad at me. They'd think I was allowing you to commit suicide if I let you fight me."

"How about we give it a try, old man?"

Wolf bristled. "Old man! Why, you young pup."

To Kara's amazement the two men lunged at one another. She couldn't tell if they were fighting or hugging, but both were laughing.

Finally, Wolf Hayward yelled he'd had enough, and Jonathan backed away.

The giant took a deep breath. "You sure didn't forget how to fight while you were away. I was afraid all that traveling around made you soft."

"One of these days I'll take you to the ground and then you won't feel the need to protect me."

Jonathan glanced at Kara and to her amazement, he winked, silently telling her that all the talk between the two men was just that . . . talk.

"Wolf, this is our new bookkeeper for the ranch."

Wolf looked confused. "Bookkeeper? I thought she'd been hired to—"

"I think she'll go along with a plan I've thought of for Fort Elliot," Jonathan interrupted. "But I didn't want to tell her the details until we were closer."

"What details?" asked Kara. She suddenly had a feeling that there was even more to this job than the bookkeeping or Wells.

Wolf growled at Jonathan as if he couldn't believe Kara hadn't been told about the stop at Fort Elliot. Jonathan only looked angry. "I'll tell her later."

"You'll tell her now," Wolf insisted, "before the train leaves." He tipped his hat to Kara. "I've got to load my horse and gear, then I'll be back. Make sure he tells you every detail, miss. The decision is yours to make, not something you feel talked into no matter how much easier having you along might make the job."

The huge man disappeared the way he'd come. Jonathan turned toward the window, his hands pressing along the frame as though he could somehow push the opening wider and escape.

Kara waited. "What is it?" she finally asked.

"Wolf's right." Jonathan faced her. "You have a right to know what you're getting into before we go any further." His clear blue eyes met hers. "I do need a bookkeeper, and Clark did think I should hire one here in Kansas City because of the trouble with Wells. But there is another reason I needed a woman with me on the way back to Texas. Wolf saw it the minute he looked at you. It took me longer to figure it out."

Kara waited, wondering if his reason could possibly be horrible enough to make her get off the train and face the killer hired by the McWimberlys.

Jonathan sat across from her and leaned forward, his hands almost touching her knees when he steepled them in front of him. "For most of my life," he began slowly as if not wanting to tell her or anyone else the story, "I lived with a tribe of Apache. They'd traded for me with a band of Comanche who'd raided my parents' homestead. The life we lived was hard, but they were fair to me. Among them I had one true friend, Quil. When I was almost fifteen, a group of trappers raided our village. They beat me half to death before they noticed my blue eyes. Then they took me to a fort south of Dallas and left me with the Texas Rangers stationed there. That's where Wolf found me and took me to my sister."

Kara didn't have to ask; she knew Jonathan had told this story very few times in his life.

"Quil was the only one in his family who survived the raid. He was taken to a reservation in Oklahoma. I thought he'd disappeared or died until a few months ago. I was heading back to Texas, hoping to get home before my grandmother died. When I passed through Fort Elliot, I saw him among a group of renegades being shipped back to the reservation."

Jonathan lowered his head to his hands for a moment. "I almost didn't recognize him. But he knew me, and I could see the hatred in his eyes. He blamed me for the raid that killed his family. I tried talking to him, telling him how hard I'd fought those first few years to get back to him and what was left of his tribe. But he didn't believe me."

Jonathan leaned back and closed his eyes. Sadness hung thick in the tiny room.

Kara's imagination molded his words into images in her mind. "What happened?" she whispered.

"I told him where to find me if he ever needed me. Even ripped the label off my saddlebag with my name burned into the leather along with the Catlin brand. But I knew I'd never hear from him. He told me he'd kill me if our paths crossed again. I have a sister I barely remember and a grandmother who died before I got to know her well. Quil was my only family. I tried to help him, but he wanted nothing from me. We'd been boys together, but now we were men in different worlds."

Jonathan looked out the window while his mind searched back in time. "I can't undo what the Comanche did to my people or what the trappers did to Quil's family. But, a few weeks ago when I was at Catlin Ranch, a message came from Fort Elliot."

"What did it say?" Kara was almost afraid to ask.

"It didn't say anything. It was only the label that I'd torn off, but I knew what it meant. Quil needed me."

"You're headed there now?"

Jonathan nodded. "I went through there on my way to Kansas City and now I'm headed back."

Kara frowned. "But why do you need me to go help? What can I do?"

"You have black hair." Jonathan's answer was so short and simple it was almost a slip.

"But . . ."

"I saw Quil on my way up here. His wife had died in the corral the army calls a holding cell."

Tears bubbled in Kara's eyes. "Oh. I'm so sorry. Is that why he called for you, to share in his grief?"

"No," Jonathan said slowly so that every word registered. "His wife died in childbirth." His eyes stared into her very soul. "We'll be making a stop on our way home. I was hoping you'd be going with me to see Quil. And you'll be walking out of that corral with a baby in your arms. A baby with hair as black as yours."

Kara began shaking her head, but she couldn't make her mind form the words. She knew nothing of the West, of Apache or forts or babies. But there was no doubt in her mind that what Catlin was asking of her was illegal. It made no sense to save the McWimberlys a bullet and let the army kill her.

Jonathan moved beside her on the seat. "You have to," he pleaded. "Quil told me once they begin the journey back to the reservation the men and women will be separated. He could never take a newborn with him.

Even if he could get a woman to take care of the baby, he'd never be able to find them again. The odds are strong the child would die."

Jonathan stared at her with unreadable emotions smoldering in his eyes. "I know what I'm asking is illegal, but Wolf and I will be right beside you all the way. Once we're back at the ranch, there will be others to take care of the baby. All you have to do is get from the fort to the train with the child in your arms."

"Can't you find someone else?"

"There's no time, and if I ask anyone in Texas, there's always the chance of someone finding out who the baby belongs to. No one knows you. They wouldn't question you having a baby. Your fair skin and green eyes may be different but, if we're careful, no one will see more than the baby's black hair. Hair the same color as yours."

His face was so close she could feel his breath along her cheek. His fingers brushed a damp curl from her forehead. "If you want to back away, I understand. I'll give you a month's salary and you can keep the clothes. You can step off this train and say good-bye. There aren't many who would do what I'm asking for an Apache child."

Kara remembered when she'd been tiny and her mother told of carrying her from doctor to doctor along the fringes of the slum where they'd lived. They were stopped three times at the office doors and told that the doctor inside didn't have time to treat Irish children. "They never can pay," one woman said, "and if one dies, there'll just be another born come spring."

"I'll do it," Kara whispered.

"Name your price." Jonathan pulled his hand away.

"No price." She stared directly into his intense eyes. "No price can be put on a child."

SEVEN

KARA SAT SILENTLY STARING OUT THE WINDOW AS the train moved through the rain. The job she thought was so perfect when she first heard about it now appeared muddled and complex. She hadn't just been hired because of her skill or the interview, but partly because of her black hair.

Jonathan seemed to relax as the train migrated into open country. He looked younger with the man called Wolf by his side. Kara knew Jonathan was far more a man and less a boy than Wolf's treatment might imply. Both men knew it also, yet they each played their part, she assumed out of comfortable habit. She wasn't sure she'd call them friends, but there was no doubt the two men respected one another.

Kara watched Jonathan Catlin out of the corner of her eye. Whatever bothered him lay all the way in the core of his being. It almost seemed that he wanted to be a spectator in life but kept colliding with the cast. She had to admit his dark good looks attracted her, but his formal manner silently warned her not to step too close.

"We'll need a reason for going into the Apache camp." Wolf rubbed his beard. "We can't just drop by for a visit."

"I've thought about that." Jonathan looked directly at Wolf, leaving Kara out of the conversation. "We wrap a shawl up like a baby bundle, and I'll tell the guards my wife wants the medicine man to take a look at our baby. When we walk out a few minutes later with a real baby, it won't seem strange. Quil told me he'd be watching for me to return. I've no doubt that if the guards show any interest in the baby, Quil will draw their attention."

Wolf shook his head. "Fort Elliot has got an army doctor stationed there. No settler is going to have a medicine man look at a baby when there's a doctor available."

"What if I say my wife's out of her head and insists on seeing the medicine man?" Jonathan looked at Kara for the first time in several minutes.

"Oh, thanks," she snapped. "How about we just say my husband is crazy."

Wolf looked from Kara to Jonathan. "It's a close call. Neither of you have all your brains if you're even considering this. The army won't take kindly to removing folks they've put under guard. Even little ones."

"I have to try. I promised Quil."

Wolf nodded at Jonathan. "If it means that much to you, I'll go along. Besides, my Molly would never forgive me if I didn't try to save a baby. I don't know about helping Quil though. From what I've heard, he's been nothing but trouble for the army."

"I don't care about that," Jonathan answered. "If you'd seen his eyes like I did, you'd understand. It took a great deal out of him to ask for help, from me or anyone. That baby's all he's got left to live for. His family is dead, his wife, hell, his whole way of life. His child is all he has left. It's what keeps him breathing."

Kara turned back to the window remembering her own loved ones and wishing she'd been allowed to stay and fight. She didn't want to think her father might already be dead and she didn't even know it. If he was, she hoped she never found out. Somehow it was easier thinking of him just living away somewhere apart from her, than knowing he might be cold in a grave.

The men continued to make plans to get in and out of the stockade without causing suspicion. Most of the captured were Comanche, but the army had called it an Apache camp. According to Jonathan, the captives knew they were in no great danger and would simply be shipped to reservations, so there was no need for a heavy guard.

Wolf finally came up with the idea that Kara would be looking for her long lost brother who'd been kidnapped by the Indians. Jonathan was along as an interpreter, and Wolf would fit in because families looking for relatives often contacted the Texas Rangers. He'd played out this scene for real so many times it should be no problem making believe this once. With a ranger and an interpreter along, the guards would never bother accompanying them past the gate.

Kara drifted into sleep with her head resting against the cold window. She dreamed of being home where there was always a warm fire. After her mother died,

Kara took over the cooking and cleaning for her father. She always thought of him as her family, but he talked of his wife as "all he'd had in the world." He became more and more involved in work, expecting Kara to work part-time at the bakery and take care of the house.

As the train rolled on, she dreamed of working at the bakery in the predawn hours . . . of walking home with bread so fresh the aroma filled her lungs with every breath . . . of making tea before waking her father and sitting by the fire, warming while she had her bread and tea.

Kara awoke slowly from the peace of her dream. Memories of home faded as the smell of leather drifted across her senses. She moved slightly and felt the softness of Jonathan's coat against her cheek. Raising her head slowly, she looked up into his sleeping face. He seemed to have had no objection to her using him as a pillow. As carefully as she could, she straightened away from him, trying not to wake him.

The rain still fell, making the day beyond the window gray and the compartment seem smoky. Kara blinked in the dim light and looked across the small space to where Wolf was stretched out on the other seat. He looked relaxed, or as relaxed as a man wearing an arsenal could. When her gaze reached his face, she was surprised to see him awake.

"Have a nice nap?" Wolf asked with almost a laugh. "You must have a clear conscience, little lady, because you sleep solid as a rock."

"What do you mean?" Kara had always been kidded about how solid she slept.

Wolf stretched. "Well, we made two stops and not

even the whistle woke you. After the first stop, Jonathan just rolled you beneath his arm so you'd be more comfortable, and you didn't even stir."

Kara blushed. "How much farther?"

"Another hour. Maybe two with the rain."

Wolf's low, southern voice was friendly enough, but he made her nervous watching her. He was not a man easily fooled, she'd guess. He might be able to see that she was running from something rather than looking forward to going somewhere.

"You said you were a Texas Ranger?" she asked, not wanting him to be the one to ask any more questions.

Wolf nodded. "I tried to retire. My wife hates for me to be gone from home. But last year the Legislature created two new forces of rangers to deal with the trouble along the frontier. Raids are still a problem, but it seems the greatest threat to Texas is Texans. We got as many outlaws as we got buffalo."

He straightened and leaned closer to her. "All the newspapers tell of the Indian raids that killed almost a hundred last year in the Panhandle alone, but there are towns where the sun can't come up unless there's been at least one shooting."

Kara didn't know whether to believe him or not. She had a hard time picturing a state filled with outlaws. She'd never seen a buffalo and, until yesterday, she couldn't remember ever meeting a Texan.

"Are you sure you want to do this, Miss O'Riley?" The way he said her name made her think he was already counting her as an outsider in their game. "Jonathan and I can get Quil's son out somehow if you don't feel right about going along."

"I agreed." She glanced at Jonathan. "Did Mr. Catlin tell you someone took a shot at us when we left the hotel?"

"He did," Wolf answered. "Said it might be his neighbor, Wells. The old man's tall as an elm and crazy as sap. He's too mean to die, and if he's the one causing all the trouble on Catlin's ranch, it's only a matter of time before we catch him."

Kara had to be honest. "What if it were someone else? Someone who wanted me dead."

Wolf smiled. "Why would anyone want you dead?"

The last words of her father drifted back to her. Trust no one. Her need to tell him the truth battled with her father's warning. "I don't know," she lied. "But it's a possibility."

"More likely just a case of mistaken identity. Jonathan said it was raining. Maybe the shooter took you for someone else. Kansas City ain't half rooted in civilization on a good day."

Kara nodded. She wanted to believe the lawman, but even in the downpour, when she'd glanced up, it looked like the man with the rifle stared straight at *her*.

"Don't worry. You'll be safe from now on. I'll stay with you until you reach Catlin land. Once there, your biggest problem will be trying to straighten out the books. Trust me, that will be no small task."

"I'm not a very good bookkeeper," Kara admitted. "I only got out of school two weeks ago and this is my first job."

Wolf grinned. "Don't worry. I have a feeling you'll do just fine. Don't let Jonathan frighten you none. It's been a hard road for him, but he's grown into a good man. The last thing he wanted was to get saddled with the responsibility of the Catlin Ranch, but he's handling it just fine."

Kara asked questions about the ranch. Before she thought an hour could have passed, they were pulling into Fort Supply. From there, they boarded a coach and headed southwest to the newly organized Fort Elliot. The stage made great time until the last few miles, where it caught up with a mule train that had left Fort Supply two days earlier. Those last miles, following a hundred-wagon caravan into Fort Elliot, were torture.

This new fort had been built beside an encampment called Hidetown. As Jonathan helped Kara from the stage, all she saw around her were soldiers and huge men covered in leather.

"Buffalo hunters," Wolf explained. "They smell worse than the buffalo."

They walked a few yards to a saloon. While Jonathan went inside and booked them rooms in the newly finished hotel, Kara looked around. The bustle of a newborn town was all around her, along with the smells of rotting meat, unwashed bodies and whiskey.

The men left Kara at the hotel while they went to talk to the fort commander. Within an hour, they were back with permission to walk around inside the camp looking for her lost family. They'd told the commander that Mrs. O'Riley was still weak from childbirth, and they'd bring her as soon as she'd rested. The commander offered a wagon and driver as transportation for the lady.

Wolf insisted on waiting until it was almost dark.

Kara folded her new white shawl ten times trying to make it look like a baby blanket with a newborn inside.

Jonathan paced.

As they stood to leave, Jonathan stepped in front of Kara, hesitated a moment, then removed her glasses.

"Now everything's a blur past a few feet." She reached for the glasses.

"Trust me, this time it could be better that way." He handed her the empty shawl with such care she could almost believe there truly was a baby inside. "I'll be there to guide you."

The area where the army imprisoned the Indians was as Jonathan described it—little more than a corral. Armed guards stood about every ten feet. There were several cooking fires and a few small tents on the grounds. Women prepared a meal of soup with some kind of flat bread while the men sat around one main campfire. Beyond a few feet the shadows blurred for Kara, but the smells were strong enough to tell her that Jonathan had been right. Maybe it was better not to look too closely.

Before tonight Kara had only seen drawings of the Apache. These people looked nothing like the pictures she'd seen. They were not the brave savages, powerful and proud. Most of the men and women before her were survivors of a storm that continued to rage across their lives. She kept her eyes down as if she could make herself invisible among them.

With his hand firmly at her elbow, Jonathan pulled her quickly around the outskirts of the group. She saw him nod slightly at a tall man who looked about his age. The man walked ahead of them for several feet, then stepped aside without a word. Quil, Kara thought.

When Jonathan reached a tent made of hides, he drew

her close and whispered, "Only the women will be in here. Go in and get Quil's son. There is one who speaks English who will give you the baby."

Kara nodded and folded into the tent as though already carrying a baby in her arms.

The inside of the tent was even darker than it had been outside. Kara stood very still. She could sense others in the darkness, but couldn't see anything clearly. As her eyes adjusted, the rounded forms of women huddled around smoking coals in the center came into view. Embers floated toward the night sky, glowing like fireflies as they escaped through an opening at the top of the tent.

Slowly, she stepped over sleeping children until she could stand straight without hitting the top of the tent. Women in blankets rocked and shifted, whispering in a language she'd never heard. A few had turned her direction when she'd let the cold wind in. But none seemed interested enough to follow her progress.

Finally one woman near the back stood and walked toward Kara carrying an odd basket Kara recognized from pictures she'd seen. A cradleboard. Apache women strapped their young inside, then laced the basket to their backs or one of the lodge poles. Kara read a story once about how baby girls' cradleboards were packed with inner bark of the cedar as stuffing to absorb soilings. Baby boys were strapped in with the bottom of the board left open to drip when needed.

"You are Quil's friend's woman?" The stranger raised a wrinkled finger almost touching Kara's cheek.

Kara stared at the woman before her wrapped so tightly in a blanket that her face was completely hidden.

"Yes," Kara whispered back. Afraid to say more or try to explain. If this old one was expecting her, she'd need no other greeting.

"When I lived among your people, I was called Raven." The old woman sat the cradleboard down. "But, that was many years ago."

Kara knelt beside her, opening her shawl to receive the baby when he was removed from the board. "It is nice to meet you," she said, thinking how the empty words meant nothing; they only filled the silence between them.

Raven turned and covered Kara's hands to still them atop the shawl. "The boy child of Quil." Aging fingers gripped Kara's hands for a moment. When she released her hold, she spread her hands palms down before Kara and brought one hand over the other again and again as if trying to make a sign that would explain. "Son of Quil has gone under," she whispered.

Kara felt a chill as surely as if the north wind had blown the tent down.

The blanket slipped away from the woman's face, revealing eyes so filled with sorrow no amount of tears would wash them clear.

"No one knows but the two of us. These women are Comanche. They care not for Apache. The child has gone under," she whispered once more in broken English. "He walks across the stars."

Kara began to shake as the words registered. The old woman's grip grew tighter on her hands. "I have lived in both worlds. My man was a mountain man many, many years ago. When he go under, I moved back to my people. But I know both."

Kara tried to quit shaking and concentrate on the old woman's words without looking at the cradleboard resting between them.

"Quil is a brave man," Raven whispered, "but he will not stay tied to the earth if he knows his son has gone on like all others in his family."

Kara knew what she was trying to say. Raven didn't think Quil could take another round of grief. Kara had seen that happen more than once when a man lost all of his family to death. Strong, young men who buried their families would drink until they rotted inside, or take chances waiting for their luck to run out. She once saw a woman who'd lost baby after baby in the birthing turn her face to the wall and die.

Tears clouded Kara's already poor vision. "I'm so sorry." She gulped back a cry. "I wish there was something I could do." The thought that in a few minutes she'd have to walk out of the tent with empty arms shook her heart with pain. Quil would see. He would know.

"There is something you can do." Raven let loose of Kara's hands. "You can go from this place with the child in your arms."

Kara shook her head. "No. I couldn't. I couldn't."

Aging hands began to unlace the cradleboard. "If you walk out holding the child as if he is still alive, it will do no harm to the boy. But Quil will not know of his son's death, and he will live another day."

"But he'll find out." Kara watched as the woman gently lifted the baby out of the cradleboard.

"One day, far away, maybe. But not this day." She held the baby up and waited for Kara to open her shawl.

Fighting back cries, Kara opened the white shawl with trembling hands.

Raven brought the baby's cheek against her own. In the shadows of the tent the child could have been only sleeping. "Son of Quil will be free tonight. Free from this place. Free from the earth. Son of Quil will walk proud into the next life."

Gently, as if not to awaken the child, the old woman wrapped him in Kara's white shawl. He was so tiny, her bundle didn't look any larger than when she'd carried it in.

"You must not cry," Raven said as she handed the baby to Kara. "My mountain man said there are those called saints who watch over the one who carries the dead with honor."

Kara slowly stood and curled the child next to her heart. By the time she stepped from the tent, all tears were gone from her eyes. She walked the few feet to Jonathan. Without a word, he took her elbow and guided her out of the camp.

As they passed the one she knew was Quil, Kara saw him straighten and nod slightly at Jonathan. She was thankful he didn't look at _her_ face. She wasn't sure she could hide the sorrow she felt.

EIGHT

THE THREE OUTSIDERS MOVED AWAY FROM THE
Apache camp and onto a converted hospital wagon the
commander had provided. Kara sat next to Jonathan on
the rear seat of the wagon for the ride back to the hotel.
The bench offered little comfort, as they moved down
uneven roads. She hardly noticed.

Wolf talked to the driver, embellishing their story—
saying how they'd looked from fort to fort for relatives.
When the driver said that maybe it was better if they
didn't find anyone alive, she felt Jonathan tense by her
side.

"You know once they've been captives, they ain't
nothing but wild savages." The driver spit a stream of
tobacco the same color as the muddy road. He continued
talking around the wad of leaves still soaking along his
jaw. "The boys are never right in the head . . . and the
girls, well, it's always better if the girls die. Nobody
wants them after they've lived with the Apache."

Wolf changed the subject, but the driver's words left

Jonathan silent. She felt him shifting angrily. When his leg accidentally brushed hers, the muscles felt more iron than human.

Kara held the baby close as if she could protect him.

When they reached the hotel, Jonathan helped her down from the bench, then hurried ahead to open the hotel door. He didn't bother thanking the driver. Wolf said good night to the soldier. The southern warmth had left his voice. Only cold formality remained.

Kara walked slowly to her room. Jonathan and Wolf followed.

As soon as the door was closed, Jonathan moved closer to Kara and brushed the shawl with his hand. "He's so quiet. Is the baby ill?"

Wolf didn't look at the child. He only stared at Kara with knowing eyes.

"I had the maid bring up a few cans of milk. That will have to do until . . ." Jonathan stopped.

Silence draped the air in sorrow. Kara held the bundle close as if she could somehow pass her warmth to the child.

"What is it?" Jonathan demanded, glancing from her to Wolf and back.

Kara stared at him and said the old woman's words: "Quil's son walks among the stars."

Jonathan took the blow without flinching. He'd learned years ago to take whatever came without showing any sign of pain. Anger was the only emotion he allowed himself to feel. Anger surrounded him now, smothering all other feelings.

He didn't need to ask why she'd carried the baby out. He knew what Quil would do if he thought his son dead.

But Jonathan hated the fact that he had become a part of a lie against his only friend. Quil asked for his help, and the aid he'd given was deception.

Jonathan barely listened as Wolf asked all the right questions. Kara told what happened in the tent. He knew judgment would come someday. Quil would find him. Ask for his son. The old woman wouldn't be there, or the little bookkeeper, or Wolf. Jonathan would have to face his friend alone and tell him the worst thing a father could hear.

"I'll make a box." Wolf scrubbed his eyes. "And check about buying a plot. This fort may be new, but in these parts, there's usually a cemetery growing faster than the town."

"No." Jonathan knew his voice was hard, but he couldn't soften it or he might fall apart completely. "Make the box, but we take Quil's son with us. The boy will be buried on Catlin land. I don't know what Quil would want, but I know he wouldn't want his son left here at a fort built beside a buffalo hunters' camp."

"All right." Wolf nodded. "I'll make the arrangements. I spoke to the owner's wife earlier. She seems a good person and she's half Comanche. She'll know how to dress the child."

Kara sat in a rocker near the window. She still cuddled the baby in loving arms. "I'll rock him until the woman comes."

All three knew the action made no sense. No one mentioned the fact.

The walls closed in around Jonathan. He needed to breathe. He needed to run. Without a word, he stormed out of the hotel room and rushed down the stairs to the street. Almost-running, he hurried to the edge of town and kept going until the night sky was all he saw before him and the racket of so-called civilization lowered to a whisper.

Low clouds made the night dark and stars only spotty. A sliver of a moon blinked between thin, velvety clouds. The smell of buffalo and blood floated in the air like sour perfume.

Jonathan crumpled to one knee and took huge gulps of the cold air, trying to cleanse the hurt from his chest.

"Don't feel," he whispered. Fog painted his breath. "Don't feel anything." The command had kept him alive when he was five with a wound in his shoulder and no one to help him. It was the one action he could take, pushing away physical pain as well as the tightening in his heart.

"Don't feel!" he ordered himself, or the agony would surely kill him.

All the times he'd said the words flashed through his mind like withered leaves falling. His heart chilled. He'd stood, his shoulder bleeding, and watched his mother's body piled atop others for burning. He'd seen his second family slaughtered with casual callousness. He'd stood a hundred times against pain and, every time, he'd won because if he didn't feel, they couldn't kill him. They couldn't hurt him. He wasn't alive inside.

It took several minutes, but finally he won the battle. He stood, turned and faced the town. As always, he'd won. He'd made all feeling disappear.

Two hours and several drinks later, Jonathan hit the floor of the saloon so hard he heard ringing in his ears.

"Get up!" yelled the soldier who'd driven them to the

stockade. "Get up, mister. Take a little of what you've been dishing out."

Two other soldiers grabbed Jonathan by the arms and pulled him into a standing position while a third pounded on him. Jonathan didn't make a sound. In truth, he didn't feel the pain. He'd asked for the fight, knowing it wouldn't be a fair one.

When he hit the floor again, the soldiers shifted places. It was another's turn. They pulled Jonathan to his feet once more, and the blows rained. Jonathan didn't bother to open his eyes. He no longer cared.

As the world began to dim and fade, the strikes stopped suddenly. Jonathan swayed, fighting to stand as the two men holding him moved away. Suddenly, in the midst of the fight, a giant intruded.

"Let the man go!" Wolf roared. "What kind of fair fight is four to one?"

It was now two to four, but the soldiers backed away. They'd taken several blows each from Jonathan and were in no shape, even with the odds, to challenge Wolf.

"He started it!" the driver yelled like a boy in the school yard. "Coming in here, telling us how we should think."

"Well, I'm finishing it." Wolf bent and folded Jonathan over his shoulder. "Any of you boys object, you know where to find me."

The four soldiers stepped out of the giant's way.

Wolf marched from the bar without another word. Jonathan faded in and out of consciousness.

When they reached the hotel lobby, he heard Wolf mumble, "Try not to bleed all over the rugs."

By the time Wolf climbed the stairs, Jonathan was

awake and demanding to be put down. Wolf dropped him off his shoulder as if Jonathan were no more than a sack of grain.

Jonathan staggered to keep his footing. "I didn't ask for your help."

"You never do, do you?" Wolf shoved him through Kara's hotel room door. "I thought you'd outgrown brawling since you went back East. Thought you might have smartened up since taking over the ranch. But no. First time I've seen you in two years, and your eye is black. I should have guessed yesterday that you hadn't changed. You're still the fiery kid looking to get yourself killed."

"And you're still the hairy guardian angel trying to save me."

"Somebody has to keep an eye on you. Those four would have left you for dead if I hadn't come along. I could hear the blows plowing into you from the street."

"The man deserved to have his face pounded in." Jonathan leaned against the dresser for support.

"They always do, don't they, Kid? Just like in some crazy way, you think you deserve getting the guts kicked out of you," Wolf raged. "Ever since the rangers pulled you out of that Apache encampment, you've been fighting the world."

"Don't give me that speech again about it not being my fault everyone close to me dies. I'm not in the mood. And stop calling me 'Kid.'"

"Stop acting the part. I've hauled your bleeding carcass out of half the bars in Texas. And I'll tell you—"

The smack of a leather ledger case against the side of his head silenced Wolf. He turned in time to see Kara, dressed only in a nightgown, double back for another swing. "What . . ." was all he got out before she hit him again.

Wolf looked at her as if a mosquito had just decided to wage war against him.

"Get out of my room!" Kara yelled. "What do the two of you think you're about bringing your fight into my room? I'll have none of it." She might be a foot shorter and less than half his weight. But she was a furious warrior in full advance.

"Your room?" Reason dawned in Wolf's eyes. "Begging your pardon, miss. I thought . . ."

The poor man looked so honestly confused, Kara almost felt sorry for him. "I suppose you just forgot that your room is across the hall?"

"Well, yes." He jerked his hat off and began mutilating it in his huge hands. The giant stood before her, an arsenal on his person, looking like he'd rather face a whole town of outlaws than apologize to one woman. "I didn't . . ."

Jonathan's body hit the floor with a thud, ending Wolf's agony.

Kara rushed to Jonathan's side and lifted his head. His handsome features were bloodied and bruised. The old wound she'd inflicted blended with new ones.

"What happened?" Kara asked as she motioned for Wolf to help her get Jonathan to the bed.

"I'm not sure, but when I got there it was four against one. The kid looked like he'd held his own long enough to bloody all the others."

Kara's Irish accent returned. "And that's something to brag about, is it?"

Wolf looked embarrassed. "No, ma'am."

"Well, help me get him on the bed so we can see if it be doctor or bandages I'll be needin'."

Wolf followed orders as they checked Jonathan for broken bones. Wolf removed Jonathan's shoes while Kara opened his shirt.

"I've had little practice treating wounds the size of a fist, but I've watched a few times when my father brought home men who'd been in fights." As she calmed, the accent disappeared. "Get me bandages for his ribs and whatever salve you can find for the cuts. Nothing appears to be broken."

Standing, Wolf hurried to follow orders.

"And by the way, Captain Hayward, Jonathan didn't get the black eye he sported yesterday from a fight. I gave it to him when we collided the day we met."

Wolf looked doubtful, then glanced at the ledger case she used as a weapon only a minute ago. He didn't question her as he disappeared to get what she needed.

She began washing away blood. To her surprise, most of the blood didn't seem to be Jonathan's, but a bruise along his ribs indicated he'd been hit several times in the same spot.

He moaned when she ran her fingers over the injury but didn't open his eyes. As she worked, she noticed numerous small cuts over his body and a deep jagged scar along his left shoulder. For a young man, he had enough scars to have served several careers as a soldier.

Wolf returned with bandages and a black salve he'd bought from a man in the bar. It claimed to cure everything from warts to poisoning of the blood. He watched as Kara worked. "As soon as you're finished, I'll move him across the hall."

"No, leave him here. I'll move across." She pulled on her robe. "I'll sit with him a while to make sure he's resting."

Wolf agreed and brought in Jonathan's things. "I need to make arrangements for tomorrow. Will you be all right here?"

Kara nodded without pausing in wiping the blood from a wound along Jonathan's arm.

With Wolf gone, the room grew quiet and she became aware of being alone with a man she hardly knew. She tried to tell herself that she was just doing what anyone would do for an injured man, doctoring cuts, wrapping wounds, cleaning off blood. But slowly, she realized it was more. She was touching this man. Except for holding the hand of a man while she danced, or kissing a friend on the cheek, Kara had never touched anyone other than her family.

She slid her fingers along Jonathan's arm and over the scar on his shoulder. The flesh was warm, inviting.

Without wondering why she felt such a need to make contact with another, or that the "other" she'd chosen was her employer, she continued. Spreading her hand wide across his chest. Moving the tips of her fingers over the contrasts at his throat, touching his hair where it curled slightly behind his ear. His skin was smooth and tanned by the sun until some of the warmth seemed to stay in the flesh. She never dreamed touching a man could be so exciting.

She checked each bruise and cut, resenting the damage to his body probably more than he would. She would never care for this cold man with his quick temper and angry eyes, but still the need to feel him remained. Maybe like touching the untouchable. Maybe because she'd been so alone for the past months. Maybe because, in a way, he was perfection in form. A statue of muscle and skin and bone. Even though wounded and damaged, the beauty showed through.

Kara almost laughed aloud. He was only a man. Nothing more. If she let her imagination run away this time, she'd get herself in true trouble. If she dared to dream of him as anything other than her employer, she would never be able to look him in the face again.

Straightening, she moved her hand an inch away before Jonathan's powerful fingers caught it in his grip.

She looked up into angry eyes burning with the fire of a challenge.

"What were you doing?" he snapped.

"I . . . I . . ." She couldn't possibly tell this man she was just taking her time feeling him. His stare told her he'd never believe she'd just been treating his wounds. If he was awake, he'd surely felt her every touch. "I . . ."

Pulling at her fingers, she tried to get away. "You were hurt. There was blood." Her words fell over one another as anxious to get out of her mouth as she was to escape Jonathan.

Suddenly, she was running toward the door. She had to get away. Maybe he'd be too hungover in the morning to remember. Maybe, with time, she'd be able to think of an explanation that made some kind of sense. But right now, she needed to flee from his questioning gaze.

Her fingers gripped the knob. The door didn't budge. For a moment, she panicked, jerking the knob as her gaze raised along the door looking for a lock.

She saw only his hand holding the door closed. He hadn't made a sound when he'd followed her, and now he blocked her exit. She could feel his breath brushing against the side of her face and the warmth of him only an inch away from her back.

Kara closed her eyes and faced him. Let him yell at her. Let him get it over with. Fire her if he wanted. She wasn't going to try and explain what she was doing, and she wasn't going to say she was sorry.

He didn't say a word.

She waited, tensing. Surely he wouldn't strike her?

Kara opened her eyes. If he hit her, she'd fly into him like a wild . . .

All thought vanished as she watched him close the distance between them. His body leaned into her completely, unlike anyone had ever done while dancing or even with a hug.

Before she could speak, his mouth covered hers totally, kissing her in a way she'd never known a kiss could happen. A flood of sensations exploded inside her, vanquishing any thought of objection.

He tasted of whiskey and need. When she breathed, he moved with her, making it seem as if they communicated with their entire bodies. His mouth was warm and demanding and giving, all at the same time. He gathered her in his embrace, holding her as if her life depended on his steady grip.

When she didn't protest, he moved his hands into her hair, holding her head in a caress as he explored her mouth. Her awareness of him made her dizzy. The warmth of his body penetrated her clothes and made her skin feel like she stood an inch too close to the stove. She didn't move. Afraid he wouldn't stop. Afraid he would.

His kiss fed her very soul. He was taking what he needed and giving back a pleasure she hadn't known she longed for.

Then, as suddenly as he'd started, he pulled away.

A moment later, she was in the hallway, running for her room. She didn't even breathe until she'd locked the door behind her. For a long while Kara stood, her back to the door, trying to slow her pulse.

She'd tasted the wildness in him and knew that the door and the tiny lock wouldn't stop him if he chose to follow. She'd also felt tenderness in his kiss, a holding back, as though he were protecting her even from himself.

Her mind filled with a hundred thoughts, a hundred feelings, but one kept pounding strong as the beat of her heart. Jonathan Catlin kissed her. The coldest man in the world kissed her with a fire that would surely have consumed her if she'd stayed any longer in his arms.

NINE

❦

Kara didn't bother to close her eyes. There was no need. Sleep would elude her as surely as smoke slips from a grasp. She wasn't sure she would ever be able to sleep again. The memory of Jonathan's kiss made all her senses come alive. Thinking about it, she relived each detail slowly and somehow the warmth of his nearness heated her all over again.

She thought of Devin and the times he kissed her. A few pecks on the cheek. Once lightly on the lips. They hadn't touched anywhere except their lips, and then only for the briefest of moments. "I'll marry you one day," he'd say. But he never truly asked her. When he came to call, it had always been to talk with her father. Visiting with her always seemed an afterthought.

Kara slipped from the bed and curled up on the floor by a small fireplace. Watching the flames always helped her think.

How strange that the coldest man in the world kissed her with more passion than Devin probably ever would.

Jonathan had changed her life, even if they never spoke of it again. For after his kiss, Kara knew she'd always hunger for more. It had been like magic, like an explosion of the senses.

As the warmth of the fire reminded her of how she'd felt in his arms, Kara closed her eyes and let herself dream of kissing like that once more. No matter how hard she tried to force the direction of her daydream, the arms around her were Jonathan's, not Devin's.

As dawn lightened her room, she dressed in her new navy skirt and slightly wrinkled white blouse. Through a dirty window, she watched Wolf guide a buggy to the front of the hotel. Fighting back the tears, Kara saw Jonathan carefully pack a tiny coffin into the back of the buggy. As though for warmth, he packed blankets around the box.

As light softened the sky, the day reflected her mood in varying shades of gray. How could she face Jonathan Catlin with the memory of the way he tasted still thick in her mind? What happened last night had all been her fault. If she hadn't been touching him like a bold harlot, he wouldn't have kissed her.

In all her life she'd never done something so bold. She'd thought of doing daring things, but until last night her thoughts had stayed in her imagination, coming out only in daydreams. Last night thought had crossed over into action.

Well, she couldn't put off seeing him any longer. If he were angry, he might as well fire her and be done with her. She could take the train back as easily as she took it here. Surely he wouldn't be so mad that he'd refuse to give her return passage. Though, she wouldn't blame him. What kind of bookkeeper touches her employer like she did? Even now, she could still feel the warmth of his flesh on her fingertips.

Kara lifted her bag and walked down to join the men. Wolf greeted her. Jonathan didn't act like he even noticed her.

"I rented a buggy for the two of you." Wolf took her bag and strapped it to the back. "I figured it would be more comfortable for you and, with Jonathan's ribs, he'll ride easier." Wolf glanced at Jonathan. "Not that he'll comment one way or the other. He probably wouldn't have two words to say if I roped him and dragged him for the next hundred miles. The man's been a mute this morning."

Wolf helped Kara into the buggy. "Hotel man said someone was asking about us last night. Might not be a bad idea to hightail it out of town before folks wake up."

Kara didn't comment. She didn't want to think about the possibility of someone following her this far. Surely, not even the McWimberlys, who'd been known to carry grudges all the way across the ocean, would track her down this far. After all, she was only the daughter of O'Riley, not someone of any importance to them.

Stepping up onto a huge roan, Wolf mumbled, "Muteness seems to be an epidemic this morning."

Jonathan climbed in beside Kara without looking in her direction. As usual, he was angry and this time she could guess what about. Dark hair uncombed and shadows beneath his eyes made her wonder if pain in his ribs had kept him awake or whether it could have been the kiss? Yet, when she glanced at the hard set of his mouth, she found it impossible to imagine his lips could soften enough to kiss a woman.

Kara felt like she suddenly became more invisible, as if that were a possibility. She sat back and watched the barren countryside pass by her. They traveled on a road used by supply wagons. In most places, the ground was hard and packed. But now and then, for no reason, the dirt turned sandy and treacherous.

Jonathan drove the buggy with great skill. One gloved hand held the reins while he used the other to brace himself against the side of the buggy. He seemed to be doing what she was, trying to ride on a bench built for two without touching. Even when his jacket brushed the side of her skirt, he pulled it away.

The effort not to touch grew tiring. Every time the buggy rocked, Kara grabbed the side so that she didn't accidentally lean in his direction. She couldn't relax a single muscle for fear that she might unintentionally touch him. The longer they didn't touch, the more critical the game became.

Wolf was the only one who made any effort to talk as he rode beside the buggy. By midmorning, he had to be aware of the tension between Jonathan and Kara. He kept switching sides, keeping first one, then the other company. Kara guessed that, on a good day, Wolf was no great conversationalist and today was definitely not a good day.

"Something wrong?" Wolf finally asked, reining his horse beside the buggy.

"No," she lied.

"What about you, Kid? Everything all right?"

"Fine." Jonathan almost spit the word.

Wolf shook his head. "Well, since everything is just fine between you two, I think I'll ride on up ahead and tell Morgan we're stopping for lunch at his place. The old stagecoach station manager claims he's out of food if you arrive after noon. Which is a lie, of course. Anyone who's had his stew knows it always tastes like it's been warming for a week on the stove."

Wolf didn't wait for an answer from the pair. He kicked his horse into action and was out of sight before Kara could think of some way to ask him to stay.

She tried to move a little farther from Jonathan and still be comfortable.

He snapped the reins to coax the horses into a faster pace. She could feel anger simmering within him and guessed it was somehow directed at her. She thought of reminding him that she hadn't acted alone last night. He'd been there also.

The buggy rocked. Kara caught the side and held on tightly. Jonathan swore under his breath. Without warning, he jerked the reins. Suddenly, Kara found herself fighting to keep from falling forward.

Jonathan reached to steady her but stopped short of touching her. He wrapped the reins around the break lever to hold the team and faced her.

"Enough!" He said the word as if it were a swear word.

Kara could think of nothing to answer in reply. She watched him, wondering what he would do next. In her whole life she never felt the need to arm herself against a man, or even be afraid of one. It occurred to her now that any sensible woman would probably be afraid of Jonathan Catlin. The eyes she once thought of as smoky and full of mystery seemed now made of winter ice. And there was no way the hard line of his mouth could have ever softened into a kiss.

He pulled off his gloves and ran his fingers through his unruly hair. "There are things that need saying."

Kara agreed but didn't know where to start. Should she apologize for touching him? If she did, she'd have to admit to doing such a thing. She couldn't. She wouldn't put her actions into words. After all, a woman engaged to be married doesn't go around caressing strangers.

Jonathan seemed to be having a great deal of trouble starting the conversation. For someone who demanded they talk, he didn't appear to have anything to say.

"Is it fired I am?" She'd take the consequences. There was no need for discussion. The man would torture her with his silence no longer.

Jonathan looked surprised. "It's fired you're not," he snapped.

Kara took a breath. So he wasn't going to fire her, and if he planned to ravish her here on the road before lunch, he was sure taking his time. She suddenly felt better than she had all morning, even though their talk hadn't been much of one. She wasn't fired. She had a job and a place to stay. She'd be safe for a year.

"I didn't mean for last night to happen," he said more to the back of the horse than her.

She wondered which part he hadn't meant to happen, but didn't think it would be polite to ask. She was pretty sure he hadn't planned the fight, or getting hurt or the kiss. To her way of thinking, he meant all of the happenings and she had a part in only one. She thought of agreeing, but saw little point.

He didn't look at her as he continued, "I don't want you to be afraid of me or think I'm some kind of madman who goes around doing that kind of thing."

Kara looked at him more closely, realizing she was far more curious than she'd ever be afraid. Embarrassed, shy, but never afraid. "I'm not," she answered. "And I don't know you well enough to judge your sanity."

"Good." He appeared relieved. She couldn't be sure since he still stared at the horse's rump while adding, "Because I want you to know that what happened last night won't happen again."

He was apologizing, she realized, though if he didn't look at her soon, she'd start wondering to whom.

"From now on, you have nothing to worry about. In fact when we get to the ranch, you'll be seeing very little of me. From this point on, I'm sure we can maintain a strictly business relationship."

Kara figured she would never get another chance to ask. "Do you always kiss like that?"

Jonathan finally looked at her. "Like what?"

"So completely. Like the world is ending, and you have to taste life one last time before it's gone."

Jonathan studied her. She couldn't read any emotion in his stare. "I don't think we should talk about this," he said slowly.

"You brought it up." She refused to back down. "I was just wondering. I've never been kissed like that before."

A smile touched the corner of his lip. "Doesn't your husband-to-be kiss you like that?"

"No. Should he? Was that a married kind of kiss?"

"Not necessarily." Jonathan looked frustrated. "We shouldn't be talking about this."

"Oh." Kara smiled, thoroughly enjoying his discomfort. "So it's all right to do; however, we must not speak of it. Do people go around kissing like that and then never mention it? Do they just forget it happened?"

"Yes . . . no . . . I don't know." Jonathan pulled on his gloves. "I should have never started this conversation. I just wanted you to know you'd be safe. I swear I'll never touch you again."

"That will help me sleep better. But why did you kiss me in the first place last night?"

"I don't know."

"If you don't know, how do you know you won't do it again?" She relaxed into the worn leather folds of the seat, for the first time taking her half of the bench. "Maybe you *are* mad and the insanity will strike you again someday. Out of nowhere I'll be kissed again. For all I know, every woman at your ranch has suffered the same fate." Her imagination took hold. "They travel the hallways and paths in twos for protection. Be they young or old, you'll appear suddenly from nowhere, crush them against you and kiss them. Maybe you jump up from the dinner table and chase the cook around. You can't help yourself. It's an illness for which there's no cure. Maybe . . ."

"Enough! Kissing you wasn't like a twitch. I said it won't happen again." He caught her stare with eyes that had turned smoky blue-gray once more. "And you didn't look like you were suffering."

"How will I know for sure? I didn't know such a kiss existed until last night."

Jonathan frowned. "What are you, some kind of new torture sent to drive me loco?"

She opened her mouth to argue, but he held up his hand. "Wait. I give you my word, I'll never kiss you again, unless, of course, you beg me. I'm not a man normally given to such foolishness. Believe me, I only want a bookkeeper in my life. Not a woman. So stop asking questions about anything else."

"Fair enough." She finally got a word in. "I understand. I want no man in my life. All I want to do is serve out my year and return home."

"To Devin," he added.

"To Devin," she echoed in just as dull a tone.

He picked up the reins and encouraged the horses into action.

Kara waited a moment then added, "There's no need for you to apologize, Mr. Catlin. If the blame is to be sliced, I have to give myself a piece."

Jonathan glanced at her and raised an eyebrow but didn't say a word. By the time they reached the stage-coach station, a silent truce had formed between them. Though nothing was said, he offered his hand to help her from the buggy and she accepted.

Wolf had bowls of stew waiting for them. While Morgan fed and watered the horses, Wolf told Kara they'd be on Catlin land by nightfall. He spoke of the place as though it were another country they were going to and not just a ranch.

Back on the road, she wanted to stay awake and watch, but the meal, the winter sun and her lack of sleep combined. As the day aged, Kara began to fight to stay awake.

The sun disappeared behind clouds that looked like a mountain range banking one side of the endless prairie. The horse's trot beat an endless rhythm against the low whine of the wind moving across the land.

Jonathan pulled a lap quilt over her without saying a word. She tried leaning against the side of the buggy, but couldn't get comfortable. Finally, half asleep, she leaned against his shoulder and gave way to dreams.

TEN

❦

JONATHAN UNHARNESSED THE HORSES IN THE DARK-ened courtyard. The Catlin Ranch Headquarters was a fortress with several buildings inside a thick adobe wall. Since he first saw the place years ago, he'd had the feeling of being locked inside more than locking out the world. The main house had been built in the early 1800s to withstand attack from Indians or Santa Anna's army. The bunkhouse was added later, then added on to, as the number of hired hands grew through the years. Inside the walls were wells and stores of food and ammunition to last a full siege.

If a man had to be closed in on the plains, there were worse places than here, he guessed. A fountain bubbled in the center of the yard. Smells of winter sage and evergreen had replaced the heavy fragrance of flowers that weighted the air all summer. The faint sounds of the horses in the corral and the cowhands in the bunkhouse were little more than a whispered melody in the night air.

As he turned the team over to a hand, Jonathan glanced at Jason Newton, the foreman. "All well on the place?" It was the same question he'd asked once a day since he'd taken over.

Newton nodded. "Some trouble, but nothing that can't wait until morning. Except old Gideon tumbled over a harness left on the back door and broke his leg while you were gone. He swears the harness fell on him, but I don't see how that could have happened."

"He all right?" Gideon had been the caretaker for almost fifty years. His granddaughter, Angela, ran the house just as her grandmother had until she died. Gideon and his wife were from Mexico City, but Angela had been born on the ranch.

"Yeah," Newton answered Jonathan's question. "It was a clean break. Luther set it for him." Newton hesitated. "Strange thing was no one remembers putting the harness there. It don't make no sense, it just appearing. A man would have had to make a special trip from the barn to put a harness there."

"Accidents happen," Jonathan said, puzzled by the same thoughts.

"Maybe." Newton didn't say more as the two men walked toward the house.

Jonathan heard Luther Ice and Willis Miller whispering as they curiously peeped inside the buggy. Like all the retired lawmen and rangers who acted as guards, they saw everything on the ranch as being their business.

"What d'you reckon she is?" Luther asked. Age cracked his voice.

"Wolf said she was a 'wee little bookkeeper,' " Willis answered. His deep tones had matured into hollow sounds as if he were speaking from the bottom of a well. "Ain't guess I ever seen one before."

"She sure is pretty. You think she's alive?" Luther sounded worried, but then folks said Luther caught a case of worry back in '61 and never recovered. The few times he hadn't been worried about the state of the world, he was surprised he'd survived to be so old. Like an old cottonwood, he'd twisted considerably with age.

" 'Course she's alive. They wouldn't bring us a dead bookkeeper." Willis's laughter made a hiccuping sound in his throat.

"Well, they brought us a dead baby, didn't they? Wolf said that's what was in the box he set on the porch."

"You're right about that," Willis conceded as he glanced at the coffin Wolf had carefully place on a bench by the front door. "Touch her. See if she's alive."

"I don't know about that." Luther shook his head so hard it appeared loose. "Maybe we could holler at her?"

Willis jingled as he shifted nervously. "You holler and you'll scare her for sure. I heard of women being scared plum to death."

Luther sounded frustrated. "Well, I ain't never heard that. And I ain't gonna sing to her."

Jonathan had listened to enough from the two retired Texas Rangers who lived on Catlin land. His grandmother used to call the worn-out lawmen, who drifted in from all parts of Texas, the Old Guard. Jonathan never thought to question their presence. They just came with the ranch he inherited. He saw them as his responsibility, just as they saw him as theirs.

Moving between them, Jonathan said, "If you two

gentlemen will step aside, I'll take care of our 'wee little bookkeeper.' "

Willis jumped, always skittish of anyone standing too close. From the rattle of his spurs to his watch chain, he jingled. He reminded Jonathan of an old cat someone tied a bell around to give birds fair warning.

Luther took longer to move aside. He relied heavily on a cane as he shifted his left hip that no longer co-operated as part of the whole. Like many of the men, he'd been wounded in his younger days and now the mended body suffered.

Jonathan debated whether to awaken Kara. She'd spoken to him a few times, asking questions before she fell asleep, but he wouldn't exactly say they were on friendly terms. When he'd carried her before, she hadn't known. She was sure to guess this time when she woke up in a strange room.

Carefully, he lifted her from the buggy. As she'd done the first night he met her, she curled into his chest without waking. He found himself wondering how many hundreds of times a father or brother must have lifted her while she was growing up.

With Luther and Willis as escorts, Jonathan carried her up the steps to the huge ranch house built by Catlins three generations before.

The ranch foreman leaned against the front door as Jonathan neared. Though the two men were within a year of the same age, Jason Newton was a head shorter than Jonathan and twice his width. He wore a twin set of Colts which added even more to his girth. "Might want to toss her back." The foreman couldn't hold in his laughter. "And hope for a bigger catch next time."

"Quiet down." Luther swung at Newton with his cane. "You don't want to wake up the bookkeeper, do you, Jason?"

Newton ignored the advice. "So that's what she is. I know the ledgers are in bad shape, but did you have to knock her out to get her way out here?"

"No." Jonathan frowned as he passed. "She just sleeps soundly, that's all."

Newton joined the procession up the stairs. "My grandmother slept soundly like that. We buried her."

Jonathan had the strangest feeling that he wanted to protect Kara. He wished he hadn't pushed so hard to get here early. Maybe he could have carried her in peace if they'd arrived after midnight.

"Where we gonna put her?" Luther asked. "I don't know if Angela fixed up one of the spare rooms. She didn't say nothin' about anyone coming. And you know Angela. If she knows anything, she shares it with the world."

"Hold her head up more," Willis grumbled at Jonathan. "She can't breathe the way you're carryin' her."

Jonathan groaned. Everything on the ranch had to be a committee decision. If Snort and H. B. were here, they'd be adding their advice to the mix. "I'll put her in my room. I know it's ready. I'll sleep downstairs on the couch tonight. Tomorrow, she and Angela can pick out a room for her."

Everyone nodded, happy to share a plan. Newton held the door, Willis jingled over to light the fireplace and Luther watched from the doorway.

Jonathan laid her carefully in the middle of his own bed, then frowned. She wouldn't have to worry about him kissing her again. With the Old Guard around, there was little chance the two of them would ever be alone again anyway.

Jonathan removed her shoes and spread a quilt over her. Everyone else backed out of the room as if turning around might cause undue noise. He brushed his finger lightly along her cheek, wishing he had the nerve to kiss her there. Strange thing about this woman . . . she could drive him crazy with her questions, but damned if he didn't think the idea of kissing her again sounded good. And tonight he was stone-cold sober.

Thoughts of her drifted through his mind as he moved about the shadows of the barn an hour later. He saddled a horse and roped a mule, then carefully tied the tiny coffin and a shovel onto the mule. The moon would provide all the light he needed for what he had to do.

He rode out silently, but Jonathan couldn't shake the feeling that the guards were watching him and knew what he was about to do. Deep into Catlin Ranch the land turned rocky and veined with canyons. It would take him hours to find the right place for Quil's son, but find it he would. A place high on a bluff where all four views were endless. A place where the wind would blow across the grave and the sun would shine without shadow from dawn until dusk.

A place where Quil would know his son would forever be free.

Dawn melted into the room between slats of huge oak shutters, awakening Kara slowly. A chill thickened the air, daring her to move from beneath the covers. She smiled at the whispered tick of a clock half a room away and the distant aroma of coffee.

Stretching, she looked about. Books were everywhere. Piled on tables, crammed into shelves, arranged like tiny foothills surrounding an armchair near the floor-to-ceiling windows. Big books, little books, old books with their covers falling off, new ones with oiled leather bindings. In her home in Pittsburgh, they had only borrowed books. From the time she could read, Kara would first borrow her teacher's books and then go to the library. For an only child left alone, books were like friends.

Now, she saw hundreds, and all looked like they'd been here forever. She could think of no more welcoming sight. Suddenly, the year didn't seem so long if she could read.

Slipping from the bed, Kara felt along the nightstand for her glasses. She couldn't remember putting them there last night. For years, the last thing she did before going to bed was to place her glasses within easy reach. At dawn, when the light was poor, she needed them more.

But this morning, Kara couldn't remember arriving at the ranch. It must've been late. She tiptoed around the room, letting her fingers glide lightly over everything. The thin-framed glasses would be hard to see against the dark wood in the shadowy light. Years ago, she learned to find them by touch each morning.

The furniture, simple in design, was well made. Kara didn't have to ask; she knew she was at the Catlin Ranch. The place where she would serve out her year before going home. That is, if there was a home to return to. Another few weeks and she could send the first telegram or letter. With luck, her father would respond.

Since she was still fully dressed, she knew someone must have carried her in here. Kara fought down the blush that threatened her cheeks. There was no real question of whom. Her bag sat next to Jonathan's just inside the door.

Closing her eyes, she took a deep breath. This had to be his room. It smelled of leather and wool. The books, though, were a surprise. He didn't seem the kind of man who could sit still long enough to read.

She pushed the door open. Maybe someone had carried in her handbag and ledger case. She would probably find her glasses downstairs with them.

Kara didn't bother to look for her shoes. She didn't want to be responsible for waking anyone.

Dark shadows haunted the hallway, angling across like barricades, warning her to stay put. A light shone from below, flickering through the carved spindles of the staircase.

In a strange way, she liked the look of the world without her glasses. All lines were softer; tiny imperfections were invisible.

Kara wondered why no one had opened the shutters. She saw the long thin outline of windows closed to any light. Surely the house wasn't meant to remain in darkness all day.

Moving slowly down a wide staircase, she felt a chill, as if the house were occupied more by ghosts than flesh and blood. The wind murmured through tiny cracks in doors and windows, fabricating a conversation just beyond the forming of words.

"May the saints and guardian angels watch over me

double today," she whispered, suddenly remembering the frightening stories her cousins used to tell around the fire late at night. If every person was only allowed a part-time guardian angel, she'd wear hers out before half her life was done.

The stairway spilled into a wide passage bordered with doors. Thick rugs were warm beneath her stockinged feet. Two massive doors stood open, inviting her into a great room with its carved, backed chairs and needlepoint cushions, rich oak paneling and a fireplace almost tall enough for her to stand in.

Kara walked around the shadowy room, seeing it more clearly by touch than by sight. Fine furnishings greeted her, still perfection even though aged.

She brushed the wood-carved design of the hearth. Most of the fire had died within the fireplace, but the warmth still penetrated her clothes.

With a start, Kara noticed Jonathan sleeping on one of two long couches several feet away. He'd removed his boots and used his coat as a blanket. He looked like he'd just collapsed there moments before. In his vest pocket she could barely make out the tip of her glasses.

Kara crept toward him, planning to get her glasses and be gone without waking him. But when her hand brushed his coat, Jonathan's fingers closed over hers.

She looked at his face and saw no sign that he'd been asleep.

"What do you want?" he asked without turning loose her hand.

"My glasses," she answered calmly over the pounding of her heart.

He let go of her hand and sat up. "Oh." He handed them to her. "I forgot I had them."

Kara's cheeks burned as she adjusted the glasses on her face. "I'm sorry I fell asleep before we arrived. If it ever happens again, please wake me. There is no need for you to carry me. I'm not a child."

Jonathan grinned. "And how does one wake you?"

"Grab me by my shoulders." She reached to demonstrate, but his cold stare made her hesitate. "Just shake me while you call my name," she finished in a whisper.

He swung so swiftly off the couch, she rocked back. The man had a way of moving quickly without giving any hint that he was about to do so. He crossed to the fireplace and stood, his back to her.

His coldness iced the air between them. Kara changed the subject. "Do we bury the child today?"

"I already did," he said without turning around. "I found a place deep into a part of the ranch we never use."

Kara brushed her hand along his shoulder. "I would have helped if I could have."

His muscles tightened beneath her touch and she pulled away. For a while he was silent and she wondered how often he'd been comforted in his life. An ocean of pain seemed locked inside him and he wanted no one to share it.

"If we are to work together," he finally said without turning around, "I think it best we establish a few rules."

Kara straightened, wondering if the man ever faced anyone directly in conversation. "Is this about the kissing again?"

"No." He shifted so their eyes met. "This is about you

always . . ." He hesitated, choosing his words carefully. "I'm not accustomed to a woman . . . to anyone being so close. I like to keep my distance from people. *All* people."

He ran his fingers through his hair. "If we are to work together, we need to maintain certain boundaries."

For a moment, Kara didn't understand. She'd grown up in a neighborhood where people hugged a greeting, held hands at funerals and weddings, patted one another as a part of conversation. Except for a few times, she'd been no closer to Jonathan Catlin than she was to anyone.

"Until I took over this ranch, I traveled. I was always surrounded by strangers. I didn't mean to startle you by moving away. I'm not used to people patting my arm or slipping things from my pocket. Or trying to comfort me."

"But those were my glasses and I meant—"

He didn't let her finish. "I prefer not to be so close to y . . . to people. I think if we are to maintain our strictly business relationship, we should both remember that. Unless politeness or necessity demand, I think there is no need for me to be within several feet of you, Miss O'Riley."

"All right, what else?"

"Else?"

"You said rules."

Jonathan nodded. "Rules. Well, I think we should be completely honest with one another. If I do something that bothers you, I'd like to be aware of it."

"Agreed." He hadn't said he'd change, she noticed.

"Is there anything you need to tell me before you begin your first day of work?"

Kara took a deep breath. "No."

"Then breakfast will be in an hour. The dining hall is directly across the foyer. I'll see you then, Miss O'Riley. We'll begin on the books immediately after breakfast."

Kara nodded and walked from the room. Before she even had time to look at her new home, Jonathan set down the rules. He acted like she was some silly girl going around touching him all the time. Didn't he know that the most difficult part of her job was going to be putting up with him? At least he said he'd be gone most of the time. Then she'd know some peace from his stare.

She didn't even like the man, much less want to be close to him. His imagination must be as overactive as hers if he thought otherwise.

Suddenly, the coldness in the house reached all the way to her bones. It was going to be a long, long year.

ELEVEN

∞

AN HOUR LATER, JONATHAN WATCHED KARA DE-
scend the stairs. He never liked the old house he inherited. It was drafty and full of cracks. But with a woman
inside, it seemed almost like a home. And a home, Jonathan reminded himself, was the last thing he wanted.

After his parents' place was destroyed and burned,
he'd made a new life with the Apache, only to have their
village raided and trampled to the ground. When he was
barely fifteen, he swore he'd never call a place home
again. Jonathan had managed to drift for years before
his grandmother died and left him the ranch.

He told himself he didn't want the place, that he'd
get rid of it as soon as he had it running smoothly. He
told himself he didn't care about the land. But three
generations of Catlin ranchers flowed in his blood, and
Jonathan wasn't sure he could run far enough or bleed
fast enough to purge them from him.

As he watched Kara, for the first time in years he
forgot about wanting to be somewhere else. Her mid-

night hair was now tied properly in a bun, and she looked fresh scrubbed and pressed. He was surprised to find himself a little saddened by the transformation.

He'd never tell her how beautiful she'd been earlier that morning still new from sleep, her hair wild and free around her shoulders, her stockinged feet showing beneath her skirt. He probably had no right to see her like that. After all, in a year she'd be another man's wife. She would marry her Devin O'Toole and live in one of those tiny row houses he'd seen by the mills in Pittsburgh. In five years she'd have five little Irish brats and more backbreaking work than she could endure. Her year in Texas would be only a faraway memory.

Jonathan turned and stormed into the dining room before she noticed him staring. He must be crazy. He didn't want to see her as anything but a bookkeeper. The last thing he wanted was to get involved in any way with her as a woman. If he had to set a hundred rules, or a thousand, he'd make sure he got no closer to Miss O'Riley.

To his surprise, everyone waited in the long dining room. Jason Newton, his foreman, stood by the windows talking with Gideon, the man who ran the grounds. It didn't appear his crutches had slowed Gideon down much. He was still yelling orders at his granddaughter Angela, who served as cook. Angela was long past the age to have moved out from beneath her relative's thumb, but an old maid has little options. At thirty she was too old for the young cow hands who worked the range and too young to be interested in any of the old men who guarded the place.

Gideon kept a close eye on the girl. His daughter,

Angela's mother, had fallen in love at sixteen, gotten pregnant and died in childbirth. Gideon would see that such a thing never happened to his only grandchild. Word was he'd sworn to shoot any man who even looked at her too long.

Four of the Old Guard were also present for breakfast. Luther, the nearest the ranch came to having a doctor, leaned on his cane. Willis, a former cavalryman and Texas Ranger, rattled coins in his pocket as he paced.

Snort, who'd pulled a night watch, would be headed to bed as soon as he ate, but he would come to breakfast first. Snort considered it part of his responsibilities to keep up with all the happenings on the ranch.

H. B., the oldest and meanest of the men who'd settled on the ranch, stood by Snort's side like an armed guard. Jonathan remembered how his grandmother always called the man "my H. B." like he was a house pet. Jonathan's opinion differed. He half-expected H. B. to start foaming at the mouth any minute. The man was as tough as they came in Texas.

The group of men paid little notice to Jonathan as he entered. For a moment, he didn't understand why they weren't seated. Usually breakfast was an informal meal with men eating as soon as they arrived. But today, they all waited, watching the door.

A few seconds later, they fell silent, as if someone had rung a bell all heard but him. Jonathan didn't have to turn around. He knew the moment when Kara entered the room. All the men straightened and grinned with whatever teeth they had left. Snort even made an effort to comb his hair down with a wide swipe of his palm.

"Gentlemen." Jonathan didn't look back at Kara. "May I introduce the bookkeeper?"

One by one, the others moved toward her and introduced themselves. All seven men waited for the lady to sit down. Jonathan had never seen such strange behavior. They were acting like the Queen of England had come to breakfast.

When Angela entered with the food she served Kara first and, to his amazement, none of the men complained.

"I'm Angela," the old maid said as she deposited food on the table. "I'm also Gideon's granddaughter, but I don't like to be reminded of that."

Gideon groaned at her attempt at humor.

"If you need anything, Miss Kara, you just let me know. I'm here from dawn 'til dusk."

"Thank you, Angela." Kara smiled politely.

Jonathan watched Kara and wondered if she had any idea that Angela had just been nicer to her than he'd ever seen the old maid be to anyone. He drank his coffee and listened to the others.

Conversation at meals had always been reports about the ranch or complaints. Suddenly they were asking how Kara liked the weather, if she slept well last night and what could they do to make her happy? It was enough to sour the milk.

The only time Jonathan got a word in was when she looked directly at him and asked about Wolf. Jonathan quickly explained that Wolf never stayed a day longer away from Molly than necessary. He'd left before dawn with a saddlebag full of food and a good horse. With luck, he would be in Austin by nightfall.

"Like the McLains always say, Wolf will keep an angel on his shoulder and his fist drawn until he's among family once more." Jonathan mumbled more to himself than anyone. "Wolf's their brother by honor if not by blood."

Before Kara could ask more about the McLains, the Old Guard, inspired by the tale of Wolf's hurried departure competed with stories of their ranger days. Days when they'd traveled twice as far in half the time with no food at all. Snort finally topped them all by adding that his horse died and he had to carry the carcass the last twenty miles.

Jonathan waited quietly until Kara finished her meal and then stood, declaring it time to work. All the men scrambled to their feet and bid her good-bye. Snort even waggled his fingers in as foolish a gesture as Jonathan had ever seen a seventy-year-old man make.

Jonathan thought he heard Kara giggle as she followed him into the study with her ledger book in hand.

The study was the only room in the house Jonathan liked. It was small, with floor-to-ceiling books on two sides and a wall of windows facing the courtyard. He had the feeling that, in years past, the ranch had been run from this room more than any other.

"Near as I can tell," he said as he directed her to the desk, "we've never had anyone here who can keep books. Several years ago, my grandmother tried, but she went blind. No one took an interest after that."

"Is that why the house is kept so dark?" she asked.

He hadn't really thought of it before. Most of the time he spent inside was after dusk. "I guess so. I remember Angela saying bright light bothered Victoria's eyes." Jonathan pulled out the desk chair for her and waited.

Kara hesitantly sat behind the massive desk.

He continued, "Since my grandmother became ill, Newton kept every receipt in this box. Somehow, by the end of our year here the books have to show a profit or the ranch will no longer be mine." He shoved the box toward her.

"Why would she make such a rule?" Kara asked.

"She wanted me to work it. Maybe even fight for it. She thought I wouldn't see its value if I didn't live here."

"And do you?" Kara looked up at him.

"Not really," he answered honestly. "This place is not what I want, but I'll give it my best effort."

"And what do you want, Mr. Catlin?"

It was an easy enough question, but the answer was impossible. "I don't know," he said. "I'd like to feel someplace was special."

"Or someone," she whispered, looking away.

As he stared he thought, for a moment, he could read her mind. She'd never been special to anyone. Maybe no one ever had or ever would value her dearly. The thought made him uncomfortable. She deserved better than this Devin O'Toole who could let her go away for a year without making her believe he valued her.

Jonathan changed the subject. "There's a safe to your left that usually stands open. We put money from the sales of cattle into it in the fall, and Newton, Gideon or myself take out whatever is needed to run the place or pay the men."

"The safe is never locked?"

Jonathan looked amused. "No one would steal from the headquarters. The Old Guard may look useless, but my guess is a thief would be dead before he could get off the land. You only met the four old men who choose to live at the bunkhouse. There are almost a dozen more scattered over the land who prefer to be alone."

"So, all your money is guarded by retired rangers?"

"Not all. There's an account in Henrietta, another in Dallas. If Brady, a little settlement an hour from here, ever gets big enough to have a bank, I'll put some there. So far all they have is a mercantile, a saloon and the telegraph office. And a stage that runs once a day to Fort Worth." Jonathan watched her write something down. "You'll find all the information you'll need in the box. We could ride over to Henrietta one day and check the accounts or even to Fort Worth."

When she didn't ask any questions, he reached for his gun belt draped over a chair by the window.

As he strapped it on, she found her tongue. "Aren't you going to stay and help me?"

"No. If anyone comes in needing payment for a bill, pay them. If you're unsure, Newton should be around somewhere. I told him to check on you. I'm riding over to the Wellses' place and see if they know anything about that shot taken at us in Kansas City."

Kara looked worried, but he couldn't tell if it was from being left alone or that he planned to face Wells. Before he could say anything, Angela entered with a steaming cup of coffee. To his surprise, the woman walked right past him and offered it to Kara.

"I brought the lady coffee." The housekeeper leaned forward. The desk looked low next to Angela's six-foot frame. "If you prefer, I'll make you tea. I make wonderful cookies for tea. Miss Victoria, Jonathan's grandmother, used to have them every morning."

Kara smiled up at the woman. If she'd been shorter, people would have called Angela plump. At six feet, large was the only word that came to mind. "Thank you. Coffee will be fine."

Jonathan frowned. Angela treated Kara like she was the mistress of the house. She didn't even notice him standing in the middle of the room.

"I might like a cup of coffee," he mumbled.

Angela looked up at him as if he interrupted something important. The woman feared no man, but her smile showed respect. "You don't have time, Mr. Catlin. Snort and H. B. are already waiting for you in the courtyard. Snort said he wouldn't sleep knowing you were riding alone. They're going with you to see Wells." She turned back to Kara and asked about what time she'd like lunch.

He was being dismissed, Jonathan thought. One bookkeeper seemed to be all everyone could think about.

"Open all the shutters in the house, Angela. It's far too dark here." He stormed out of the study, not giving either woman time to answer.

Before he reached the front door, Kara caught up to him. She grabbed his arm with her hand. Jonathan stopped as if she held him with iron.

"Be careful," she whispered, her green eyes filled with worry.

He was in no mood to be ordered, or mothered. Staring at her fingers on his sleeve, he hissed, "I thought we agreed not to touch."

She pulled her fingers away and locked her hands behind her. "I'm sorry. I forgot."

He almost felt guilty. "You have no need to worry.

I'm not going looking for a fight. I've only met Wells a few times. He never struck me as a wise man. If he had anything to do with someone shooting at us, I'll be able to see it in his eyes."

Kara straightened, her voice suddenly formal, almost void of the Irish accent. "Should I tell Angela to keep lunch ready for you?"

"No." He shoved his hat low. "Or supper either. The Wellses' headquarters is half a day's ride away, and we'll stop in town on our way back."

She nodded and watched him walk out the door. He was a cold, cold man. But he was the only one she really knew here. Everyone else, though nice, was a stranger.

Suddenly, she felt very much alone. The only person she felt she knew for hundreds of miles was Jonathan Catlin, and he didn't even want her touching his arm.

As she moved to the doorway and watched him swing up onto a horse like he'd been born for the saddle, Kara had the feeling she was being watched. The hair stood on the back of her neck, and air colder than that outside drifted past her. She remembered something her father used to repeat about houses having moods. He'd laugh and say, "Some homes welcome you with a 'come in and sit a spell,' while others seem to be waiting for you to leave."

Kara tried to shake the feeling. She could see no one looking at her as Jonathan and the others rode out. When she turned, the foyer and the study were empty. Yet, the coffee she had left steaming only a few minutes before was cold. Not lukewarm or tepid, but cold, as though it had been stored in snow while she was gone.

She poured the coffee into the planter beside her desk

and hoped it didn't kill the weedlike plant that struggled to survive. Then, with little idea of what she was doing, Kara went to work. She sorted the receipts from the box by date and recorded each carefully in the ledger. Since she had no beginning balance, all the numbers were negative for several weeks. Finally, she found a sales sheet for cattle and the books began to balance.

Angela brought in lunch. Kara continued to work as she ate. By midafternoon, she'd reached the fourth month of ranch operation and the scratchings on the receipts began to make sense.

Jason Newton dropped by every hour. After being bombarded with questions several times, his visits grew further apart. He wanted to help, but he wasn't a man who took to book work. Every time Kara asked him to read something or figure out the exact numbers scribbled on a scrap of paper, he looked like she was asking him to take medicine.

Finally, he didn't even step in the room when he passed by to tell her he had business on the range and would be gone for several hours.

Angela was no help, saying she "never took no reading or writing." The Old Guard seemed to have disappeared completely, as well. Shadows grew into evening, and Kara felt alone in the huge house. If she listened carefully she could almost hear whispering. Maybe it was just the wind. She tried not to listen.

Just before sundown, Angela appeared to tell Kara that her supper was in the kitchen and a room had been cleaned for her at the opposite end of the hall from where she'd slept last night.

"Only Jonathan will be in the house after dark. I stay

no later," she explained. "Jason and the others are in the bunkhouse across the courtyard. Miss Victoria insisted I have my own place. My little house is on the other side of the garden. My grandfather was against it, but Miss Victoria insisted a woman needs a nest of her own by the time she's twenty."

"No one else will be here?" Kara asked, realizing when Angela left, she would be alone.

Angela nodded. "Like my grandfather always tells me, bolt your door. If anything frightens you in this old house, scream for Jonathan. He'll come running to your aid."

After the woman left, Kara let the warning roll around in her mind. Why would she need to bolt her door in a house inside a fortress where even the safe sat open? Jonathan was the only one close enough to reach her. If she were to encounter trouble, he was the one who would save her. Nothing—the warning, the bolt, the empty house—made sense.

TWELVE

KARA WORKED UNTIL HER EYES NO LONGER FO-
cused on the numbers. Pulling off her glasses, she
rubbed at her nose. She'd thought to wait up for Jonathan, but realized he might not be coming back tonight.
He was not a man accustomed to answering to anyone,
and certainly not a bookkeeper.

She moved through the shadows to the kitchen. Soup
and bread sat atop a stove that had been banked for the
night, providing just enough warmth to keep the supper
heated. Kara carried a bowl to a long counter and
hopped onto a stool.

She could remember eating very few meals alone, in
the past few months. Most of the places she'd stayed
included two meals with the rent of a room. They were
always served in crowded little dining areas. Everyone
answered the dinner bell immediately, or was left with
cold gravy and fat to eat.

Somehow, tonight, the silence wasn't lonely. Angela's
touches were everywhere in her kitchen, making this the

only room in the house that seemed lived in. The house-keeper was a matter-of-fact woman who saw little use for conversation. She seemed far older than thirty. Kara guessed that was because she'd been raised by a strict grandfather. But here in Angela's kitchen there was warmth and color and smells that welcomed.

Halfway through the meal, the back door opened. Jonathan came in with the wind, dusty and looking tired, with his hat pulled low. Kara wondered if the man ever slept more than a few hours a night.

He didn't notice her right away. The jingle of his spurs on the brick floor was almost musical. The soft brush of leather against leather contrasted with the hard lines of his lean body.

As she watched, he lifted an empty coffeepot and let out a long breath of disappointment.

"I could make you some," Kara volunteered.

Jonathan turned loose of the handle. His fingers were on his Colt before the pot clanged against the stove.

He whirled to face her so quickly she felt as though she'd blinked and he'd shifted positions without her seeing him move.

His angry eyes softened slightly when he saw her. His hand moved away from his weapon. "How could I not have noticed you there?" He stared at her, worry lines cutting deeply into his face.

She jumped from the stool. Something haunted him, and she knew it wasn't the lack of coffee or her presence. A sadness lingered in his smoky eyes that almost made her catch her breath every time she met his gaze. Yet, she knew it would be a waste of time to ask. "I'm sorry." She moved toward him slowly. "I didn't intend to startle you. I worked late and was just finishing a meal."

He stood frozen as she neared.

Trying not to brush against him, Kara leaned around Jonathan and picked up the coffeepot. "How do you like your coffee?"

"What?" he managed to say as she crossed to the sink.

"Strong, I'd guess. Anyway, that's the only way I know how to make it." She filled the pot with grounds and water without looking toward Jonathan, who seemed to think of himself as a kitchen statue. "There's little soup left, I'm afraid."

When she passed him to put the pot on the stove, she had to gently shove him out of the way to reach more wood.

As her hand pressed against his arm, he stepped back quickly, suddenly aware of what she was trying to do.

"Have you had dinner?"

"No." Jonathan walked to the sink and washed in cold water from the pump.

Kara didn't ask any more questions. She collected pans and food. She knew a hungry man needed to eat, and without knowing much about the kitchen and its stores, there were few options of what to cook.

While a skillet heated, she mixed several eggs with milk. When butter sizzled in the pan, she cut two thick slices of bread and placed them on one side to brown. The eggs cooked on the other.

With his back to her, Jonathan propped his foot on a bench by the door and unstrapped his cowhide chaps and silver spurs. He hung them on a hook, then got a cup from the cupboard and claimed the stool she'd been sitting on. He watched her without comment.

In only a few minutes, she sat a plate of fried bread and scrambled eggs before him. It wasn't much, but in her part of the world it was often considered a feast.

"What's this?" He looked at the food.

"Dinner." She poured coffee. "If I knew where everything was, I could have cooked you something else. The bread tastes great with honey on it."

Jonathan cut away a bite with his fork. Without a word, he tasted first the bread, then the eggs. "You can cook," he mumbled between bites.

"Of course, I can cook. But this is hardly a meal. I used to make this for my father when he had to pull a late shift." She moved another stool across the table from him and climbed on it. "Until three months ago, I made three meals a day for him. Now, I guess he eats at his cousins' house down the way, or at a pub."

"Why'd you leave?" He didn't look up from his food.

The question could almost have been casual and simply to make conversation. But Kara guessed nothing about Jonathan was ever casual. He wasn't the kind of man who bothered making small talk.

Kara busied herself getting more coffee. After she was settled once more, she answered, "My father thought I should see some of the country before I marry and settle down. He sent me to school in Kansas City. When I finished, I just decided not to go back." It wasn't all a lie. Everything she'd said was based on scraps of truth.

Jonathan made no further effort at communication. She drank her coffee and watched him finish everything before him.

When he carried his plate past Kara to the sink, she asked, "Would you like more?"

He walked to her side before answering. For a moment, he hovered as though trying to figure out just how close he should stand to her. "Not tonight," he finally said as though having to figure out each word in order to make conversation. "But again sometime. I like your cooking." He moved his hands out as if to help her down, then pulled back. "This stool is too high for you. You'll break your neck jumping on and off of it."

Kara tried to remain calm. The rule he'd made of not touching bothered him as well. She'd never been aware of how frequently people touch inadvertently. She guessed no touch of Jonathan's would ever be casual. "I'm used to everything being too high for me. I can barely touch the floor from your chair in the study." She tried to relax. "I'm sure the work table and stools fit Angela fine. I think she may be the tallest woman I've ever known and her grandfather, Gideon, couldn't be more than five-five."

"Maybe her father's side of the family was tall." He said the words as though he knew the answer.

"Maybe." She didn't want to pry.

"My sister, Allie, is small like you." He changed directions. "Her husband, Wes, is taller than me. He kids her about her thinking his name is 'Get me,' because she's always saying 'Get me this or that.'"

Kara laughed and stepped away. It seemed strange to think Jonathan might have a sister, someone he cared about. "Do you have brothers as well?"

He hardened before her eyes, and she wasn't sure if he planned to answer. Finally his words came fast, matter-of-factly. "I had three Catlin brothers who were killed in a raid by Comanche. I was so small they took me alive to trade. When I went to the Apache, I had two brothers in my adopted family. Quil and one other who was killed the day I was rescued." He said the last word like it left a bad taste in his mouth.

She didn't have to ask. She knew what he'd just told her, he'd told very few people in his life. "I'm sorry," she whispered.

"Don't be. That's the way life is out here. There is no sanctuary." He turned away, not letting her see his eyes. "Time I got some sleep. It's been a long day."

Before he could reach the door, Kara asked, "What about Wells? Was he involved in the shooting in Kansas City?"

Jonathan slowed but didn't stop. "It wasn't Wells who shot at us. There was no surprise or fear in his eyes when he saw me. Only hatred. The man wants not just me, but all trace of the Catlin Ranch destroyed. But he's no fool."

"Oh."

Jonathan turned at the door. "You seem disappointed."

Kara quickly rattled her dishes at the sink. "Oh, no. I just wish we knew who tried to kill us. Now we'll have to keep guessing." She couldn't say the possibility of it being a McWimberly lingered in her mind.

"We may have picked up a few more clues today. The north range was hit by rustlers. They didn't seem to be just after the cattle. It was like they were trying to do as much damage as possible. Trying to send me some kind of message." He sounded tired. "I covered every inch of their trail and couldn't figure it out."

He glanced at her, looking surprised he'd told her so much. With sudden harshness he added, "Good night, Miss O'Riley."

"Good night, Mr. Catlin," she said, but he'd already gone.

She cleaned up the dishes and lit a lantern to take with her through the house to her room. Except for the low fireplace glow in both the study and the great room, no lamps or candles burned to help her see her way. The hallways filled with shadows on top of shadows, all in varying shades of darkness. The house seemed to close itself away from her as if not wanting her to intrude.

The lantern's light danced along the walls just ahead of her as she climbed the stairs and walked down the long passageway. She could see a sliver of light from under Jonathan's door and knew he was still awake, but the house felt huge and empty. She was to her room before she realized she'd left her glasses in the study downstairs.

It didn't matter, she told herself, she was too tired to read tonight, anyway.

As she opened the door to her assigned quarters, Kara smiled. The room was small with colorful quilts on the bed and rugs on the polished floor. A dainty desk sat next to the window along with a chair turned to catch the morning light for reading. The three books of Jonathan's she'd looked at in his quarters were stacked on a tiny table next to the chair. Whether by accident, or by plan, the room seemed designed just for her.

Kara ran her hand over the books, wondering if Angela or Jonathan had placed them there. "Jonathan," she

answered her own question. He would be the only one
to notice she'd moved his books the night before.

She bolted her door, as Angela had instructed, then
undressed. A few minutes later when she crawled into
bed, the howling wind and the whispers in the house
didn't matter. She slept soundly through the night.

At dawn, she joined the men for breakfast.

As the weeks passed, the meal became her favorite
time of the day. The Old Guard told stories. Newton
talked about the happenings of the ranch. And Jonathan
watched her.

In time, the watching no longer bothered her. She told
herself he was just observant. Like the books, a stool
appeared in the kitchen that had a step built into the base
so she no longer had to jump up. Since the first night,
when she'd carried a lantern from the kitchen, lamps
lined the foyer and hallway. All were lit at dusk. And a
board was fitted beneath her desk so her feet no longer
dangled.

Jonathan was a man of details, that was all. He was
a man who watched all around him.

After breakfast each morning, Kara went to the study
and worked. Most days Jonathan joined her for the first
few minutes to tell her why he couldn't stay and help.
Then he'd be gone, along with everyone else.

Kara worked alone. Alone with bookkeeping tasks she
slowly grew to hate. By the second week, she was fighting to keep from throwing away the ledgers and receipts.
She even thought of telling Jonathan they'd all been destroyed in a fire. However, he might think it a little
strange that they burned, while the rest of the study remained intact.

She knew how important her work was to him. If the books weren't in the black within a year, Jonathan stood to lose the ranch. She had to be accurate. She wrote Mary Ann Adams in Kansas City with her problems, and Mary Ann wrote back with suggestions.

After the second week, Kara took her lunch in the kitchen with Angela. The woman didn't talk much, but some company was better than no company. When Kara offered to stay a few minutes and help her finish the bread making, Angela seemed grateful. Lunchtime in the kitchen grew longer each day until Kara found herself spending her afternoons cooking.

The workings of the ranch kitchen were far more interesting than the bookkeeping. The huge bunkhouse also had a cook, a man named Smithy who thought the only bread was cornbread. Angela traded baked goods with him for smoked meats. He also rode into Brady twice a week for supplies for both kitchens.

Every Tuesday Angela cooked for what looked like an army. She filled baskets with bread and pies, and jars of stew, chili Smithy brought over and fresh vegetables from the winter stores in the cellar.

They loaded the baskets in a wagon, and Gideon made the rounds to the outposts where guards lived alone. By midafternoon, he returned with his wagon as full as when he'd left. The men sent fresh-cut pinion, freshly butchered meat, wild berries and flowers. Baskets and baskets of prairie flowers in bright yellows and blues.

One afternoon in late November, Kara wiped flour from her hands and ran to watch Gideon supervise the unloading. When he handed down the bright red blooms of Indian paintbrush, Kara laughed aloud. In a land of so little color, the sight of flowers was all the more beautiful.

"Are these for the house?" Kara hoped so. She'd love to have a few of them for the office. Anything would be better than the weed by the window that had suddenly taken a growing spurt thanks to daily coffee.

"Those are for you," Angela said without emotion as she stepped around the flowers and helped with the food. "It's the Old Guard's way of saying welcome."

"It can't be." Kara was overwhelmed. "I haven't even met the men on the outposts. They wouldn't be sending me these."

Angela stopped and stared at Kara with a frown. "They know about you. Word travels fast on this ranch. The men on the outskirts used to send Miss Victoria flowers in winter, too. There are places deep down in the ravines where they grow almost year-round. I heard one of the men tell Jonathan. I wouldn't waste my time looking."

Kara still couldn't believe the flowers were for her. "But I only work here. They wouldn't send me flowers. There must be some mistake."

Gideon and Angela looked at one another. Gideon winked. Something unsaid passed between them.

"What?" Kara felt left out of a secret.

Gideon lowered his eyes and faced Kara. "We all saw it," he finally answered as though his words made sense.

"Saw what?"

"Saw Mr. Catlin carry you in." He hesitated, as if being forced to explain the obvious. "No woman ever carried over the threshold has left."

Kara fought for words while Angela handed her two

baskets of flowers. "Oh, no. You don't understand. There's been some mistake. You're reading something into an action that meant nothing. You don't understand."

Angela and Gideon nodded their heads, showing no sign of listening to a word she said. Kara tried to explain about Devin O'Toole and how she got the job, but they just smiled like freshly fed house cats.

"Where's Mr. Catlin?" she finally demanded, realizing only Jonathan could straighten out this mess.

"He just rode in from Brady with the mail," Gideon said. "Would you like me to go get him for you, Miss Kara?"

She noticed it then. The way she'd been calling them by their first names and they called her "miss." The way they acted as if they were talking with the mistress of the house. Things she hadn't noticed came to mind. Angela always asked her what time she wanted each meal. The men waited for her to be seated at breakfast.

"No. I'll find him." Kara stormed across the yard. She'd get this corrected right now. She couldn't let the rest of the staff think there was something between her and Jonathan. Not when that was the furthermost thing from the truth.

THIRTEEN

JONATHAN SAW HER COMING FROM FIFTY FEET AWAY and climbed off his horse to wait for the storm. He had no idea what Miss O'Riley was angry about, but by her doubled-up fists and quick steps, there was no doubt she was on the warpath. And he was in her line of fire.

He'd watched Kara for weeks. The way she smiled so easily, the way she blushed when complimented, the way she tried not to act bothered when he stepped too near. He told himself watching Miss O'Riley was an interesting pastime, but he knew it had become a habit.

Kara stopped three feet from him and took a deep breath. "Mr. Catlin, I'd like a few words with you if ye have no objection."

Her green eyes danced with fire. He almost laughed, remembering the last time he'd seen them just that color. She had blamed him for breaking her shoe with his face.

"I'm busy, Miss O'Riley. Can it wait?" he said, just to watch the sparks fly. "I've got important business."

"It's waited long enough," she answered, moving a

step closer. "I'd like this straightened out now. It will only take a few minutes."

Jonathan glanced toward the bunkhouse. Half the cowhands on the place were listening. "Shall I follow you to the office, or should we walk a spell?"

Kara hesitated. "Walk." She stormed past him.

It never occurred to Jonathan to let loose of his horse's reins as they headed out the back gate of the corral. She stormed past the half-finished chapel by the Catlin cemetery and kept walking.

He didn't try to stop her when he figured they were well out of hearing range. He just let her march across the open pasture until, finally, her pace slowed.

When she faced him, anger still smoldered in her gaze, making everything about her sparkle with life. When he'd first seen her, he didn't remember thinking she was pretty. That was before he'd seen her angry.

Before she could speak, he asked politely, "Private enough?"

The sky was endless above them. Prairie stretched from horizon to horizon without a break. Wind whispering through the dry buffalo grass was the only sound. He knew she could feel the loneliness of the place. A loneliness he'd long ago begun to think of as comforting. If she wanted to talk in private, she picked the perfect place.

Kara nodded.

Jonathan waited.

Finally, she found her voice. "Everyone at the ranch thinks there is something between you and me. They . . ."

"Isn't there?" he said before she could add more. He

was worse than a kid blowing into the embers just to
see the fire flare, he decided, unable to hide his smile.

Her knuckles whitened. Her eyes blazed. "There is
not!" she snapped. "I am your employee. And, I'll thank
you to remember that I'm engaged to Devin O'Toole,
who is at this very minute waiting for me to return so
he can marry me."

"The one who's never kissed you? That Devin
O'Toole?" Jonathan asked for clarification as if he knew
of another. "The one with more important matters to
worry about than you?"

"Yes. No." She whirled to leave, then changed her
mind and faced him once more. "That's none of your
business, Mr. Catlin."

He guessed he'd hit on the truth, but Miss O'Riley
would never admit he was right about her Devin. To be
honest, he didn't want her to. In admitting she wasn't
on the top of Devin O'Toole's list, she somehow had to
accept it as fact.

"Why don't you call me Jonathan?" He shoved back
his hat, preparing to dance with a rattler. "After all, we
are living together."

The fire roared in her eyes once more, hot enough to
set the prairie on fire. He wouldn't have been surprised
if Kara took a swing at him.

But she just leaned closer and frowned. "That's another thing that's improper. No matter how big the house
is, it's not right for me to be staying there with you . . .
alone."

"Fair enough." He couldn't remember when he'd enjoyed an argument more. "Any other demands, Kara?"

"Yes. Explain to your staff that you hired me as the bookkeeper, nothing more."

"I'm not in the habit of explaining what I do to anyone. Anything else?"

"Aye."

The accent was back, warning him of her temper.

She leaned a bit closer and pointed her finger at his nose. "Stop staring at me."

He reached for her finger with his gloved hand but hesitated an inch before he touched her. "I'll try," he said aloud while mentally reminding himself not to make contact.

"Fair enough," she retreated.

"Is that all?"

She turned toward the headquarters. "Yes," she said as she started back the way they'd come.

"May I offer you a ride?" Jonathan swung into the saddle.

"I'll walk, thank you."

"All right." He pulled his hat low against the sun, wondering how long this formality would last. "Watch out for snakes."

With an exasperated sigh, she turned and raised her arms. Jonathan leaned low, circled her waist and lifted her up in front of him. He kicked the horse into action before she had time to protest.

She held on tightly until they reached the steps of the main house, and he enjoyed every minute.

When he reached the house, he pulled the reins hard, swung down even before the horse had stilled and lifted her from the saddle.

His actions were necessary, formal, he told himself,

nothing more. He was simply delivering her to safety. The nearness of her had no effect on him, he reminded himself . . . twice.

But when he lowered her, he brought her closer than necessary and he hesitated a moment before her feet touched the ground.

"Thank you, Mr. Catlin," she managed to say as formally as possible with Angela and Gideon snickering by the doorway.

"You're welcome, Miss O'Riley."

He tipped his hat and was gone before he broke out into a full laugh. The trouble was, he had no idea why.

After a few attempts, Kara gave up trying to explain anything to Angela and Gideon. The two were determined to believe something smoldered between her and Jonathan. When she tried to explain about the ride he'd given her from the prairie, they both just nodded their heads.

She retreated to the office and worked all afternoon on the books. At sunset, she went to the kitchen to say good night to Angela and eat her supper. As before, her meal waited on the stove. Angela always retreated to her house before night could fall.

Kara had just filled her plate when Snort walked through the back door carrying saddlebags over one shoulder and a rifle cradled in the bend of his arm.

"Evenin'." He grinned and sat the rifle by the door. "That smells mighty good, Miss Kara."

"Help yourself," she offered. "For some reason, Angela left far more than I can eat tonight."

Snort made himself at home. "Oh, she knew I was

coming as soon as I could get my gear together. H. B.'ll be here in a minute. He's collected too darn much to pack fast." Snort dusted his hands along his pant legs and reached for a plate as he continued talking. "When a man stays too long in one place, his pockets and bed-roll get too heavy. Pretty soon H. B. will have to have a wagon to haul his stuff, then a house to keep it in. Before he knows it he'll up and die leaving everyone else the problem of trying to figure out what to do with all he collected. A fellow has to be mighty careful about stuff accumulating."

Kara raised an eyebrow. Except for breakfast, the men always ate in the bunkhouse. Now Snort appeared in the kitchen, visiting as though he had all night.

Kara handed him a cup of coffee. "Please join me for supper before you have to go."

He accepted the drink and filled his plate. "Oh, I ain't going nowhere. We're bunking in here tonight." Snort sat on the stool across from her. "Boss told us about an hour ago that we were house guests for as long as you're here."

He glanced at her and misread her frown. "I know we ain't the most dependable pair. We do like to disappear for a night or two around payday. But don't you worry none, when we can't be here Willis or Luther will take the shift."

Before he could elaborate, H. B. banged across the back threshold. He had not only saddlebags but a huge cloth sack and a wooden box.

"Evenin'," he mumbled as he dropped everything he owned in a corner of Angela's freshly scrubbed kitchen. Dust circled above his belongings and then settled back.

He kept muttering to himself as he moved toward the stove. Kara couldn't tell if he were swearing or growling.

"Help yourself," Kara offered for the second time. "Any more of you gentlemen coming in for supper tonight?"

Snort laughed. "Nope. We're the two that lost the toss."

H. B. clanked his bowl on the table and sat down. He didn't look at anyone as he alternately ate and growled, reminding Kara of a half-wild dog afraid someone might try to steal his food. Snort bathed at least seasonally, but she wasn't too sure about H. B. He had an earthy smell about him that was probably ground-in manure and corral dirt. The little hair he had hadn't seen soap in years.

Kara looked at Snort for more explanation.

His smile stretched all the way to his gum line. "Not that we didn't want to come, mind you." Snort wiped his mouth on his sleeve. "It's just that we're used to our own beds in the bunkhouse."

"You're moving in here permanently?" Kara asked, surprised.

"Chaperones, that's what we are," H. B. said between bites. "Never in this lifetime did I think I'd sink so low."

"We go where we're needed," Snort argued, obviously trying to make the best of a terrible situation.

"What good are we gonna do? I ain't standing between two people if they wanna be together." H. B. swore again in a grumble. "No reason for us to be here, 'less he's forcing himself on the lady. Which seems unlikely, since he's the one who told us to move here."

Both men turned toward Kara. Snort whispered what

appeared to be on their minds. "He ain't, is he? Forcing you?"

"Of course not!" Kara stood. She found it hard to believe when she'd mentioned it not being proper for her and Jonathan to be in the house alone, he'd consider this the solution. "We don't need chaperones, because nothing is going on."

"If that's what you say, that's what we'll say." Snort pledged his allegiance.

"But that's how . . ." Kara stopped. She saw how hopeless her quest was. She turned and left the kitchen without another word.

After a quick check of the downstairs rooms, she knocked on Jonathan's door on the slight chance that he was already home. He moved so quietly she rarely heard him come in at night.

Kara had turned to walk away when he suddenly pulled the door open. He didn't say a word, only stood waiting.

Kara almost forgot what she'd been about to say. The man standing before her wore nothing above the waist. She'd seen bare chests a few times when she'd doctored her father and his friends after accidents at work, and she'd seen men wearing only undershirts. But she'd never thought a man would have answered the door, even in his own house, without pulling on a shirt.

She couldn't help but stare at his deeply tanned and muscular chest. The memory of the way his skin had felt the night he'd been injured and she'd taken care of his cuts . . . and she'd touched him . . . drifted through her mind. She'd felt the warmth of the sun on his flesh and the pounding of his heart just beneath.

"Are you all right, Miss O'Riley?" He folded a telegram he held.

She raised her gaze to his eyes. "I'm fine. I . . . it can wait until morning." Kara forced herself to return his stare and not look down again at the scars she'd once traced with her fingers.

"I'll be leaving in the morning," he said. "It appears I'm needed in Fort Worth as soon as I can get there. Wolf's sister wouldn't have sent me this telegram unless it was important."

"How far are we from Fort Worth?" The thought crossed her mind that enough time had passed that she could write Father James. If she could get a letter to him and the trouble was over, she could be on her way home before Christmas. She could leave this strange land and these strange people and return to all that was familiar.

"A day's ride in good weather. Two if it rains." Jonathan watched her closely, his face as unreadable as always. "Would you like to ride along? You could check out the records at the bank while we're there."

"Yes," she said without hesitation. The idea of staying with Snort and H. B. watching over her was not one she wanted to consider. And in truth, she'd be glad to leave this house with its noises and dark shadows.

Jonathan nodded. "I'll have a horse saddled for you at dawn." He closed the door without another word.

Kara hurried to her room. She had a letter to write. Her first communication with her family in over three months would have to be worded carefully, letting them know she was all right without giving away her location. A letter postmarked from Fort Worth would be safe to send. And she'd instruct them how to write back in care of the Widow Adams at Bayley's Mercantile in Kansas City. Mary Ann Adams would know how to slip a returning letter into a shipment headed for the Catlin Ranch. Kara had already sent Mary Ann a note saying anyone, except Devin O'Toole, of course, asking about a Karina or Kara O'Riley was to be given no information.

Kara slept little between worrying about the letter and fear that she might oversleep and be left behind. At first light, she was dressed and waiting in the foyer.

Snort stumbled down the stairs without his boots and trying to straighten his suspenders over his shoulders as he walked. He took one look at Kara and frowned. "Fort Worth," he mumbled. "I forgot, but as soon as I've had my coffee I'll be ready to go."

"Don't worry about it," Jonathan said from the top of the stairs. He was dressed and as always wearing a gun strapped to one leg. "We're leaving now. Willis and Newton are riding with us. We'll be fine."

Snort nodded but appeared disappointed. He was a man who looked like he believed that the greatest barn dance held in his lifetime was going to be the one he missed. "Willis is your best rider," Snort reasoned. "And Newton will have business in Fort Worth. There's probably no reason for me to tag along."

Jonathan glanced at Kara. "You ready, Miss O'Riley?"

She nodded, pulling on the leather gloves and wide-brimmed hat Angela had given her.

"We may hit bad weather." Jonathan took the stairs two at a time. "It smells like rain."

Kara pointed at the raincoat lying atop her small bag. She'd already thought of the weather.

Jonathan walked past her, picked up the bag, and opened the front door. As he'd mentioned, Jason Newton, the foreman, and Willis were waiting to act as guards. Kara couldn't help but wonder at the need for guards every time Jonathan left the ranch. She had a feeling it was necessary, but wasn't sure she wanted to ask why.

After a few moments of awkwardness, he helped her on her horse. She nodded her thanks. Silently, she agreed to a truce. There were times they'd have to touch, she told herself. It didn't have to mean anything and there was no changing what the others thought.

He tied her bag behind the saddle. "The bay is gentle." He checked her stirrup length, only brushing her ankle to insure the fit was right. "She'll give you no trouble."

Kara couldn't be sure if he was talking to the horse or her.

Jonathan looked at the doorway where Snort pouted. "We'll be back in three, four days at the most. Hold down the fort. I'm depending on you, Snort."

The old man straightened. "Yes, sir."

With dark clouds building in the northern sky, the small party rode out of the headquarters and turned west. Kara didn't dare mention how long it had been since she'd ridden, but she figured the others could tell. It took her an hour to get the feel of the horse but, slowly, the pastime she'd enjoyed as a child returned as a skill.

An hour before noon, they left Catlin land at the road and headed northwest. The weather turned ugly. Rain hung thick in the air. Jonathan stopped to check the horses and everyone pulled on coats.

"You all right?" he asked as he lowered her from the saddle so she could stretch her legs.

"Aye!" she answered, very much aware that he stood close as though making sure she had her footing. His body sheltered her against the rain, and she found herself wanting to stay beside him.

"Willis? Newton?" Jonathan slowly moved away from her.

Both men answered that all was well, even though now the storm was so noisy, Kara could barely hear them. She stroked the bay's neck while Jonathan checked the horse's hooves.

"We'll hit shelter at the Riney Place a half-mile away." He looked directly at her. "Everyone ready to ride?"

Kara fought the hem of her skirt to reach the stirrup. Before she could pull herself up, Jonathan moved behind her and lifted her with ease.

"Thanks."

He touched his gloved hand to his hat and stepped away.

Kara suddenly had to concentrate on her actions. The road became a muddy river and lightning flickered all around them, spooking the horses. She held the reins tight, staying alert as she followed closely behind Jonathan.

In a flash of sudden brightness, lightning struck the ground fifty feet in front of them, firing the earth for a second before rain drenched the spark. For a time, the storm was silent, then thunder rattled in deafening rage as though competing for attention with the lightning.

Kara pulled her horse under control, fighting to stay seated as he danced in the mud. The mount behind her stomped the ground and reared. Newton shouted at Willis. The old man lost control and tumbled from the horse. The animal circled wildly, frightened and without direction.

Newton and Jonathan were on the ground in a second, shouting and shooing the horse from Willis's twisted body.

Kara slid down as soon as she could and ran to the others. A scream caught in the back of her throat, strangled by fear.

Willis rocked from side to side in the mud.

"Where are you hurt?" She knelt beside him, trying to help him sit up.

He didn't answer. He fought a battle with a force far darker than the storm. His movements were jerky, as if he took blows from an unseen assailant.

Kara tried to hold him tight, but he rocked from her arms and twisted in the mud.

Jonathan was on the man's other side trying to calm him. "Can you ride?" Jonathan asked. "Willis! Can you understand? We have to get out of this weather."

Willis didn't answer. He raised his face to the rain, as though he didn't feel the water pounding.

"Can you stand?" Jonathan asked without expecting an answer. He glanced at Kara. "We have to get him up."

Willis melted against Kara's side suddenly, too tired to hold his head up a moment longer. He curled against her like a frightened child.

"We've got to get him out of this storm!" Newton lifted Willis slowly.

Jonathan agreed as he stood and offered his hand to Kara. When his strong fingers closed around hers, she realized how badly she was shaking, unsure whether it was from fear or cold.

Jonathan helped Newton lift Willis onto a horse. The old man seemed to be made of rags. He offered no protest, no voice in answer. The foreman swung up behind him. Jonathan grabbed the reins of all three of the men's horses and began plowing through the mud, into the rage of the tempest.

He shouted back to Kara. "Can you manage?"

"Yes," she answered as she calmed the bay.

Kara fought her skirts and climbed back into her saddle. She brought up the rear, staying close lest they disappear into the sheets of rain now washing against them like waves.

An eternity passed before they reached the Riney place, half a mile away through mud. The rain beat every ounce of energy from her. When she finally slid from the saddle, she wasn't sure she had the strength to stand. The men had more important things than her to worry about. She'd make it.

The Riney farmhouse and barn, huddling together on the plains, had long ago been abandoned. Newton explained earlier that James Riney and his wife moved to Austin when Riney had been elected to the House of Representatives. Talk was he'd run for governor someday, Newton said, maybe even president. But one thing was certain . . . he'd never come back to farming or to this hard prairie life.

While Jonathan took the horses, Newton carried Willis into what was left of the one-room house. Most of the window glass had broken out. The openings let in watery light barely better than twilight even though it couldn't be much past three. The back door flapped on one leather hinge. Half the roof had caved in on a bedroom loft, but the downstairs remained dry.

The fireplace stood intact. Newton built a fire while Kara tried to make Willis comfortable close to the hearth. The thin old man didn't appear to have broken any bones, but he couldn't move one side of his body and speech came hard and slow. A bruise darkened from his hairline to his eyebrow, discoloring most of his forehead, but there was no cut. As if calling loved ones from the past, he mumbled names she'd never heard. When Kara took his hand in hers, no grip returned her hold.

She was afraid he'd catch pneumonia if she wrapped him in a wet bedroll; all their clothes were soaked. She decided it would be better to keep him close to the fire and let his clothes dry on him. Though he kept mumbling, he didn't seem in great pain.

Kara used pieces of broken furniture to make a circle around Willis. She then placed all their wet blankets over the furniture to dry and to offer some shelter from the wind that whipped through the house.

She found supplies in a leather bag Jonathan brought in with the saddles. A small coffee pot, coffee beans, fresh bread and ham wrapped in one of the kitchen towels. If Kara were guessing, she'd say Angela had made the old man bring the supplies along just in case they were needed.

Within minutes the room warmed and filled with the

smell of coffee. She tried to get Willis to eat, but he didn't seem to understand what she wanted. The old man closed his eyes and turned his head away.

Newton drank the coffee but turned down any offer of food. He talked to Willis like the man might roll over and say something at any minute. As time passed, Kara grew more worried.

"Isn't there something we can do?" she asked.

Newton shook his head. "Even without the storm, we're hours from a doc. I'm not sure he'd live long if we tried to move him now. It'll be dark soon and we wouldn't be able to see the road. There's nothing we can do until the storm lets up."

Doing nothing wasn't an option Kara could accept. She buttoned her coat and went to find Jonathan. Surely he could think of something . . . anything . . . to do besides watching Willis die.

FOURTEEN

K<small>ARA</small> FOUND JONATHAN IN THE BARN RUBBING down the horses with old straw. She knew he heard her come in, but he didn't turn around. In the watery light, she saw him only in shadows. Long, lean, powerful shadows.

"Willis is bad," she said. "The fall must have hurt him inside. There's nothing Newton or I can think to do for him but try and keep him warm."

Jonathan never stopped working. "The fall didn't hurt him. A man like him, who's lived his life on a horse, doesn't just fall, even in a storm. The illness struck him first, then he fell. It wasn't the mount or the storm."

"How do you know?" She was surprised by Jonathan's coldness in stating what he believed were the facts.

"When I was a boy and lived among the Indians for a time, once I saw an old man like Willis is now, unable to move one side of his body."

"But why?"

"My Apache father said it was because one half of the man stepped into the afterlife. No one can live long when one half has already gone. Unless he comes back, there is nothing we can do."

"How much longer do you think he has?" she breathed the words.

"I don't know." He stopped working and looked toward her. "The old man of the tribe lingered for a while, his spirit in both worlds."

Kara shivered from sudden cold. Before she had time to think, she closed the distance between them.

He stood rooted in place as she pressed the length of her body against his, then circled his neck with her arms. Slowly, as though he were figuring out what to do, he put his arms around her.

The warmth of him passed through her, and she leaned into his chest, letting him keep them balanced. His stance widened. His grip tightened around her. He smelled of rain and damp leather and horses, but he felt wonderful so close. He was a solid anchor in the storm.

Neither moved for a long while. They just held one another, both lost in their own private fears.

Finally, Jonathan placed his arm around her shoulder and sheltered her through the rain to the house.

Newton looked up when they entered. The fire in the hearth was bright and lit the room in streamers of light.

"How is he?" Kara asked as she slipped between the curtain of drying blankets.

"Better, I think," Newton said without much conviction. He was a big man who tended to rock from side to side when upset.

Kara knelt so that she could brush her hand along

Willis's cheek. She felt no fever, only the warm tickle of his breath against her fingers. When the blankets dried, they covered him so that he wouldn't get cold. The sky turned a few shades darker into night, and the temperature dropped.

Kara sat beside Willis in case he stirred. Finally, she heard him snoring. Newton made a bed on the left side of the fire where the floor was dry. Jonathan used his coat as cover and one of the saddles as a pillow. He slept close to the door, like a guard. She debated where to sleep. The choices were few, and the memory of Jonathan's warm hug drew her. But she wasn't sure he'd welcome her a second time. He didn't have to tell her he was not a man who usually hugged anyone.

She leaned against the warm rocks of the hearth and wrapped her arms around her knees. Curled into a ball, she tried to sleep. She'd never felt so alone, so far from her home.

The letter in her pocket reminded her that she might be heading home soon. They'd get the mail. She could almost see Father James rushing it over to her father where the priest knew he had supper, maybe at the pub, maybe at his cousins' house. Everyone would huddle around to read a letter from Karina, whom they all repeatedly testified to how dearly they missed. Maybe they'd volley over who should go after her. And, of course, they'd let Devin win. After all, he would be her husband soon. He'd come for her, declaring his love forever and sweeping her off her feet in a huge bear hug. He'd take her home to a grand party in her honor. Her father would say he was sorry he'd sent her away, that he wished he'd kept her close even in the time of trouble.

Kara tugged the letter from her pocket, still lost in her daydream. All her neighbors and cousins would be fine. They'd claim the worst of the feud was her absence and the loss of her cooking. Life would return to normal. She'd go back to working at the bakery before dawn and walking home with the smell of fresh bread surrounding her. And she'd have her tea by the fire before she started her day. All just like before.

Kara looked down at the letter . . . the proof that her daydream could come true.

The paper was damp in her fingers, the ink erased by trails of water that had run like tiny rivers down the envelope.

She gulped down a sob and held the letter close as if she could forget the damage and the dream would return.

But it didn't. No one was on his way to get her. No party waited. No one knew where she was and she wasn't sure anyone even cared.

She lifted the letter and dropped it into the fire. In truth, she was in the middle of nowhere, hungry and tired, with a man who might die only a few feet from her. Did anyone really care about her? Would anyone miss her?

As the paper burned, she hugged her knees tightly to her and lowered her head against her muddy skirt. Tears flowed as silently as the rain. Her body shook with loneliness. Her arms clenched around her as though holding on, less she disappear completely.

The reality that she might not have been sent away because they valued her dearly, but because she was in the way registered against her heart. And Devin had never come to call on her . . . just her. . . . He'd always simply passed by her on his way to see her father. If she died in this abandoned shack in this wild country, no one would notice, except, maybe, some Sunday one of her cousins would ask, "Whatever happened to those great biscuits we used to have?"

She could never remember her father saying he loved her, just that she should stop questioning him. Or Devin saying anything to her except that he'd marry her one day. When he had time, she thought. *If* he had time.

Exhaustion and fear struggled within her as her imagination visualized the worst. Kara fought back the sobs. She wasn't weak, she told herself. She could face the truth. What if no one cared? What if even the angels no longer had time to watch over her?

From the blackness of her world, strong arms lifted her. Jonathan pulled her up to him, letting her tears fall against his chest. Then, he held her tightly as though the bands of his arms could protect her against the world, against her dreams, against her fears.

"Kara," he whispered near her ear, no louder than a prayer.

The warmth of his voice brushed her cheek.

She wrapped her arms around his neck and let him lift her. He didn't ask a question or offer advice. He didn't tell her to stop being foolish like her father would have. He simply carried her away from the burning letter and into the shadows.

She wanted to apologize for crying, but he didn't seem to want, or need, words. He carefully placed her atop his coat and pulled her damp raincoat over them both. Then, he wrapped his arms around her and whispered, "Go to sleep, darlin'."

Kara had never been more awake in her life. She could hear Jonathan's heart pounding beneath her ear. One of his arms rested just below her breasts. And his hand gently touched her cheek as his breathing slowed to the rhythm of sleep.

Her imagination turned from wallowing in an ocean of self-pity to jumping onto a ship of fear. What if he moved in his sleep? Only an inch and he'd be touching her breasts. If she let herself fall asleep, there was no telling what might happen. What would Newton think if they were wrapped up together at dawn?

The warmth of his body calmed her. His slow steady breathing relaxed her. She stayed awake as long as she could, then finally decided if Jonathan Catlin planned to take liberties, he was sure taking his time about it. Maybe she should sleep.

Jonathan slipped away from Kara's side just before dawn. He checked on Willis, who still slept soundly, then hurried to saddle the horses. He wanted to be on the road as soon as possible. They were still three, maybe four hours out of Fort Worth.

Twenty minutes later, Jonathan watched the sun lighten the sky from what was left of the Rineys' barn loft. The world sparkled with dampness, making everything around him seem newborn. He never tired of the ever-changing weather. Somehow, in its inconsistency, the weather was one of the few constants in his life. No matter where he was, the seasons, the storms, the sunrises and sunsets were a constantly shifting canvas that spread like a balm across his soul.

He wished his life could have a new dawn with all the past washed away. What would it be like to wake up one morning with no memories haunting him? He would give all he owned to be fool enough to believe in forever . . . or to love and think it might last . . . or to build a home and know it would stand. Experience had taught him otherwise. Nothing lasts and the more you care about something, or someone, the more it hurts when they're gone.

Then why had he held Kara last night?

He told himself it was because she looked so pitiful crying by the fire. There was no doubt she'd been frightened and alone. He told himself he'd only been trying to help her. She mattered little to him. No more than any employee. He hadn't asked for the burden of the ranch and all its people and problems, but he'd accepted it.

But why did he have to call her "darlin'?" An endearment he'd heard men use for women they cared about? A word he doubted he'd ever said aloud in his life.

Jonathan was tired of arguing with himself. He was obviously conversing with an idiot. There were more important matters with which to contend. Like getting Willis to a doctor as fast as possible and reaching Wolf's sister while there was still time to help. If Nichole McLain needed him, he had to get there as fast as possible.

When he turned from the sunrise, he noticed Kara standing behind him, her fists balled at her waist, her stance wide. She was preparing to fight, and he wasn't in the mood.

"About last night," she began.

"Last night never happened," he hissed as he brushed past her. The last thing he wanted was to have to tell her why he'd held her. If he did that, the next thing he'd be admitting was how many other times he'd almost touched her and how the boundaries he'd insisted on were imprisoning him far more than her.

The squeal and Irish swear she let out made him smile as he climbed from the loft. He almost reconsidered not taking time to argue. She was obviously in a state this morning.

When he saw her five minutes later in the house, he knew she was furious with him. She wouldn't even look at him directly and addressed all her questions to Newton.

Jonathan didn't try to explain. He reminded himself he never explained. Let her be mad. The angrier she was at him, the better their chances of staying away from one another. She wanted, all women wanted, something he couldn't give . . . tenderness . . . forever.

Willis had improved, but was very weak. Jonathan and Newton decided it would be better to take him on to Fort Worth. There, Nichole's husband could take a look at Willis while Jonathan found out what Nichole needed. She wouldn't have sent for him unless it was important. Her husband, Adam McLain, was the finest doctor in the state.

Jonathan and Newton decided to take turns riding double with Willis. With luck they could be in Fort Worth by noon.

Jonathan locked his arm around Willis and held the reins in his other hand. He watched Kara struggling with her skirt as she climbed onto her horse. He wished he could help her. If she took to riding, he'd have the low bench brought out from the barn. His grandmother once used it as a step to mount. The old men said Victoria Catlin could ride like a champion when she was younger. He'd like to see Kara ride just for the pleasure of it.

She handled a horse well for one not used to doing so, but what amazed him was that she never complained. They'd gone through hell yesterday, and she hadn't said a word. Yet when he'd held her and kept her warm, she'd been ready to fight. He found the contrast interesting.

They rode in silence for an hour. Willis would straighten and try to take the reins, then tire and fall asleep. Jonathan held him securely in the saddle.

An hour outside Fort Worth, Newton traded horses and took a shift behind Willis. As Jonathan swung into the saddle, he saw three riders coming fast from the direction of the town.

He pointed with his head, making Newton aware of them also. Both men unstrapped the leather loop holding their weapons in place.

As the riders neared, Jonathan recognized one of the men. A ranger who'd traveled with Wolf years ago.

"Catlin?" The ranger pulled his horse to a stop. Two men hung back several yards, their hands near the grips of their sidearms.

"Yes." Jonathan noticed the ranger carefully studied

them. He'd have to be blind not to see that they had an injured man. "It's Ranger Davis, isn't it?"

Davis smiled, knowing he had the right party. He signaled his men that all was well. "I was sent to locate you. You've changed considerably in the years since I've seen you. You were expected last night at the McLain place."

"As you can see, we ran into some trouble." Jonathan remembered Davis had been with Wolf and Wes one night when they'd hauled him out of jail at Fort Griffin. He wasn't surprised Davis had trouble recognizing him. Jonathan had changed, at least on the outside. "We've got a man in need of care."

Davis moved his horse closer. "I've orders to escort you as fast as possible to the springs known as Willow Brakes, south of town. Mrs. McLain will meet you there."

Jonathan sensed something was wrong. Nichole McLain rarely left her husband's side. "Where's Adam McLain?" he asked. Adam was one of the few doctors in Texas who just might be able to help Willis.

"He's in town. There wasn't time for Nichole to tell him she was leaving. He was at the hospital when the jail break happened. Nichole followed the prisoner and I followed her." The ranger looked like he was afraid he would say too much in front of the others. "My men can get the old fellow to Dr. McLain, but it's imperative you come with me."

Newton interrupted. "I'll ride with Willis to town, Boss. You go with the ranger."

Jonathan nodded. He and Newton had known the

McLains for years. If they called for help, it was time
to ride and ask questions later.

Davis's gaze took in Kara. "What about her?"

"She goes with me," Jonathan answered. He had no
idea what he'd be riding into, but Newton would have
his hands full with Willis. There was no way to get Kara
back to the ranch safely, so she'd have to stay with him.

Davis nodded, then moved back to talk to his men.

Jonathan swung from his horse and walked to Kara.
He knew she'd been too far away to hear the exchange,
but to her credit, she didn't look as frightened as he
guessed she might be.

Jonathan placed his gloved hand over hers where they
rested on the saddle horn. "The man with Willis and
Newton is a Texas Ranger named Davis. He's a friend
of Wolf's. He asked me to go with him to meet Wolf's
sister, Nichole McLain. She's a fine lady." Jonathan tried
to keep his voice calm. The last thing he wanted to do
was frighten Kara. "She asked for my help, and I'd like
you to ride along with me."

He thought he'd done a fine job of laying out the
facts.

She nodded slowly. He guessed she knew her choices
were limited. The men with Davis looked rough. They
were probably hard-riding rangers, but to Kara they
could have been robbers or killers. This was not a country where it was easy to tell the law-abiding from the
outlaws. And, with rangers, it was always hard to tell
the saints from the sinners. Jonathan learned long ago to
judge a man by his actions and not his appearance.

Within minutes, they were following Davis across
open country. The ranger kept the pace fast. Jonathan

slowed, putting Kara between him and Davis. If she tired, he wanted to know it before she fell off her horse.

In less than an hour, they reached a line of willow trees that marked the springs. Jonathan knew the place well. As a boy he camped by the springs with the Apache. It was not on any road or near any town, so the land was still untouched. He could almost feel himself stepping back into the time of his youth.

"They're over here." Davis guided his horse into the willows. He swung down and tied his horse to a tree.

Jonathan did the same, then helped Kara down. They walked toward the sound of water.

Kara kept close to Jonathan. She felt like she was entering a world she hadn't known existed. She'd grown up walking in parks and visiting in the country around Pittsburgh from time to time, but none of the land looked like this. Something about it seemed wild and untouched.

As Jonathan passed between two branches, he took her hand. His fingers were firm. Kara made no protest. She had no idea what they might walk into as they moved deeper among the trees until even the sun was held at bay by the branches.

Suddenly, staying home with Snort and H. B. didn't seem like such a bad idea.

As they moved toward a clearing, Jonathan pulled her close. "Stay back in the tree line and you'll be safe," he whispered. "I'll let you know when it's safe to step out."

He glanced at Davis who nodded agreement.

"I'll stay out of sight as well," Davis whispered. "I wouldn't want to frighten the prisoner more, if that's possible."

Kara hadn't heard about any prisoner, but she was too frightened to ask questions.

Jonathan took another step. His fingers tightened for a moment, then let go of her hand. She strained to look around him.

The sight shook her to the core. A woman, dressed in a black shirt and trousers, perched on a rock the height of a chair, a Colt strapped to her side. Her gloved hand held the end of a rope. A younger woman with wild hair knelt beside the rock. A blanket circled around her thin shoulders. The other end of the rope hung about her neck.

Kara watched in horror. The woman in black stood when Jonathan stepped into the clearing. The young woman huddled further into the blanket, pulling on the rope like an animal.

"Thank God you're here," the woman in black said to Jonathan. "I only had my horse's lead rope with me. I didn't know how long I could keep her without handcuffs or chains."

"I came as soon as I could, Nichole." Jonathan didn't say a word about the rope. "Does she speak any English?"

"No," Nichole answered. "She must have been captured very young. All she wants to do is escape and go back to what she believes are her people. But as near as I can find in the records, the tribe she was traveling with has been moved to the reservation in the Oklahoma Territory. The Indian Agents would never let her in, even if we could find the people she'd been living with."

Jonathan nodded, as if he'd heard the story before.

Kara looked closely at the young woman on the

ground, who couldn't have been out of her teens. If her hair had been clean, it might be more blond than brown. She huddled into a ball, as if protecting something in her lap. She showed no sign of understanding what the others said. For a moment Kara thought the creature must be simple-minded, or insane. She'd heard of people going mad and thinking of themselves as animals.

When Jonathan squatted several feet in front of the young woman, she let out a low sound and pulled the blanket around her. Only the rope about her neck kept her from running.

"Who had her?" Jonathan asked Nichole.

"Apache, we think. I would have asked your sister to come in and try to talk to her, but Allie's too far along with child to travel. This woman showed up at Fort Supply a week ago. They brought her down to Fort Worth because they'd heard I've had some luck with finding families. Somewhere along the line someone put that dress on her, because I'd bet she wasn't captured in it."

Jonathan agreed. "The rag looks like others I've seen. Well-meaning women of the forts force them on both Indians and girls thought to have been kidnapped from settlements as children. The soldiers' wives seemed to believe that once the children have on proper clothes they'll forget the years they've lived and return to 'civilization.' "

Kara didn't miss the bitterness in his voice and wondered if there was a time he'd huddled on the ground with a rope around his neck.

"She's done everything to escape." Nichole rubbed her eyes, exhausted. "I'm afraid if she tries again, she'll kill herself. If it wasn't for the child, she'd probably have already ended her life."

"Child?" Jonathan leaned closer.

Nichole nodded. "She's cradling a little one in that blanket. A girl, I think. Adam tried to get a look at her to make sure she was all right. Our little mother here went crazy. I thought I could help. I waited until the jail was quiet and tried to get close to her. She broke and ran. I followed, trying not to hurt her but not letting her free."

"If you had let her go, chances are good she'd die out here all by herself without supplies. The baby would never make it."

Nichole held the rope to Jonathan. "Can you help?"

He didn't take the offering. "I'll try."

Kara watched in disbelief as he sat down a few feet from the wild creature. He talked to her in a language Kara had never heard.

At first the woman appeared to argue. She shouted and waved her hands and cried out as though she were swearing at the world.

Then, slowly, she began to listen to Jonathan.

Finally, she turned her head toward Nichole.

"She thinks we will kill the baby when we see that it is Indian," Jonathan translated.

"Is it hers?" Nichole asked.

Jonathan nodded. "But she thinks the soldiers, and now us, will take the baby from her."

A sob escaped Kara. She realized by what Jonathan and Nichole were not saying that there was a possibility the woman's fears were true.

"We can't take her back to the fort," Nichole finally

said. "The sheriff can't find any kin who'll claim her. She's so wild, I think they are considering the hospital in Austin for the insane."

"They'll take the baby for sure then," Jonathan added. "And she'll be treated like an Apache child." He hesitated and finished the scenario, "And the mother *will* go insane."

"Can you talk to her?" Nichole asked.

"I'll try, but you were right about her wanting to kill herself. She saw her husband die in the raid. If it weren't for the child, she'd already be with him in death."

Jonathan turned back to the woman and spoke to her once more. Slowly, as the shadows grew long, she calmed. She didn't panic when Jonathan untied the rope about her neck.

He motioned for Kara to enter the clearing and appeared to introduce her to the woman. Davis had disappeared a few hours before. He now returned with supplies, but he stood at the tree line and handed them to Kara.

When Kara offered water to the captive, the young woman drank a little and gave the rest to her child.

Nichole smiled at Kara, but they didn't speak. There would be time to talk later.

Finally, Jonathan stood. "You lost her in the woods," he said to Nichole. "She got away without a trace."

Nichole nodded.

"She got away?" Jonathan asked, then turned to Davis knowing the ranger would understand what he asked.

Davis agreed to the lie.

"I'll take her back to the ranch with me. No one will

look for her there. At least for a time the child and she will be safe."

"What then?"

Jonathan looked torn. "If, in a few months, she still wants to go back with the Apache, I'll take her to Indian Territory myself."

"It won't work, Jonathan. She belongs here." Nichole closed her eyes for a moment but when she looked up the sadness was still there. "She can never go back. Even if you could find what's left of the tribe, they wouldn't accept her. They might even blame her for the raid. There are those on the reservation who hate enough to kill her."

"She can't go back, and her baby can't stay." Jonathan lashed out at Nichole. "Why don't you just cut the woman in half now and save her the pain of having to rip herself apart." The fury in his voice shook the clearing.

To Kara's surprise, Nichole didn't look the least upset. She stood slowly and wrapped her arms around Jonathan's shoulders. "It's all right," she whispered like a mother. "We'll find a way. Jonathan, we'll find a way."

He nodded, but his eyes told Kara he didn't believe Nichole.

FIFTEEN

Darkness settled over the clearing. Davis built a fire and brought in the rest of the supplies he'd picked up in town. Kara made coffee, then sliced meat and bread. Jonathan talked with the captive.

Kara walked to the stream to wash the coffeepot.

Nichole followed. She was a tall, beautiful woman—every ounce a lady, even in her strange clothes. She had an easy, southern way of talking that made Kara like her instantly. Though ten years older than Kara, she didn't make her feel like a child.

They both had black hair and green eyes. If it weren't for the fact that Nichole stood a head taller, they could be sisters. Everything about Nichole silently said she was a woman of worth, valued by both family and, judging from Davis's respectful tones, the community.

Kara felt comfortable as they knelt side by side at the stream.

"I see your influence on our Jonathan," Nichole com-

THE TEXAN'S DREAM 169

mented casually. "The anger is not as great within him when he looks at you."

"It's not me," Kara rushed to explain. "I'm only the bookkeeper on the Catlin Ranch. I don't matter to him."

Nichole raised an eyebrow. "I suggest you stop looking in the mirror and look into his eyes. You'll see yourself far more clearly."

Kara changed the subject. She had no idea how to respond to Nichole's advice. "Will you come with us to the ranch?"

"No," Nichole answered. "I have to get back to Fort Worth, but Adam and I will come as soon as we can. The child inside the folds of that blanket looks healthy enough, but I'd like Adam to examine her, as well as the mother. After she's talked with Jonathan a while maybe she'll let us near her child."

They moved back to the clearing and said their goodbyes. Davis stood, preparing to escort Nichole home. She didn't move toward the captive, but crossed her hands, palm up, in a sign of peace as she'd seen Jonathan do.

The captive held her crying baby close and gave no sign in return.

After they left, Kara wasn't sure what to do, but she wanted to help. She pulled a comb from her bag and moved behind the woman.

At first, the filthy woman was suspicious. Slowly, she let Kara work the tangles out of the ends of her hair. Kara tried to be gentle but it must have been days since the hair had been touched.

The woman talked to Jonathan, and he laughed.

Kara glanced at him with a raised eyebrow. "What did she say?"

"She said my woman is kind. You will make a good mother." Jonathan hesitated, then translated. "She said I should keep your belly rounded with my sons."

Kara blushed.

By the time she got all the tangles out of the captive's hair, her arms ached. Jonathan cut two strips of leather from his saddle and handed them to the woman so she could braid her hair.

"What do we call her?" Kara asked him.

"By her name. It translates simply to Dawn." He repeated his words in Apache.

The woman nodded. With her hair combed and fear gone from her eyes, she looked even younger.

"I have a change of clothes in my bag. Should I offer them to her?"

Jonathan shook his head. "She'd see it as an insult. I promised her leather to make new clothes as soon as we get to the ranch. I think that might keep her from running, at least for tonight. She doesn't want to go back to her people in what she calls 'white women's rags.' "

"Does she know she can't go back?" Kara wondered if her own situation was the same. If her father had been killed in a fight, there would be nothing to return to. The thought of moving into her cousins' homes seemed little better than starving. Not that they wouldn't be kind. But she'd seen how homeless relatives were treated by everyone. For the rest of her life she'd sleep where there was room and do the work no one else in the house wanted to do.

"I'll tell her there's no going back later. Right now,

we need to let her know she's safe with us."

He pulled a knife from his belt and offered it to Dawn, handle first, saying something Kara didn't understand.

Dawn nodded and spread her blanket beside the fire. She cradled her child close and lay the knife within easy reach.

Kara gathered her traveling bag and walked down to the spring. It had been two days since she'd combed her own hair. She guessed it might look almost as bad as Dawn's had. She unwound it from the bun and combed her long strands free. The strokes felt good running along her scalp. Then, she removed her jacket and opened her blouse so she could wash with a tiny ball of soap she'd found on the washstand in her room one night.

The water was cold against her skin, but felt wonderful. The soap smelled of roses.

She glanced toward the clearing. Jonathan sat with his back to her.

Kara unbuttoned her blouse and continued washing. She was careful to leave on enough clothes so she could quickly become presentable if she heard someone coming.

When she finished, she pulled her hair over her shoulder and twisted it into one long braid.

"I like your hair like that," Jonathan said from just behind her. He'd moved close without making a sound.

Kara stood. Her fingers fumbled as she frantically tried to pull her blouse together. "I didn't hear you."

"I just wanted to thank you for all you did today." With the fire at his back, she couldn't see his features.

"I didn't do . . ."

"You did more than you know." He watched while she buttoned her blouse as though he found the action fascinating. "You have a way about you. Dawn was right, a mothering way. In your worrying over whether everyone is fed or cared for, you make people feel comfortable. I think it's a gift."

Kara didn't know what to say. She'd mothered her father and sick cousins from age eleven after her own mother died. No one had ever thanked her for it. It was just something she did. Most young girls would have hated the routine of running a house, but Kara found it calming, satisfying.

She thought it strange that no one except this man ever took the time to notice or to appreciate. Even her father would come home to a clean house, with a meal on the table and ask her what she did with herself all day.

"Were you like Dawn?" she asked before she lost her nerve.

"Worse," he answered. "Far worse. I fought everyone. At one point Wolf tied me to the floor in a barn for days. I hated him for it, but looking back I see how his action might have saved my life. But at the time, all I wanted was to be free. To run wild. I was like Dawn. I wanted to get back to my people and a way of life I understood."

"But eventually, you calmed down and made a life."

"No." His laughter sounded sad. "I'm still the same inside. And my chains are the 'white man's rags' I still wear."

Though he said the words calmly, she watched him, knowing there was more than a grain of truth in what he said. He used the "touch of a savage" others thought they saw in him to keep people away. But what if it were really a part of him?

She moved beside him and saw his face in the firelight. Her heart slammed into her rib cage. Smoky eyes cried out with need, a longing so great it frightened her.

She moved to pass him. She wasn't sure she wanted to see the savage in him. He both drew her near and frightened her as no one ever had in her life.

When she stepped around him, his hand closed over her arm. "Stay," he whispered. "Stay with me."

She jerked free, tasting panic in her throat.

As she hurried away, she heard him whisper, "Then stay away."

The ride back to the ranch was made in almost complete silence. Kara tried to figure out the two different men who lived inside of Jonathan. One was kind, thoughtful, considerate. The other sharp, angry, savage.

It crossed her mind that he might be mad. But, if so, she seemed to be the only one to bring it out in him. His men respected him. Nichole and Wolf loved him like a brother.

Maybe she was the one going mad. She'd been in this wild country too long. Except for the night he kissed her so passionately, he never made advances. And as far as she could remember, she had touched him first that night. Maybe she was like some kind of poison that infected him?

He'd been the only man who ever acted like he wanted to kiss her, and here she was thinking he must be mad. If Devin O'Toole had ever made an advance, would she have tried to have him committed?

The thought crossed her mind that maybe the next time he asked her to stay, she'd linger a little longer and see if it were the wild man or the tender one who moved closer.

She pondered the possibility for most of the journey and finally decided she'd probably never have the opportunity to find out.

They made good time and reached the ranch house well before sunset. Jonathan talked Dawn slowly into the house while Angela ran upstairs and got the room next to Kara ready for the woman and her child. The hands and retired rangers stared from the safe distance of the bunkhouse, but no one said a word.

An hour later, Jonathan, Dawn and Kara sat by the fireplace in Dawn's room and ate supper off a tablecloth spread on the floor. Once in a while, Jonathan would tell Kara what Dawn said and how strange she thought everything was, but mostly they spoke in Apache.

When the baby cried, Jonathan stood and offered his hand to Kara. "Maybe we should say good night?"

Jonathan showed Dawn how to work the lock so she would feel safe. She shook her head until, finally, he gave her his knife, and all was right.

After Dawn closed her door, Kara and Jonathan stood alone for a moment in the hallway, both tired, both wondering what to say to the other.

Jonathan finally broke the silence. "I've some work to do before I sleep. I'll have a bath sent up if you like."

"That would be nice." She didn't meet his eyes. "Good night."

"I'll be downstairs if you need me," he said and

turned away. "Call me if you hear anything from Dawn's room."

"Like what?"

"Never mind. If she's leaving, you'll never hear her go. No one will. My guess is she'll stay, at least for a while. I'll notify the guard that no one goes near her if she ventures from her room. I don't want anyone frightening her again."

The cold, angry man was back, she thought, and wished there was something she could say to mend things between them.

H. B. and Snort's voices reached her and she noticed the pair heading up the stairs. Kara hurried to her room. She didn't feel like answering any questions tonight, and Snort looked like a man wanting answers. He'd been a sheriff in San Antonio and questioned everything and everyone around him.

An hour later, as she bathed in warm water, the stress of the past few days seeped from her. Kara dressed for bed, then sat at her tiny desk rewriting the letter to her father.

When she finished, the house was silent. Kara slipped on her robe and tiptoed down the hallway, thinking if she left her letter in the foyer where Angela always put the supply list, it might go out early with a rider headed toward Brady. The mercantile clerk would put it in a mail bag loaded onto the stage. All mail was transferred to the train in Fort Worth. In less than a week it would be in Kansas City where Mary Ann would forward it on to Father James. So many steps. So many chances for one small envelope to be lost. She'd take that chance, Kara reasoned. She had to contact her father.

The sounds of a mother comforting her child drifted from Dawn's room. Snort and H. B. were both snoring. No light shone from beneath Jonathan's door, so she guessed all were asleep. The lights in the hallway helped, but something bothered Kara about the house. The dark hallways and shadowy corners never welcomed her.

She hurried through her task, returning to her room as quickly as possible. As Angela suggested, Kara locked the door behind her, feeling as though she'd run through a haunted house.

Kara had the same feeling when she walked the hallway two weeks later with a letter to Mary Ann in her pocket. Jonathan had kidded her that she spent all her salary on stamps, but almost every time the mail went out, a letter went to Kansas City. And one of Mary Ann's always seemed to be in the mail coming in.

Tonight she'd written her friend all about what Christmas would be like on the Catlin Ranch. From the moment Angela had told her, Kara looked forward to the day. The McLains would come, along with Wolf and his family. For once the old house would be filled with life.

Kara placed Mary Ann's letter on the table and started back toward her room. When she reached the door to the great room, a sound caught her attention. A muffled thumping came from the area by the windows.

Deciding it must be a loose shutter, Kara felt her way across the room. On most nights, the glow from a dying fire would have lit the room enough to make crossing easy. But no one had built a fire tonight. She brushed the furniture as she moved slowly toward the pale moonlit windows.

As she leaned out to pull in the shutter, something moved across the courtyard. She froze, not believing what she saw.

An outline of a man shifted again, working his way across the yard from building to building. The shadow was tall and lean, yet crouched and darted like a thief.

Kara's mouth opened to scream. She whirled to sound the alarm.

Strong arms encircled her. A hand covered her mouth. Her attacker pulled her close against his chest. Panic climbed suddenly into Kara's heart.

"Easy now, darlin'." Jonathan's words brushed against her ear as he pulled her away from the window and into the velvet folds of the drapes. "We don't want to frighten away whoever it is."

Anger overrode fear. She kicked Jonathan hard.

The oath he swore was in Apache, but she knew she'd hurt him.

One arm pulled her closer. His hand tightened about her mouth. His words came in an angry rush against the side of her face. "You're a hard woman to save, Miss O'Riley. Maybe I should just let the trespasser shoot you when you screamed. Then I'd know who he is and be rid of one Irish pest to boot."

Her foot struck again. Her fingers clawed his hand from her mouth. "You frightened me far more by grabbing me than a shadow moving in the yard did." She shoved at his chest suddenly, angry and embarrassed. "There's no need to continue holding me. I've no intention of screaming now that I know observing a trespasser advance across the yard seems to be your pastime."

Jonathan inched away, his hands sliding to her waist.

"You're right. I have been watching our shadow for quite some time. He circles the courtyard then disappears behind the bunkhouse almost every night at this same time. I've tried to follow him and confront him, but the man must have Apache blood, for he moves swiftly without leaving a trail. I left the shutter open hoping he'd enter the house and I'd find out who he is. But he passed it by. Apparently, whatever he seeks isn't in here. Unless, of course, he saw you and was frightened away."

Jonathan leaned forward, rubbing his shin. "Maybe he's encountered you before in the dark."

Kara straightened. After a moment of silence, she said, "If you're waiting for me to say I'm sorry for springing your trap, you'll be waiting a long time, Mr. Catlin." She couldn't see herself apologizing for closing a window. "If you like, I'll reopen the window."

"No." Jonathan sighed. "He's gone. Whoever our shadow is, he darts off at the slightest sound."

Kara let out an angry breath and shoved once more at his chest. The man stood entirely too near to be proper.

But instead of backing away, Jonathan leaned closer, burying his face against her neck. "You smell delicious tonight, Miss O'Riley. Like roses."

She felt his face moving across the side of her throat, tickling her senses alive.

"Angela leaves little balls of red, rose-scented soap in my room." She wasn't sure he heard her as he drank in her nearness.

Leaning back into the velvet, she tried to put a little distance between them before she enjoyed the sensation too much.

Stay, she whispered inside her mind. *Stay and discover the true man behind the smoky gray eyes.*

When she didn't slip away, Jonathan's arm circled her hesitantly, pulling her sideways while his free hand caressed her braid and tugged her head gently. Now the neck and throat he admired was exposed.

He whispered her name almost as if he were the one surrendering and not advancing.

She didn't move as he brushed his cheek from her ear to the lace of her collar. The heat of his breath made her tremble. Slowly, as though he had all the time in the world, he brushed his lips across her throat.

Kara closed her eyes and leaned her head back further, willingly drowning in the newly discovered pleasure. Never had she imagined a man's slight touch could make her feel so wonderful. When Devin took her hand or patted her cheek there had been nothing like this. She knew she could easily slip from Jonathan's grasp, but she stayed.

His next journey, from the bottom of her ear to her collar, planted light kisses along the path, then he returned, tasting her skin before she had time to cool.

He released her slowly, holding her in place by only the warmth of his body so near hers.

"You taste," he whispered in a kiss against her ear, "even better than you smell." While he spoke, his fingers unbuttoned the collar of her gown. He pushed the lace aside and moved lower.

Her hands reached behind her, gripping the heavy drapes. As he unbuttoned another button and found the hollow of her neck she couldn't stop the sigh that left her lips.

Nothing had ever felt so good. She should stop him, step away, scream, remind him they'd agreed not to touch. But just as she needed to be held nights ago during the storm, now she needed to be desired and he was consuming her, one breath, one taste, one inch at a time.

His hands braced the wall on either side of her head as his mouth moved slowly back to her ear. "Free me from my promise," he whispered. "Beg me to kiss you."

"No," she answered as his jawline stroked hers, his rough day's growth of beard against her freshly scrubbed cheek.

He continued his advance. She trembled against him with pleasure as he brushed her skin with warm kisses. His fingers slowly opened the gown more, daring her to stop him. Daring her not to.

When she said nothing, he stroked the valley between her breasts with his fingers, making her cry out softly in pure enjoyment. His mouth followed the fingers' journey downward.

When she sighed with pleasure, he leaned into her, pressing her against the curtains with the warmth of his body, letting the velvet encompass them.

His hands crossed behind her, drawing her fingers to his chest. Gently sliding her hands over his shoulders, he leaned down once more and pulled one side of her gown open, revealing the rise of her breast.

"Beg me to kiss you," he mumbled as his mouth brushed against her flesh.

"No," she whispered as he moved lower. Her hands stroked his shoulders and she rocked with the waves of heat spreading through her body.

When his kisses reached the swell of her breast, his

hand delved beneath the cotton of her gown. The feel
of his gentle grip spreading over her competed with his
tongue sliding between her breasts.

When he leaned against her once more, she could feel
the pounding of his heart next to hers.

"Beg me!" His hand never left her breast, but caressed
her as though he held a treasure.

"Kiss me . . ."

His lips covered hers before she could finish. The kiss
burned across her mouth as before, only now there was
a fire of need deep within it.

She crossed her arms around his neck and hung on as
the tidal wave hit her. There was something wild about
him, making her hunger for more as he parted her lips
and tasted her mouth.

As the kiss continued, she could tell he was fighting
to be gentle, tender. His hands cautiously touched her
hair, and moved ever so lightly against her throat already
made sensitive by his attention. His effort touched her
heart, where his passion couldn't have.

When finally he broke the kiss, he took huge gulps of
air, brushing against her with each breath. She could feel
his every breath, his heart pounding.

"I've never known it could be . . ." she tried to say
and breathe at the same time.

"Neither did I," he answered as he cupped her face
and kissed her lightly.

When she responded to his feather kisses, his lips softened into a tender kiss. The warmth of his mouth on her
spread through her body, creating a hunger for more.

When he reluctantly ended the kiss, he held her
gently.

Kara pushed to be free. For a moment, he resisted her. Then he let go and stepped aside.

She looked up into his blue eyes and saw what Nichole had told her to look for: passion, need, hunger and love.

The last frightened her the most, mixing reality into what seemed a perfect dream. "We shouldn't be doing this."

He reached for her, but she darted away. "It's not right. I'm going to marry another man." She'd only meant to linger. She'd stayed too long . . . far too long.

Her head was filled with a sensual fog. How could she enjoy the closeness of another man when she'd never kissed Devin O'Toole? Would he kiss her like that when they married? Would anyone ever kiss her like that again in her life?

Kara ran from the room. She didn't want to think, and she'd spent far too much time feeling in the past hour.

She ran past Snort's room.

The old man appeared in the doorway wearing his longhandles. "Ever'thing all right, Miss Kara?"

"No." She fought back tears. "Not at all."

Before he could ask more, she slammed her bedroom door.

SIXTEEN

❦

"NOW, IF YOU'RE MAKING THE LITTLE LADY FEEL UN welcome . . ." Snort began, his crooked finger pointing in the general direction of Jonathan.

Jonathan stared over Snort's head at the windows. Low clouds moved in the west, almost as dark as his mood. The ranch was losing cattle. He had no idea how much money he had in the bank. Willis was hurt, maybe dead in Fort Worth, and all Snort worried about was Kara's feelings.

"Yeah, or maybe you're talking to her too rough." H. B. added his thoughts. "Women seem to mind yelling and swearing. They want to be asked how they're feeling and the like, even if it don't matter a flea to you."

"That's right." Snort fell into step. "And they like having someone spend time with them. Near as I can tell, if a woman has her druthers, she would never be alone. Even old widows travel in flocks ever'where they go. You'll see an old man sitting in a saloon having a drink all by hisself, but you never see one old woman alone, not even in church. I think they're converted in rows at most revivals just to fill the pew."

Jonathan lowered his stare to the two old-timers in front of him. Suddenly these two retired rangers, who'd never been married and only presumably had mothers, were experts on women. "I didn't do anything to make her cry," he said for the tenth time.

"Well, you must have done somethin'," Snort accused, lifting his gunbelt a few inches as if getting down to the business of investigating. " 'Cause I seen her running down the hall, water dripping off her face like she was a natural spring."

"And she didn't come down to breakfast," H. B. pointed out. "That's something she's never done before. Not since I've known her."

"She hasn't even been here but a few months," Jonathan reminded them, but it didn't seem to be a factor. "We've more important things that need discussing besides Miss O'Riley's moods."

In truth, he'd been thinking about her most of the night instead of sleeping. He went over and over what had happened by the windows when they'd been wrapped in velvet and the night. She'd been as willing as he. She even asked . . . no, begged . . . him to kiss her.

"What?" Snort pulled Jonathan back from his thoughts.

Jonathan moved closer to the two men and lowered his voice. "I saw the shadow moving across the courtyard again last night."

"Sure it wasn't just some cowhand out for a walk? You know, Lefty can't go a night without at least one trip to the privy ever since that time he was shot down by the Rio Grande."

"Where was he shot again?" H. B. asked.

"Right south of El Paso. He was riding with Walker, crossing back and forth over the river getting rustlers when the army wouldn't touch them."

"I was on a few of those raids. One time . . ."

"Gentlemen. It wasn't Lefty." Jonathan shook his head. "He moved from shadow to shadow, hiding, making sure all was quiet before he moved again. Whoever our night walker is, he didn't want to be seen. And he's good at what he does. Otherwise, we'd have caught him by now." Jonathan looked at Snort. "How many new men did Newton hire last week in Brady?"

"Three," Snort answered. "Two of them were local boys who've worked for the ranch before. The third seems like a nice fellow. Irishman. Tired of working the railroads, he said."

"Check him out," Jonathan ordered two men who knew exactly what that entailed. "And bring a few men in to pull guard duty. From now on, I want a man watching the courtyard from dusk 'til dawn, as well as one at the gate."

Almost as an afterthought, he asked, "Did we have any new lawmen come by looking for a job?" Jonathan knew it was the ranch policy never to turn one away. His grandmother knew these men usually had no family to go home to. Here, they could live out their days in peace. She always offered them a full wage and a house on the ranch borders in exchange for security. Jonathan planned to continue the policy for as long as he owned the ranch.

"One," Snort answered. "A fellow by the name of Cooper who was a deputy in Houston. He arrived about the same time you got back from Kansas City. He said they let him go 'cause he busted his hand up, but a cowhand saw him target shooting and said he can blast away just as good with the other. He's gray headed, but even unarmed, he's not a man you'd want to cross."

"Check around, see if anyone remembers him." Jonathan added, "And keep an eye on him after dark."

"We'll get right on it." They both snapped to attention like old bloodhounds forever ready for the call.

"What about Miss Kara?" Snort asked, determined not to forget about the lady.

"I'll talk to her," Jonathan promised. "Maybe she's just homesick."

Both men nodded. That seemed a logical explanation.

"We'll have Angela cook her something Irish," Snort suggested.

"Ain't nothin' Irish but potatoes, and we have that ever'day," H. B. complained.

The men left trying to think of a food that would remind Kara of home.

Jonathan took the stairs two at a time. Kara's quarters were open, everything in her room neat and tidy. He stepped next door to Dawn's room.

The door was unlocked. As he let himself in slowly, he saw the two women sitting on the floor with the baby between them. The remains of a breakfast rested by the fire.

"Good morning," Kara said formally. "We were just having breakfast and talking."

Jonathan raised an eyebrow.

Kara laughed. "Well, kind of talking."

Dawn said something in Apache, and Jonathan answered her. When he finished, he translated. "She wants more leather I promised her."

Dawn spoke again.

"And," Jonathan relayed the message, "she likes my woman."

"Tell her I'm not your woman," Kara said. "Tell her I'm just the bookkeeper."

"There is no word for bookkeeper in Apache."

"Then tell her I enjoyed our breakfast, and I will return this afternoon to help her sew her dress." Kara stood.

Jonathan said something to Dawn, and they both laughed.

Kara brushed past Jonathan before he could explain. It took him a moment to realize she was gone.

He said farewell to Dawn and followed Kara to the study. She stood next to the window where he'd been earlier. Before he spoke, he closed the door hoping they'd have a small degree of privacy.

Kara moved as far across the little room as she could, then faced him. He couldn't miss the slight puffiness around her eyes. Her lips looked pouty as well, and he wondered if she had slept any more than he had last night.

He found himself standing in the sunlight, looking at her across the room and wishing he could kiss her. The realization angered him. Parts of his mind and body were mutinying against all he thought logical.

"Before you start, I want you to know I don't blame you for what happened last night." She stared straight

ahead at his chest as she continued. "It was as much my
doing as yours. And don't ye dare say nothing happened.
I don't think I could bear that. I'm not sure what it was,
but it can't be put, in any way, into the category of
nothing."

Jonathan waited for her to take a breath. "Are you
finished?"

She nodded.

He had no idea what to say next. He wanted to swing
her into his arms and tell her everything was all right.
But if he touched her it could make matters worse. He
told himself the last thing he wanted was a woman in
his life, and she obviously didn't want him. So there
shouldn't be a problem, right?

Right! Then why couldn't he stop staring at her lips?
He was five feet away, and he would swear he smelled
her hair. He must be catching some dreaded disease.
She'd filled his thoughts and was now spreading like
bindweed to his senses.

Jonathan was relegated to accepting H. B.'s advice.
"How do you feel?" he asked without much conviction.

She lifted her head. "Fine," she lied.

"Good." Jonathan waited. So much for H. B.'s suggestion.

He decided they couldn't live under the same roof and
not speak of what happened. There were things that
needed saying between them, and he'd listen to none of
her objections. He'd have his say, clear the air and then
never speak of it again. "I want you to know I've never
felt like I did last night when I kissed you." He paced
as he thought of just how to tell her.

"It must never happen again," she whispered more to the window than to him.

Jonathan was planning his words, not listening to hers. "I'm not saying I haven't kissed a few women. More than a few, to tell the truth. But not like that." He scrubbed at his lips with his fist.

She didn't notice. "It should never have happened in the first place." She nodded at her own reflection in the windowpane. "It took us both by surprise."

He stared at the ceiling before closing his eyes. "You filled a hunger in me, Kara. I never thought a woman would do that. Every touch keeps running over and over in my thoughts."

"Never again." She pressed her cheek against the glass, wishing it would cool the blush of her cheeks.

"It was like I couldn't get enough. Like I became addicted in one touch."

"No matter how often we're together," she swore.

"I know you felt it, too. Somewhere destiny binds us together and saying it won't happen again is like denying the wind."

"The saints as my witness."

"The saints as mine, too," he finished, wondering what she'd been talking about.

Angela tapped on the door, then opened it awkwardly as she carried a small tray of coffee and cookies. "I thought I'd find you in here, Mr. Jonathan. I brought you both a cup."

"Thanks." Jonathan noticed Angela looked like she'd been crying. Frustrated, he plowed his fingers through his hair. The entire female population seemed to have caught a weeping affliction. "Is something wrong, Angela?"

"I just heard Snort say we have a prowler."

"Don't be frightened." Jonathan had a hard time believing Angela, at over six feet tall, was ever frightened by anything, much less the shadow of a prowler.

"Snort said they might just have to shoot him and ask questions later." She wiped her tears with her apron. "You wouldn't let them do that, would you? I don't want to think of a man dying in our courtyard for no other reason than he went out walking at night."

Jonathan had never known the woman to care much about anything except her baking. "Angela, do you know anything about this man?"

She shook her head and hurried to the door. "I never seen any man sneaking around late at night, but if I did, I wouldn't shoot him until I knew he was trouble."

She was gone before he could ask more questions, but Jonathan bet she knew more. Maybe the prowler was simply a secret lover? But of Angela's?

Jonathan turned back to Kara. "What do you think?"

Kara smiled. "I think she knows more than she's saying. And I think it would be most improper of you to question her further."

Jonathan nodded. "I agree, unless I want to find another cook. But that doesn't mean I won't question the prowler."

"Who else might he be?"

Jonathan shrugged. "Someone wanting to kill me. Maybe the same man who shot at us in Kansas City. Who knows? Except for the slight chance that Angela has a lover, I assume the fellow is up to no good. There's a way out of the headquarters behind the bunkhouse. We found it unlocked this morning. The shadow could be one of my men, disappearing back into the bunkhouse, or a stranger leaving through the gate."

"What if someone wanted to kill me?" Kara whispered so softly he barely heard her.

Jonathan moved to touch her, but stopped a few feet away. "If it were someone set on harming you, he'd have to pass through me first. Don't you believe you're safe here, Kara?"

She tried to smile, almost believing him.

He moved closer. "There's no reason for you to be afraid of a prowler . . . or of me," he added.

Tears threatened to bubble over her eyelids. "I'm not afraid of you." She swallowed. "I'm afraid of me when I'm with you. I'm promised to another and all I want to do is go back home."

The heartbreak in her green eyes startled him. He knew how she felt. Most of his life he'd wanted to go home, but for him, there had been no home to return to.

He straightened slightly. If she wouldn't let him touch her, at least he'd keep her safe and when the time came, he'd make sure she got back to her home. He'd take her back to her Devin, a man who would never cherish her the way Kara deserved. If the man had such ability, he'd never have let her go in the first place.

"If that's what you want," he said, wishing other words were coming from his mouth. "You'll be safe here until you tell me it's time to take you home." There were reasons she wasn't going back, but he wouldn't pry.

She smiled for the first time that morning. "After last night can we still be friends?"

He didn't think they were friends before last night, but he thought it wise not to bring up the matter. "Because of last night, we'll always be friends."

She lifted her hand, and he took it in his.

He didn't leave the office all morning, but stayed and worked with her. He listened to the numbers she quoted, looked over her shoulder as she worked, got everything in order to take to the bank. Through her work, it was obvious something was wrong. The money for cattle sales didn't add up to the expenses.

Maybe because of what they'd shared over the past few days, they relaxed around one another for the first time. Both were surprised at how much time had passed when Angela brought in lunch.

They talked of the ranch while they ate. Jonathan relayed stories the rangers told him of the history. They both laughed when he told her his grandmother's hobby was burying husbands.

After lunch, a rider brought in several more leather hides. They took them to Dawn, who seemed delighted. Jonathan tried to get her to move to a larger room to work, but the woman wouldn't budge. She had set up camp in the tiny bedroom and planned to stay there until she left for good.

He gave Kara his grandmother's old sewing box. He considered staying to interpret, but learned the women no longer needed him. Sign language served them fine.

He checked the grounds, restless. The storm that showed promise that morning became a threat to be dealt with by midafternoon. Cowhands rode in from the ranges, and began tying things down and boarding up for a winter storm.

When he passed through the kitchen, Angela was bringing in plenty of wood and stores from the cellars. The cowhands might be stuck at headquarters with little to do, but her job never ended. If the ranch was snowed in, they'd be playing cards. She'd be cooking.

At dusk, Dawn didn't want to stop to eat. Jonathan finally talked Kara into joining him downstairs for dinner. They left Dawn working by the fire with her baby asleep beside her.

He offered his arm at the stairs, and Kara accepted. For the first night since she'd been here, Jonathan insisted they eat in the dining room. They filled their plates from the stove, then sat at one end of the long dining table.

Kara asked him why Angela always left the main house before dark and refused to spend the night in the place.

He shook his head. "I have no idea. Her mother and father were both dead before she had time to remember them. She's been raised by her grandfather, Gideon, who was very strict. Except for a few trips to Brady, I don't think she's ever been off the ranch."

"How did her mother die?"

Jonathan shrugged. "She never recovered from the birth of Angela. She was very young, I think."

"And her father?"

"I heard someone say he was killed by accident by the guards."

"Maybe that's why Angela is so upset about Snort shooting a prowler."

"Maybe." Jonathan hadn't thought of it. "Who knows?

There'll be snow by morning," he said, changing the subject, listening to the wind howl through the chimney.

"You think so?"

"Want to see it coming in?" Before she could answer, Jonathan took her hand. "I've my own private balcony to watch."

He led her up the stairs to a ladder that he pulled down from the ceiling of the second floor. "They used this as a lookout when the Indian raids were bad."

She followed him up to a tiny balcony built into the roof of the house.

"It's called a widow's walk. I have no idea why. My grandmother used to say that a man could see a hundred miles from this point."

The wind whipped through them with icy force, but the beauty was breathtaking. The last light from the sun was dying, turning the earth over to darkness. Huge clouds fought one another for space along the horizon while thinner ones raced across the sky above them, sending out an alarm.

"It's beautiful," Kara whispered.

Jonathan moved behind her, blocking the wind with his body as his arms circled around her loosely to offer warmth.

They stood, silently watching the night and the storm moving closer.

From the corner of her eye, Kara thought she saw a lone figure slipping away from the headquarters and into the night.

But when she looked, no one was there.

SEVENTEEN

THE STORM LASTED TWO DAYS, BLOWING SNOW across the plains in icy drifts. By morning of the second day, Jonathan walked the halls like a caged animal. He seemed on a quest to wear out the tile flooring.

Kara watched Dawn sew, worked on the books and helped Angela cook, but Jonathan's pacing wore on her nerves. The fragile truce between them strained at times. They made an effort not to migrate toward one another when they were both in the same room. But, invariably, they ended up in the same room at the same time. Again and again, they brushed in passing, or accidentally touched when reaching for the same thing.

She found herself looking for him, listening when he talked with others, waiting until he neared.

All the workings of the ranch stopped for two days. The third day dawned clear and cowhands rode out to break the ice. Cattle, if still alive, had to be able to reach water.

They returned by midafternoon, with news that a hundred head or more had disappeared from the north pasture. Not frozen, or drifted across downed fences, but disappeared.

Jonathan took the news with fury. With guards posted along the borders of his land, there was no way that many head of cattle were moved unseen, not even in a snowstorm. And, anyone moving cattle in bad weather would not only have to be a trained cowman, he'd have to know his way, for he'd be herding blind in a storm.

An hour later more bad news rode in with the last of the men. The body of a guard named Russell, who lived on the west border, had been discovered in a gully beside his cabin. The cowhands reasoned he must have slipped on the snow and ice and tumbled to his death.

Jonathan went with the other guards to pay their respects to Russell. He questioned the two men who found Russell's body, making sure they'd seen no tracks or cattle, or horses near the place. Both men said they would have noticed tracks in the snow when they rode up to Russell's place if there had been any.

When Jonathan and the guard returned, the men met in the dining room.

Jonathan's first theory about the cattle was that one of the guards had been bought off by Wells. Snort and H. B. assured him that was impossible. They both said they'd stake their lives on the loyalty of any man along the line.

Maps were needed to prove Jonathan's second theory. As evening crept across a cloudy sky, Snort, H. B. and Luther spread maps out across the dining table. Most were old, few were accurate. Several looked more like paintings of the land than actual maps. But what kept

Jonathan searching was something he'd heard Angela say to Kara. She'd commented about the flowers, saying there were ravines where the Indian paintbrush and blue-bonnets grew year-round.

It had to be true. The flowers were proof, but no record of them registered on the maps.

"If they exist?" Jonathan asked as he tried to ignore Kara moving behind him lighting lamps. "Isn't it possible the cattle were driven through them and off Catlin land?"

His men took turns scratching their balding heads. They were fighters, not surveyors. Only two men knew the ranch well enough to find the flower ravines: Newton and Gideon, who made the rounds to the outposts.

Newton was in Fort Worth with Willis, and because of his broken leg, Gideon could only travel in a buck-board. With the snow, it might be days before a wagon could make it across wet land.

Gideon could, however, point to the likely spots on the map.

"Saddle my horse at dawn," Jonathan said between yelling for Gideon. "I have to find the ravines, if they exist, before the snow melts. It will be easy to follow tracks. Once the snow disappears, so will the clues."

Snort and H. B. both volunteered to ride with him.

"Snort, I can use you with me." Jonathan knew how antsy the old man was after being left behind last time. "Bring along the new man, Cooper, as well. H. B., I need you here guarding the house with Luther."

"But we haven't checked Cooper out fully," H. B. mumbled.

"That's why I'm taking him with me," Jonathan said

as Gideon entered the room and they all turned back to the maps.

The groundskeeper proved to be little help. He could trace his route from outpost to outpost, but he didn't venture off the path. He'd never actually seen any ravines where the flowers grew. At best, all he could do was pinpoint the cabins along Catlin borders where guards had sent in baskets of flowers back to headquarters. Russell's cabin was among them.

Gideon thought he remembered Russell saying something about the key to the flowers was marked by a pine that grew out of a boulder. But Russell's words had made no sense.

When the man called Cooper entered the house, all talk of the ravine ceased. Jonathan moved to greet the newcomer.

"You sent for me?" Cooper asked as he removed his hat. He was polite, but there was no bowing of his head to the boss. "I'm Cooper."

Jonathan didn't expect anything but civil respect until he'd earned more. He liked a man who looked at him directly when asking a question. Jonathan offered his hand. "Jonathan Catlin," he said, as if Cooper didn't know who he was. "I haven't seen you around, but welcome."

Cooper shifted, acting like he didn't notice the offered hand. "I been pulling night watch since I got here."

Jonathan lowered his hand, noticing Cooper's right-hand fingers were curled at his side. He held his hat in his left.

"Are you up for riding with me in the morning? I need a good man."

"Yes, sir, I'm about ready to stretch my legs," Cooper answered. "Mind my asking where we're headed?"

"We're circling, looking for rustlers. Somehow during the storm they came in close to the headquarters and removed maybe a hundred head. If we find nothing, we'll be back before nightfall. If we cross the tracks, we stay with the trail."

Cooper nodded. "I'll be saddled by first light."

Every man in the room watched Cooper leave. If he were part of the trouble, they'd know soon enough.

An hour after sunset a rider made it in from Brady. He brought a telegram and was immediately offered supper and a night's stay. The kid accepted gladly. The excitement of staying at the Catlin Ranch was well worth a ride in cold weather.

Jonathan walked to his office and closed the door. He stared at the envelope for a long minute wondering if good news ever came by telegram. He also wondered why he'd let the Western Union office in Brady know that he'd pay a five-dollar tip to any man who brought out a telegram. Couldn't bad news wait a few days for a mail run?

He opened the message and read without allowing his expression to change. The paper read simply, "Bringing body home. Newton."

Jonathan crumbled the telegram and closed his eyes. He hadn't wanted this place and its people, but he'd sworn he'd do the best by them he could. Now, he'd lost not one but two men.

"What is it?" Kara asked from a few feet behind him.

Jonathan whirled. She must have been sitting at the

desk all along and he hadn't noticed her when he'd entered.

Without a word, he handed her the crumpled telegram.

She let out a little cry as she read it. "He's dead! Willis is dead."

Jonathan leaned against the desk. "I shouldn't have let him go with us. I should have known he was getting too old for that kind of ride. I should have . . ."

"Willis was old, but he loved being in the saddle," Kara comforted. "Accidents happen."

Jonathan shook his head, still blaming himself.

She moved around the desk. "With the weather, you couldn't have gotten him to a doctor any faster."

"I know all the reasons, but they don't change the facts." He moved away toward the window. He didn't want her to look at him. "First Russell was found dead near his cabin, now Willis. Two men are down on my watch. Death stalks me again, Kara. No matter how far or how fast I run, it's always a step behind, waiting to strike."

He didn't realize she'd followed him until her hand touched his arm.

With a jerk he pulled away, angry more at life than her. He'd let her get too close. He'd allowed himself to think of this place as a home. "Don't you understand? Don't get too close to me. Everyone I've ever cared about dies."

He saw shock register in her eyes, but he didn't care. Better that she know the truth. Even being his friend might draw death closer to her. She'd be safer if she kept calling him Mr. Catlin and never touched him.

"But . . ."

He saw the question in her green depths, the disbelief, the shock that he would say such a thing. She reached for him.

"No," he whispered, letting her hand move along his arm. "I'm only telling you the facts. If you value your life, stay away from me."

With a grim determination, Jonathan left the room. As he walked toward the bunkhouse, he felt sick at his stomach for telling Kara about his private demons. If she believed him, the telling would only serve to frighten her. If she didn't believe what he said, she now must be convinced he was losing his mind.

Either way, he'd made his point. She'd avoid him like the plague from now on.

Jonathan shoved thoughts of Kara aside as he walked into the bunkhouse and told the men about Willis. The young cowhands were saddened, saying how sorry they were and how much they liked the old man. But the Old Guard behaved differently. They spoke of how lucky Willis was to die quickly. Men like them never expected to live long enough to retire. To do so and then die without wasting away in bed was good fortune.

Jonathan left the bunkhouse wondering what might happen to the Old Guard if he sold the place. Where would they go? Would anyone else bother to make them feel needed?

He told himself it wasn't his problem. He didn't want ties. He didn't need people. He wasn't meant to stay in one place. But, in the end, he knew it was his problem, inherited along with the land.

The mood was somber the next morning when Cooper, Snort and Jonathan rode out after Russell's funeral.

Every man on the ranch knew that if tracks were found leading toward Wells's place, there would be an all-out war. Small towns like Brady didn't have sheriffs, and men would never be sent down from Fort Worth. Ranchers usually settled their own arguments with talk or with guns.

The three didn't speak as they rode across frozen virgin snow. A huge spread like Catlin Ranch could never be completely covered, but could be crisscrossed. A hundred head of cattle leave a wide trail in the snow. Most of the spread was flat, good range country, but there were places with wide gullies and bluffs. The canyons were confusing even for a seasoned hand. Once a man lost sight of the horizon, he often forfeited his sense of direction, taking hours to find his way out of a box canyon.

By noon, they'd found several strays and spoken to two guards along the border, but nothing else. The snow had turned to slush, slowing the horses.

Jonathan watched Cooper. The man did nothing to arouse suspicion. He had a good eye for strays and checked behind them regularly. He even made a habit of circling back when they'd taken a turn or reached high ground, so he could see better just in case they were being followed.

When Snort stopped to check his horse, Cooper signaled to Jonathan that he'd be circling back once more. Jonathan nodded and drew his canteen, preparing to wait. They were halfway back to the headquarters on high, rocky ground. They had plenty of time to make another loop, maybe two before dark.

Snort jerked off his coat and swore at his horse before

tackling a mud-packed hoof with the blunt blade of his knife.

Jonathan watched Cooper disappear behind rocks. Seconds passed. A shot rang out, popping the air like a whip. Another followed, almost quick enough to be an echo. A second later a bullet bounced off the rocks. Jonathan dropped the water and wrenched his rifle from its sheath on the saddle.

"Take cover, Snort!" he yelled as he scanned the low hills in the direction Cooper had disappeared. Jonathan slapped his horse out of the way and slid behind a pile of rocks barely large enough to provide cover.

Cooper's down, Jonathan thought, knowing he'd be running with no cover if he tried to get to the man.

"Cooper!" he yelled. "You all right?"

Silence. If the man was down, he was dead.

For a long breath, Jonathan watched the hills, searching for the glint of a rifle or any movement among the rocks. Nothing. The cold air went completely still, as though the shot came from nowhere. Cooper vanished into a cloudless sky.

"Any ideas, Snort?" Jonathan glanced in the direction of the old man's horse. The animal was skittish but couldn't run. His reins were wrapped around Snort's hand, and Snort lay, facedown, on the ground.

"No!" Jonathan forgot about cover and ran to the old man, expecting bullets to mark his progress.

But no fire thundered as Jonathan rolled Snort over and watched blood pump out of his shoulder.

"Ain't so bad." Snort slowly sat up and stared at his own blood. "I reckon it missed my heart or I wouldn't be looking."

Jonathan ripped away the old man's shirt and tied a bandage tightly over the wound. "Can you ride?" The longer they stayed, the easier a target they became. "We've got to get you back to headquarters."

"As fast as I'm losing blood, I'm getting lighter in the saddle all along. Get me on the horse. I'll beat you back."

Jonathan lifted him into the saddle and handed Snort the reins. The old man was a half-mile in front of him before Jonathan could catch his horse and follow. Even at a pounding gallop all the way, he expected to hear more fire. Nothing.

In twenty minutes, they were barreling into headquarters at full speed. Gideon barely got the gates open as they raced in. Snort rode to the front door and slid from his horse.

Suddenly, men were everywhere, closing the gates, taking care of the horses, carrying Snort inside, running for supplies. Jonathan stood and watched, almost expecting Cooper to follow them in. When he didn't, Jonathan turned and let the trail of Snort's blood lead him inside.

The old-timers seemed to have lived through times like this before. There was no discussion. Snort was deposited on one of the leather couches in the great room and supplies were brought in too quickly not to have been kept ready. He could hear Angela yelling from the kitchen that water would be hot soon. Gideon built a fire in the grate.

Luther examined Snort's wound while H. B. poured whiskey alternately on the injury and down Snort's throat.

Snort woke long enough to swallow and swear. When Kara appeared, the old man reached for her hand, seeming to need it for comfort.

She glanced at Jonathan for answers, but it was Luther who spoke.

"The bullet went right through his shoulder," announced Luther. "All we got to do is stop the bleeding. Heat a knife."

One of the cowhands slid a long bowie knife from his boot and shoved it handle-deep into the hot coals of the fireplace.

Jonathan glanced over in time to see Kara pale. Before the knife was ready, he moved to her side and drew her from the room. It was bad enough she would hear Snort scream and smell flesh burning. She didn't need to see it, as well.

"Are you hurt?" she asked, spreading her hand over the blood on his coat.

"No."

"The old man. Will he live?"

"He'll live to invent a long story of today." Jonathan covered her hand with his, trapping it against his chest. Had it only been hours ago that he'd warned her to stay away? It seemed like days.

"Will you be all right here?" He studied her eyes for the answer. She was young, not accustomed to this hard life.

"I'll be fine. How can I help?"

The sparkle of a warrior flickered in her green eyes, and he had the same sense he'd had once before that she'd fight, no matter the odds.

"I'm taking several men with me." He forced his mind

to think of other things besides her, though his body wanted nothing more than to hold her. "We need to see if we can pick up the shooter's trail before sunset."

She nodded.

"Can you fire a gun?"

She shook her head.

"Well, I've got about ten minutes to teach you."

And ten minutes was all he allowed. Snort was resting quietly in Angela's care, and the men were ready to ride when Jonathan handed her two Colts.

"Fire a shot in the air if trouble comes. We'll hear it. If necessary, level the weapon and defend yourself," he ordered. "Let no harm near, Kara. I'm depending on you. Do you understand?"

"Aye," she answered, thinking he was giving her the chance to stand and fight. The very chance her father wouldn't give her. She would not let Jonathan down.

Kara stood alone at the doorway and watched them thunder out like an army. She helped Gideon close the gate. Operating on one crutch, he hopped his way toward the bunkhouse. "I'll check the other gates," he said. "Nothing larger than a squirrel can get in here once we're closed up."

Kara still didn't feel secure. If trouble came, it would find Angela, who refused to touch a gun; Snort, who was injured and drunk; Gideon, who was crippled; and her. Oh, she must not forget the woman upstairs who thought she was Apache and who now had a knife and might kill them all if she got frightened.

Kara tried to think of something—of anything—else. She told herself that her father must have already received her letter. He could be coming for her at this very moment. But even if he'd left yesterday, or the day before, it might be too late to save her by the time he traveled halfway across the country.

She shoved one of the Colts Jonathan had given her into her right-hand pocket and began pacing around the fountain. Months ago she'd begged to be allowed to stay and fight, to defend her home. Now she'd been given that chance and she wished desperately there was a train she could catch.

In her imagination, she could almost see killers crawling over the walls of the fortress. Or maybe they were tunneling under. Maybe the McWimberlys had joined forces with whoever shot Snort? Maybe they were ten, twenty, a hundred strong by now.

She'd never been so frightened. Not even when her father shoved her on the train. She'd been a fool to think she'd be brave in a fight. All she wanted to do now was run and hide.

But she couldn't. The others were depending on her.

Kara walked back into the dining room, picked up another Colt and put it into her left-hand pocket. Twelve bullets, she thought. If they were a hundred strong, she'd at least stop a dozen of them. Like a soldier, she marched back to the courtyard and began alternately watching the top of the wall and the bottom.

An hour later, she was exhausted from carrying the weapons around and around the yard. She went back to the house and found Snort lying on one of the long leather couches in the great room with his feet propped on the arm. He was singing songs she'd never heard before about "bedding down the dogies." The bottle of whiskey was empty beside him.

Kara left Snort with Gideon and went to the kitchen. Angela stood at the counter, cutting vegetables and crying.

"Snort's going to be all right," Kara comforted. "I think he'll be fine in a few days."

Angela sniffed and attacked a carrot. "I know," she said, "but they all blame Cooper, and I know he wouldn't shoot Snort."

Kara slipped onto her stool and listened. Anything was better than listening to her own imagination going wild.

"He's a good man," Angela continued, "I don't know where he disappeared to, but there's another answer besides him shooting at them. There has to be."

Angela didn't need to say more. Kara guessed all that she wasn't saying.

EIGHTEEN

As the sun faded, the air turned colder at Catlin Headquarters. Kara pulled on Jonathan's long wool coat that she'd first worn the day they met and continued her vigil at the front door.

All was quiet inside the house. Earlier, Kara heard Dawn's baby crying, but the child must have finally fallen asleep. Snort was still passed out from the bottle of whiskey he'd downed. Gideon sat with him, keeping an eye on the wounded man. Angela had vanished before dark, as always, inside her little house.

Luther had ridden in an hour before saying Jonathan had sent him back to check on Snort, but Kara guessed it was more because the aging lawman couldn't take the ride and the cold any longer. His bones had begun to knot like branches on a weathered tree.

"Want some supper, Miss Kara?" Luther asked from the doorway. He leaned on his cane heavily tonight. "Angela left plenty. I could keep watch out here if that's what you're worried about."

"No, thanks," Kara answered.

The old man moved out into the night watching the sky, listening for any sound of the riders returning. "It sure is quiet out here at sunset. You can almost hear the stars being born."

Kara pulled Jonathan's coat tighter around her. "Back home, we lived so close to the mills that it was never quiet. No one had a clock. Our lives revolved around the whistles for the shift changes."

"Where is home for you?" he asked politely as if not wanting to pry.

Kara hesitated, then realized no one here knew, or probably cared about her problems at home. The steel mills seemed a million miles away. "Pittsburgh." She might as well have said China, for all he knew of the place. "My father had worked in the steel mills since he was sixteen. Back home, smoke fills the air, and sunsets are blocked by buildings."

"You miss it?"

Kara surprised herself by saying, "Not as badly as I thought I would."

Luther lowered his body to the stone wall framing the fountain. "I left home at sixteen, hungry for adventure. I went to Tennessee for a while, then Kansas and finally here. I was always trying to outrun civilization. Always looking for adventure."

"And did you find it?" Kara sat down beside him.

Luther laughed. "I reckon I did. But in a way I guess I shut out more things than I welcomed. Raising a family, settling in one place, growing old with one woman by my side, those might have been the greatest adventures of them all. I closed myself off as completely as Angela does each night."

Kara could barely see the corner of Angela's little house. A light shown from her window. "Does she always leave at sunset?"

Luther nodded. "From sunset 'til dawn, she bolts her door. I don't know that she'd come out even if the place were on fire."

"But why?"

"Some say it's because of her grandfather, Gideon. Thirty years ago Angela's mother used to sneak out at night to meet a lover. The boy, tall for his age, was killed one winter night by a man on guard who thought he was a rustler. Angela's young mother was heartbroken and lived just long enough to give birth to Angela. Some say she was too young to have a child. Others claim that she just plain didn't want to go on living. The boy was a neighbor's son and probably wouldn't have married her anyway, but she believed what he told her."

Luther straightened his leg out carefully before continuing. "From the time Angela was little, Gideon filled her head with stories of demons who roam the night. After Gideon's wife died and they moved into the bunkhouse, Miss Victoria didn't think it was proper for a little girl to sleep in the bunkhouse even if she did have a space blanketed off from the men. So, Gideon built Angela that little house with windows too small to climb out. For years he bolted the door from the outside every night. But as she grew from a pretty young girl to an old maid, he finally moved the bolt to the inside. But if you ask me, his stories and warnings locked her in more than any bolt could."

Kara stared at the long, thin windows of Angela's house and the pieces of her story began to fit together. "The boy was Wells's son, wasn't he?"

"Yep," Luther answered. "That was the start of the bad blood between the Catlins and the Wellses. Strange thing is everyone agreed when Angela was born that we'd never mention her to Wells, or anyone outside the ranch, for that matter. She was dark like her mother. No one would know that she wasn't part of Gideon's family who came from Mexico City years ago. But as she grew, the extreme height of the Wells came through. None of her kin are over five six or seven, but, much as Gideon hates it, Angela has her father's blood, as well."

A silence fell between Luther and Kara. She thought about what he'd told her. Now that she knew the history, it seemed very unlikely that the prowler from several nights ago had been Angela's lover.

From far away, like the sound of distant thunder, she heard horses coming. Three shots rang out in the night.

Luther hurried to his feet. "That's the signal to open the gate after dark."

Before he could move more than a few steps, Gideon limped from the house. Between the two of them, they managed to get the gate open before the men rode in.

Kara stood frozen in the shadows, not knowing what to do as horses danced in the courtyard and men shouted. The place had gone from calm to chaos in the twinkling of a star.

Jonathan's voice rang above them all. "Luther, get the supplies. We've got another man hurt."

She watched as men carried a body into the house. When the light from the foyer washed over them, Kara gasped. "Cooper!" The new man's face was streaked in blood. Kara fought down a scream.

Jonathan brushed his hand across her shoulder and turned her toward the house. "Are you all right?"

She nodded, not trusting her voice. She'd traveled half a country to escape violence and somehow it found her.

"Luther may need help with the doctoring." Jonathan's voice was low, but hurried. "Can you handle the job?"

Kara didn't meet his gaze. "Aye," she answered as she pulled away from his warmth and followed Luther and the others into the great room.

Luther's mind was still sharp, full of the knowledge he'd gained from countless battles, but his hands were no longer steady. As the night aged, he needed Kara to do the work while he gave instructions.

Cooper had a deep gash across his forehead that plowed an inch into his hairline. The wound had to be cleaned and stitched, then doctored to prevent infection. Unlike Snort's wound, Luther said it would be better to let Cooper's injury bleed. The man was in no danger of bleeding to death, and the more blood that seeped from the wound the less chance of poisoning.

Kara did everything Luther told her while she listened to the men talking. They'd found Cooper's horse first, but it took them an hour to find the man. He must have tried to make it back to headquarters, but tumbled from the mount. The trail of blood indicated he'd crawled a quarter of a mile before passing out.

There was now no question about Cooper firing the shots at Jonathan and Snort. All guessed that, of the two shots fired in the rocks, one hit Cooper, the other Snort.

The men all came close, one at a time, and patted Cooper on the arm as though silently apologizing for doubting his loyalty. He was no longer the new man, he was one of them.

Though his hair was gray, his face looked more lined by the sun than age. Kara hadn't taken the time to look at him earlier. Now that she did, she realized he was a man not out of his forties. If his hand hadn't been crippled, he might have served as a sheriff for another ten years, maybe longer.

Cooper mumbled as Kara changed the bandage across his forehead. She couldn't be sure, but she thought he called Angela's name.

When she leaned closer, he whispered, "Tell her I can't come to her window tonight. Tell her I tried to make it back."

Kara glanced up. No one else had heard his words. "I'll tell her," she whispered.

Ten minutes later, as the men ate supper in the dining room, Kara slipped out the kitchen door and ran through the barren winter garden to Angela's house.

Kara tapped on the door. No answer. Then she circled to the high windows running along the side of the house and tapped again.

The window opened a few inches.

"Angela?" Kara whispered.

There was no answer, but she knew the old maid must be on the other side of the opening. "Angela, I came to tell you Cooper's all right. He's hurt, but he made it back, and he wasn't the one who shot Snort."

"I knew that," came an angry voice from the other side. "I never for one moment thought he was."

"Do you want to come see him? He's in the great room resting now."

"No." Angela's voice softened a little. "I'll die if I step foot out at night. My grandfather says it is written in the stars since my birth. I have to stay here."

"But you'd like to see Cooper," Kara tried again.

"He's been very kind to me. He's the only one who stops by to thank me for the meals I send over to the bunkhouse and sometimes he stands where you are now and talks to me."

"I'm sure he'd like to see you now. He's in some pain. Having you to talk to might help."

"I can't," she whispered. "I told you, I'll die."

Kara guessed how Angela's imagination, since childhood, had built on the fear her grandfather planted. The woman wasn't just afraid, she believed her words.

"Tell him I'll see him in the morning. I'll sit with him then."

"I'll tell him." Kara fought back tears. Fear bolted Angela inside, and there was nothing she could do to coax her out.

Kara walked back to the house. She sat by Cooper until he finally came to enough to understand her words. Then, while no one was listening, Kara leaned close and whispered, "She wants to come, Cooper. But she's afraid. She says she'll see you at dawn."

He nodded. "I know. I'll wait."

He took a long breath and added, "Miss, she ain't as cranky as she lets on."

"I know," Kara answered, wondering what these two found to talk about.

Luther's cane tapped on the floor, announcing his presence. "How's our patient?"

"Resting," Kara said. "As you should be. It's late. I'll sit up with Snort and Cooper for a while."

"No, let me," Luther mumbled as he fell back into a comfortable chair between the two wounded men. "At my age, my body sleeps even when I'm awake. They're both resting quietly and out of any danger except fever. I'll take this shift."

Kara didn't argue. She washed her hands in the basin set up by the windows, added another log to the fire and left the room.

She thought to go straight to bed, but as she passed Jonathan's room his door opened.

He looked as surprised to see her as she was to see him. For a moment they stared at one another, neither knowing what to say.

For once, Jonathan broke the silence. "I was just going up to the widow's walk to look out. Want to come with me?"

She nodded and followed.

Once they climbed the ladder and were alone on the walk, Jonathan pulled the trapdoor closed so that no light came from the house. "I know I can't see anything on these moonless nights, but I keep hoping. My men are being shot, and there doesn't seem to be a thing I can do about it. I don't even see the why of it all."

Kara listened, knowing he needed to reason out his own thoughts.

"I think the first shot today was meant for me, but ricocheted off the rocks and hit Snort. Then, Cooper must have surprised the shooter and taken the second shot. But why didn't the man behind the rocks take aim a third or fourth time? He could have finished us all off." Jonathan paced back and forth in the little space. "From the tracks and the few words Cooper said when we found him, the shooter must have panicked and ran."

Jonathan slammed his fist against the railing. "It doesn't make sense. If he wanted to kill us, why didn't he finish the job? Cooper was down, half-blinded by blood. Snort was hit, and I stood in plain sight."

"Maybe the man shooting didn't want you dead, only frightened."

Jonathan looked her direction as he leaned on the railing. "That's the only answer I can come up with. But what could be gained from trying to scare me off? He must not know me very well to think I'd run so easily."

Kara watched him closely. "What does frighten you, Jonathan?"

He faced her. "It's good to hear you finally call me Jonathan. I was beginning to think I'd be Mr. Catlin to you until the day you left."

Kara smiled. "You're avoiding the question. What frightens you?"

"Nothing." His smoky stare watched her closely even in the moonlight. "Nothing at all," he whispered.

NINETEEN

KARA THOUGHT ABOUT WHAT JONATHAN SAID FOR most of the night. How could someone claim he was afraid of nothing? Was he lying to her? Or to himself?

Of late, she felt like she was afraid of everything—most of all the way she felt about Jonathan. She fell asleep thinking of the way his arms felt surrounding her.

Breakfast consisted of burned biscuits, watery gravy and half-cooked eggs, but no one commented. Angela hovered in the great room while making a production of caring for Snort and Cooper. She seemed as cranky as ever, but Kara noticed she patted Cooper's hand every time she passed him. The old lawman was battle-scarred and cynical, the old maid withered and misanthropic, yet somehow they connected.

Jonathan stormed through the dining area in his usual hurry. He downed a cup of coffee as he gave orders to everyone.

Kara watched him from the doorway. As always, he was dressed in leather from his chocolate-colored vest to the tawny-colored chaps laced to his legs. His collar was open with a navy blue bandanna tied about his throat. Before, in the pictures of cowboys she'd seen, she'd thought the bandannas were worn for flair. Now, thanks to a discussion with Snort, she knew they had much more practical purposes. They were masks against a dust storm, bandages for small cuts, pot holders around a camp fire and wash clothes when needed.

The clothes she'd thought looked strange only a few months ago now seemed suitable. If she saw Jonathan in his button-on collar and black suit she'd think it wasn't right for the man. She'd grown used to noticing the mold of his powerful legs wrapped in leather and the way his gunbelt made his waist and hips leaner and his shoulders wider.

Jonathan's eyes met hers. He'd caught her staring at him.

Not just staring, but analyzing, admiring.

A blush climbed up Kara's cheeks. He only smiled, an almost lazy smile, before he downed a gulp of coffee and got back to work.

She tried to act as if nothing had happened between them as she filled her plate and took a seat as far from him as possible.

"I'm going out with the ranch hands today," Jonathan informed her a few minutes later. "I want what's left of the guard staying around headquarters."

An uneasiness settled over Kara. If Jonathan were leaving the guard here, he must expect trouble to strike at the headquarters next.

"The ground's drying," he continued. "The boys and I will be able to make some time riding today. By nightfall, we'll know for sure that the cattle have been stolen and not simply disappeared into one of the box canyons."

H. B. grumbled. "Don't you think I'd better ride with you?" None of the guard took to nesting, but H. B. was the worst of the lot. For the lanky old fighter, staying home rated right up there with a prison sentence.

"With Willis gone, Snort and Cooper wounded, and Newton not back from Fort Worth yet, I need you here." Jonathan slammed his coffee cup down and stormed across the room, not waiting for H. B. to answer.

"Miss O'Riley," he snapped as he passed her chair. "I need to see you for a minute."

Kara followed him to the study wondering what could be the matter. She didn't have long to wait.

As soon as the door closed, he turned to her and said, "It's not me they're trying to kill. It's the guard!"

He was right. The moment he said the words, she saw what had been the obvious answer all along.

"But why?"

"I don't know. Maybe just to get them out of the way so they can rustle cattle. Maybe someone hates lawmen."

Jonathan paced as he talked. "The harness left on the back porch wasn't meant for Gideon, but for one of the Old Guard when they came out after breakfast. Willis said the morning we left that his horse had been acting funny, like someone fed him locoweed. He'd wrestled the animal all day before he fell. Russell could have been pushed off the bluff behind his cabin. A man doesn't just walk out from a house he's lived in for ten years and forget where the cliff starts."

Kara hugged herself. "You're frightening me, Jonathan," she whispered. "These are not easy men to kill."

"That's why two of them are still alive. A shoulder wound and a blow to the head should have killed them both. Only, whoever did it may not know that either man is still alive. If he thought them dead, that might explain why he rode off without taking a third shot at me."

Jonathan pulled her against him as if the air had grown suddenly cold in the study. "I'll leave two ranch hands on guard. Newton should be back today. When he gets here, tell him what I suspect. Until then, be careful. I've got to take care of the cattle or there'll be nothing to sell come spring. If I hear even one shot, I'll be riding this way at breakneck speed."

"How many guards live in cabins near the borders?"

"Eight, I think," he whispered against her hair. "I'll call them all in. If my theory is right, we may not have much time before the shooter strikes again."

He kissed her forehead. "I'm glad you're here, Kara. There's something calming about having you around. This may be far from over."

"Be careful." She raised her head and lightly brushed his lips with her mouth. A friendly kiss, she told herself, nothing more.

"I'll be back before dark." Jonathan pulled away and left the study without another word.

He was a mile away from headquarters before he could think of anything besides the way her lips felt when they brushed his. There had been no passion in it, only caring, and that affected him far more. He could handle passion. Hell, he could buy passion by the hour if he wanted it. But caring. That was never for sale.

Jonathan tried to keep his mind on his job. He was

riding with cowhands now. They were mostly young men used to staying in the saddle all day, and they rode as if born to it. But they were not rangers. They lacked the edge even old rangers had for staying alive.

Pushing himself hard, Jonathan won their respect as they rounded up the herd on the north pasture. Thanks to the storm, strays were everywhere. By midafternoon, Jonathan felt like he'd pulled a hundred head out of the mud and twisted branches. The work was good for him, granting him a reprieve from other worries.

By the time the sun touched the horizon, Jonathan's body ached all the way to his bones. He'd heard no shots fired from headquarters, so all must be safe. Even in the midst of trouble, the work of ranching had to go on. And, with the work came long days.

After taking care of his horse, he walked slowly up the front steps feeling like he was wearing more than a few pounds of dirt. But it had felt good to push himself.

Kara met him at the door. She didn't say a word, but watched him closely.

He put his boot on the bench and unstrapped his spurs, then his gunbelt. "I've had a hard day of rounding up cattle, but all was quiet. I think we notified most of the guard to pack up their gear and move into the bunkhouse for a few days." He liked the way she waited for him to tell her instead of bombarding him with questions. "No sign of the missing cattle. Our best estimate is that we somehow lost a hundred during the storm."

As he slipped his coat off aching shoulders, he stopped suddenly, realizing she was helping him. For a moment he thought of pulling away and telling her he didn't need any assistance. But it felt good to let her help. Not because he needed it, but because she cared.

"Snort and Cooper are both better. Angela insists they get well." Kara's voice was low. "All was quiet here today."

"Good." He faced her. "Any food?"

Kara smiled at him. "I'll make you something while you clean up."

Jonathan only wanted to eat and tumble into bed, but he didn't argue. Twenty minutes later, he felt much better after a cold bath on the back porch and a change of clothes. He stepped into the kitchen just as she set a plate on the counter beside a platter of meat, a bowl of gravy and a basket of biscuits that smelled good enough to have been baked in heaven.

"Thanks. You didn't have to do this, you know." He pulled up a stool and took a bite of one of the biscuits while she poured coffee for them both.

"I know. I enjoy doing it for you. We're friends, after all."

He nodded and relaxed. They talked of the day with the ease of old friends. He found he not only enjoyed the conversation, but he also enjoyed watching her. He liked the way she moved. The way she talked with her hands. The way her eyes said more than her words.

When he finished, she moved to his side of the counter and picked up his empty plate. Jonathan twisted on the stool to face her and took the plate from her. "Wait," he said. "I need to give you something back that you gave me this morning."

Kara didn't move as he leaned close and lightly brushed his lips against hers.

"I know you're promised to another." He began what

he'd practiced all day. "But you're not married yet, so there could be no harm in our getting . . ." he picked his words carefully, "to know one another. Despite what you said the other night, I figure you're as interested as I am. We could . . ."

She pulled away. "We could what?" Fire suddenly danced in her green eyes as quickly as if lightning had struck there an instant before.

Jonathan fought to keep his frustration from showing. She wasn't reacting the way he'd thought she would. "I know you like being near, touching me. You enjoyed the kiss we shared by the windows as much as I did. We can't keep going hot and cold."

He wanted to say *you can't*, but he was trying to be considerate. "I think I know what we both aren't saying to one another. You're telling me you're engaged. I've made it plain that I want no ties. But we both know there's something between us. Maybe we could reach some kind of agreement."

He thought he'd come up with a logical plan, but she was getting angry before she heard the details.

"Agreement?" Her voice was low. Too low.

Jonathan didn't read the signal. "You know, something we'd both enjoy. I've never been around a woman I've wanted to hold so often. We could talk it out, set the boundaries. There doesn't have to be any ties or strings."

"Boundaries?" She said the word slowly.

He took her two words as a sign of negotiation. "I wouldn't expect you to share my bed. At least not until you're comfortable with doing so. I'm willing to go slowly."

She should have considered his thoughtfulness, but all she did was frown. "Boundaries," she whispered as though she'd heard the word once too often in her life.

"At any speed you like." He smiled, proud of himself for being the first to compromise. There was no reason for them to argue. They both wanted the same thing. He'd seen it in her eyes that morning. Felt it every time they touched. "It's foolish for both of us to fight to stay apart, to never touch. There's a kind of touching that could bring both of us a great deal of pleasure."

"And where do we start? A kiss each morning?" She crossed her arms, making him aware of her breasts.

"That would be fine." He thought about how much he'd enjoyed the way she'd touched her lips to his that morning.

"And at lunch?"

"If I'm home and we have a few minutes alone." He grinned. This was easier than he thought.

"And at night?"

"Definitely at night." He pushed away from the table. She was being practical about this. It didn't take any experience with women, he decided. It just took honesty, laying the facts on the table. He should have thought of this discussion before.

The plate hit him on the forehead first. Then the basket of biscuits slapped against his cheek, then the platter of meat and last the gravy. Jonathan was so totally taken off guard by the assault of food he didn't try to defend himself until the gravy. He managed to catch the bowl, sending gravy splattered all over him.

He watched the door slam behind Kara, more confused by her response than angry.

Before he could move, H. B. rattled through the back door with Newton just behind him.

The old man frowned, but the foreman burst out laughing.

"Well, I guess supper is over, Mr. Catlin," Newton said with no respect in his voice. "All over, if you get my drift."

"Shut up," Jonathan growled. He refused to wipe the gravy from his face.

"You and the 'wee little bookkeeper' must have had one hell of a fight." Newton hooted he was laughing so hard. "I would have paid to see it."

H. B.'s eyes narrowed on Jonathan. "You had a fight with Miss Kara? You didn't hurt her, did you? I won't tolerate that kind of behavior, even if your name is Catlin."

"I'm the one with the plate dent in my scalp and you're threatening *me!*" If the man hadn't been over twice his age, Jonathan would have swung at him.

Newton fell to his knees, still laughing.

Jonathan ignored him and faced H. B. "All we were doing was talking. She must have misunderstood something I said." *Probably everything I said,* he thought. "All at once plates started flying. She went crazy for no reason. The woman must be insane."

H. B. looked like he was already knotting the noose while he listened.

"We were just talking," Jonathan ended, almost wishing H. B. would slug him. He had no idea why, but he was sure he deserved it. "Go ahead. Kill me."

When he looked into the old man's eyes, Jonathan wasn't sure H. B. didn't plan to do just that.

Newton crawled across the floor. Every time he encountered a biscuit, he had another fit.

"You should have asked her how she felt," H. B. lectured. "I told you women like that kind of thing. Then you ask her to step out with you somewhere. And for a long while you're real careful not to talk about nothing that might be upsetting."

Newton interrupted the lecture as he tried to stand with the aid of a stool. "No, sir, Jonathan. We don't want to kill you. It'll be too much fun letting the 'wee little bookkeeper' do it."

H. B. didn't crack a smile. "Maybe I should shoot him in one or two limbs to make it a fair fight."

Newton finally managed to stand, still holding his side. "Hell, H. B., it looks like she's the one winning."

Jonathan felt along his hairline with gravy-splattered fingers. A knot the size of an egg was already forming. If he kept running into Kara, he wouldn't have to worry about anyone else killing him. Newton was right, she'd do the job.

Newton continued, "Maybe we should teach her to shoot so she won't make such a mess in the kitchen when she does murder you."

"I already have," Jonathan grumbled.

Newton suffered another fit.

TWENTY

Kara ran all the way to her room and curled on the floor against the far side of her bed. She'd never been so humiliated. Jonathan talked to her as if she meant nothing to him, like they were making some kind of deal. It wasn't as though she were a woman of the streets and he was negotiating a price for service. He expected favors because she'd said they were friends. Friends!

He didn't deserve to have a friend.

He didn't deserve to be kissed! She wished she could take them all back.

He didn't even deserve to have her as a bookkeeper. No, she reconsidered. He deserved that. In the months she'd been here she had managed to calculate the books into worse shape than they were when she arrived.

When she thought over all he had said, anger replaced tears. Where on earth would he get such a lamebrain plan? Yes, she kissed him a few times, but of course she hadn't meant to. It had always been an action she'd taken without thought, in the heat of the moment. It had always "just happened."

Kara remembered something her neighbor back home used to say about girls who claimed getting pregnant "just happened." The old woman would shake her finger at Kara and say, "Ain't nothing that just happens that involves taking off your clothes. Lightning don't strike leaving you naked."

Kara's anger turned inward. She had been a fool, lying to herself, not owning up to her actions and her feelings. No wonder Jonathan was confused. She told him she was engaged, but she didn't act the part. She'd already done what he suggested—touched him, been near him, kissed him. And all the while denying feelings were involved. If she hadn't planned it, or thought about it, then she wouldn't have to admit any guilt or responsibility.

The truth slammed against Kara's heart. She didn't love Devin O'Toole. She never loved him. He'd merely been a means to assure herself that someone cared about her, wanted her. Even when he said he would marry her one day, he'd been joking with her father and not looking at her.

Kara cried, realizing she was just as locked away in an imaginary world as Angela. She hadn't been honest about her life. Telling herself she loved Devin. Telling herself she didn't feel anything for Jonathan.

Between her tears, Kara saw her door open slowly. Dawn tiptoed in as silently as a breeze. The woman wore her newly made leather dress, complete with beads and braid. Her hair was combed free, blond against the warm leather. Before, she'd looked broken, a crumpled spirit in her "white women's rags." Now, she stood tall, radiant.

Dawn didn't say a word but knelt beside Kara and pulled her into her arms. The gesture was so unconditional in its acceptance, Kara cried even harder.

Dawn stroked Kara's hair and whispered softly. It didn't matter that Kara couldn't understand the words. She understood the meaning.

A moment later Jonathan opened the door. Both women glanced toward him.

Dawn said something sharp and angry to him in Apache.

For a second, he looked like he'd been slapped. "Wonderful! You don't understand a word and you still take her side."

He slammed the door without bothering to translate his words to Apache.

Kara gulped down a giggle. If *she* was confused, she could only imagine how Jonathan felt. He claimed he knew little about women and their last conversation had proved his words true.

In the morning she would apologize for her behavior and for her flirtations. He only offered what he thought she wanted. Tomorrow, she'd tell him how wrong he'd been. She didn't want the game of loving at all. And she didn't want the pretense as she had with Devin. She wanted real love, and Jonathan made it plain that he never wanted ties.

No matter how attracted to one another they were, they didn't match.

If it were a choice between a complete kind of loving or nothing at all, Kara would take nothing at all.

In a strange kind of way, by asking for "an agreement" Jonathan was more honest with her than she'd been with him.

Dawn smiled as she wiped away the last of Kara's tears. It didn't matter that they understood none of each other's words. They were friends.

Kara complimented the dress. Dawn beamed with pride. She tugged on Kara's hand urging her to follow. Once they were in Dawn's room, the young mother showed her the things she was making for the baby.

When Kara finally went back to her own room, she decided to pack. After making a fool of herself, she couldn't stay. She would ask one of the men to take her into Brady, and from there, catch the stage to Fort Worth where she could buy a train ticket. She knew Jonathan would be fair about paying her for the months and probably let her keep the clothes. She would promise to send money back to square the debt as soon as she found other work.

There must be a job somewhere for the world's worst bookkeeper.

At dawn, she walked down the stairs with her head held high. She felt she'd grown much older during the night. If nothing else from knowing first Devin and then Jonathan, she'd learned what she didn't want. A part-time love or a someday marriage would never do.

H. B., Newton, Gideon and Luther waited for her in the dining room. All stood at attention as she entered, then fought to see which one would pull out her chair.

For a few minutes all were silent, until Newton said, "Pass the gravy."

He fought to keep down a laugh as the other men

frowned at him, but Newton was a man who never reined in his feelings.

H. B. attempted to silence Newton by delivering a blow across the large man's chest. If Newton hadn't weighed two hundred pounds, he would have been knocked out of his chair.

Kara's cheeks burned. There was no question that the men knew about the fight. She only hoped they didn't know the details. She took a deep breath. It was either die of embarrassment, or laugh. Laughing seemed easier.

"Of course." She picked up the gravy bowl. "Would you like biscuits tossed your direction, also?"

The roar that followed shook the windows. All the men talked at once, telling Kara they didn't care what the argument last night was about. They were on her side.

"You should have seen the man," Newton snorted. "He was downright calico from head to foot. Gravy spots, meat stuck to him, biscuits hanging off him." They all roared. "And he had this look on his face as if he had no idea where the sudden food storm had come from."

"But we knew." H. B. nodded with the soberness of a judge. "It had to be an Irish storm."

Newton agreed.

Snort came into the dining room, a blanket draped over his bandaged shoulder. Newton related the story again, adding several points he must have forgotten in the first telling.

Finally, when everyone calmed down, Kara asked, "Where is Jonathan?" At this point, she wouldn't have been surprised if the men had tied him up.

"He left early to meet the supply train due in from Kansas City. One of the rangers, who rode in last night, said the wagons were camped just inside Catlin land. They should be here in a few hours."

Kara tried to smile but couldn't. A supply train from Kansas City might bring her a letter from Mary Ann, maybe even from her father. Enough time had passed for the letter to go through Mary Ann to Father James, to her father and back again. In a few hours she might have word that all was calm at home once more and she could return. The longer her father took to answer, the more her worries grew.

The wagons would also be heading back, offering her the ride she needed. Her time at Catlin Ranch was ending. She'd apologize to Jonathan, then say her good-byes.

She excused herself and headed toward the study. As she passed the great room, Kara noticed Angela sitting beside Cooper. He appeared to be sleeping. Kara watched Angela straighten the covers across his chest, then gently brush a strand of his graying hair from his bandaged forehead.

Not wanting to pry, Kara hurried to the small study she used as an office.

Three hours later, she was still trying to straighten the mass of paperwork so that some real bookkeeper could take over. She heard Gideon yell to pull the gates and glanced up to see wagons rolling into the courtyard.

Kara ran to watch along with everyone else on the ranch.

Angela told her that general supplies came in from Brady, but twice a year the ranch ordered their main goods from Kansas City. Among the delivery would be gardening tools, seeds and four dozen trees with their roots wrapped in burlap. Two new washtubs for the bunkhouse. A Franklin stove for the new wing that had been built last fall had also been included.

One wagon contained all manner of saddles and gear needed for the roundup. Another wagon hauled only rosewood planks to complete the chapel Miss Victoria had started years ago by the cemetery.

Kara stood on the porch, watching as men hurried from the bunkhouse to ask about shipments they requested.

The driver of the third wagon seemed to have most of the personal orders. When the crowd cleared, Kara ventured closer to him.

"Do you have anything for Kara O'Riley?" she asked. "A letter from a Mary Ann Adams, perhaps?"

"Fifth wagon," the man shouted as he moved his team out of the way. "The one with a covering."

Kara noticed Jonathan watching her from atop his horse, but she didn't speak to him as she ran to the fifth wagon. His hat was low against the sun but she knew he wasn't smiling. He was not a man given to smiling, and after last night he would probably never do so again in her presence.

When Kara came around the side of the fifth wagon, a tiny woman in a black shawl almost jumped off the bench. "Kara!" Mary Ann cried.

For a moment, Kara couldn't believe what she saw. "Mary Ann!" she shouted. "Oh, Mary Ann."

They hugged and laughed.

"But how? Why?" Kara had too many questions to get any one out of her mouth.

"Mr. Bayley said I could come. But I can only stay a few days. Then I have to go back with the wagons. In your letters, you talked about this place so much, I had to see it. I hope I don't crowd you up by coming so close to Christmas? I told Mr. Bayley you were my family and I just had to come."

"Oh, no, we have plenty of room." She glanced at Jonathan, who was near enough to hear the conversation.

He still frowned, but he nodded at Kara, backing up her invitation.

"The children are asleep in the wagon. They made me promise to wake them when we got here." Mary Ann looped her arm around Kara's. "We also brought you a grand surprise."

As the women rounded the rear of the wagon, a man backed out from beneath the canvas top. He wore the first wool, square-cut suit Kara had seen in months and carried a little round hat that looked out of place. His legs were stocky and short, his chest broad.

As he stepped down he sneezed loudly and reached for a handkerchief in his back pocket with worn workman's hands. He blew his nose and turned to face the women.

When Kara's gaze reached his face, her heart stopped. "Devin!" she whispered with the little air left in her lungs.

"Karina O'Riley," he said with a nod. "I've come to take you home." His words were matter-of-fact, more an order than a request. His smile one of relief.

Jonathan swung out of his saddle in one fluid movement and caught Kara just seconds before she hit the dirt. He lifted her up in his arms and turned toward the house without even a glance in the direction of Devin O'Toole. He'd watched the Irishman for the past three hours and seen quite enough of the man.

"What's wrong with the lass?" Devin asked as he followed. "She's a simpleton, that one, fainting at the sight of someone she's known near all her life."

No one listened to the redheaded man in wool. Jonathan glanced at Newton and knew the foreman's observations were the same as his. Devin hadn't offered so much as a handshake to his future bride.

Without a word Jonathan passed the command to Newton, for he had other things on his mind and in his arms at the moment.

After Jonathan carried Kara through the wide front doors, H. B. stepped in front of Devin like a huge human gate.

"Pardon me!" Devin tried to move around the old man who towered over him.

"You're pardoned, mister, but you'll not pass until the boss gives the word." H. B.'s snarl pushed the Irishman back a few feet.

"I'll have you know I'm a friend of the O'Riley family." Devin's face reddened with anger.

"I don't care if you're President Ulysses S. Grant and Julia B. is calling. No one enters the house without an invitation."

Devin wouldn't be put off so easily. "Who do you think you are?" With a deep breath he barreled his chest, like a rooster preparing to fight. The effect was ruined shortly when he had to sneeze.

"I'm Saint Peter, and you're fixin' to pass through the pearly gates if you don't back off." H. B. smiled, truly smiled, for the first time in months.

Devin backed down. "I'll wait until Karina comes to her senses. If the woman ever does."

H. B. widened his stance and remained rooted to his post.

Mary Ann watched the exchange. She shivered, huddling close to her sleeping children. If Devin O'Toole hadn't been allowed to enter, she and her children might also not be able to pass. She may have traveled all this way to spend Christmas with her friend and be left to sleep in the wagon. Kara had written about the men called the Old Guard. She'd said they were old, but she hadn't mentioned how frightening they looked.

A cowboy, who'd been yelling orders in rapid fire, stepped up to Mary Ann. Though he was easily twice her size or more, he held his hat in his hand as though bashful.

"Pardon me, ma'am. I'm Jason Newton, the foreman of this spread." He blushed beneath his tanned skin. "I understand you're Miss Kara's friend. Is there any way I can be of service to you?"

Mary Ann was almost too afraid to speak. "I'm Mrs. Adams. If no one would object, I'd like to find a place to get my children out of the cold." She looked around at the other buildings. The place was like a small town with not only a huge house but a long bunkhouse next to the barn and several other buildings encircled by a stone fence.

"Have you had any lunch, Mrs. Adams?" the big man asked.

"No." She raised her gaze to meet his. He had kind eyes. Eyes that said he'd been all alone in the world and he knew of a better place to be.

"Well, we got the best cook in the county in our kitchen," he began. "How about I take you and the little ones in to meet her? I'm sure Miss Kara is in good hands. We've got Luther, the best almost-doctor in the state."

Mary Ann smiled shyly. "And you're the best foreman?"

"That I am." Newton smiled. "That I am."

Jonathan carried Kara into the great room and lowered her gently onto the couch.

Angela rose from Cooper's side and hurried to get a damp towel. "Is she hurt?" The cook shoved two cowhands aside so she could have a better look.

"I think she just fainted." Jonathan couldn't keep the worry from his voice.

Snort, who'd taken up residence in one of the comfortable chairs by the fireplace, moved closer. He nursed his arm as he asked, "You didn't say anything to upset her, did you, Boss?"

Jonathan cut his eyes at the man. Why was it when anything happened to Kara, the blame was always placed on him?

"I didn't even speak to her. She just fainted."

Luther moved next to Snort. "She's mighty pale. She was fine this morning at breakfast." He lowered his voice. "Maybe it's her time."

"What time?" Snort asked, scratching his head.

"You know." Luther's voice was as low as he could

get it and still be speaking. "Her time of the month."

"What time of the month? What are you talking about?" Snort questioned. "You're not making any sense."

Luther looked embarrassed. "Don't you know nothing about women?"

"I know plenty. I had a mother, and I had a wife for three days before she left with a piano player down in Fort Smith."

"She left you for a piano player?" Luther said the last words as though that profession were one level above lice.

"Yeah, but he was a real good one from what I was told. I went out to have a smoke and a few drinks and when I come back, I was single again. She said at least with him, she'd always have music." Snort shook his head. "Ain't that the dumbest thing you ever heard? I missed that woman for a year before I figured out I was better off without her."

"Gentlemen, could you finish reminiscing about your courting days somewhere else?" Jonathan complained.

Angela handed Jonathan a glass of water and shooed the old men aside.

Jonathan lifted Kara's shoulders in the bend of his arm and touched the glass to her lips. He couldn't get the way she looked when she saw Devin out of his mind. He wasn't sure how to describe it, but she sure didn't look happy to see the man.

"Come on, darlin', take a drink," he encouraged.

Kara swallowed once, then opened her eyes. "I thought I saw . . ."

She closed her eyes again. Jonathan set the glass

down. He wasn't sure where to put his hand. If he closed his other arm around her, he'd look like he was hugging her. If he placed his hand at her waist, he would be reminded of what was just above. If he held her too far away from him, the guards would start lecturing him. If he held her too close, she would probably slap him when she came to.

Jonathan decided he could never win.

When she looked up once more, he whispered close to her ear, "Your fiancé. Devin O'Toole is here." From the way the man acted when he saw Kara, Jonathan couldn't help but wonder if *O'Toole* knew he was the man she planned to marry.

"He's not really here, is he?" She curled her face against his neck.

"I can get rid of him if you like," Jonathan answered.

"You can?"

"I'll have H. B. kill him."

Green eyes opened wide in shock.

Jonathan's smile let her know he was kidding.

"That won't be necessary," she reasoned. "I'll talk to him."

"I'll put H. B. in reserve, just in case you change your mind."

TWENTY-ONE

Kara stared out one of the huge windows running along a wall of the great room. Sure enough, there was Devin O'Toole looking as out of place as a goose egg in a wolf den. She watched him for a while, wondering why she ever thought him handsome. His face was pale, pinkish really, his movements awkward, not smooth and fluid like Jonathan's. He didn't even look balanced without a Colt strapped to one leg.

"What are you going to do about the Irishman?" Snort asked from just behind her. "He means to take you home."

"I know." She didn't add that her bags were packed and waiting. Until the wagons arrived, she planned to leave. Now, she wasn't so sure.

"I think I'll have a word with my friend before I ask Devin in," Kara announced. "Angela said Mary Ann is in the kitchen."

Snort nodded his approval. "No need to bring the Irishman in before dark."

Kara left before she started laughing. Snort talked about Devin as though he were a houseplant.

In the kitchen, she found Mary Ann and her children drinking hot cocoa and eating Angela's cookies. Newton entertained them with stories as if he didn't have a ranch to run.

Kara hugged her friend again. Somehow, over the months of writing, they became close. She wasn't sure why, but she'd written her feelings boldly when she might have hesitated had she been speaking directly to Mary Ann. And Mary Ann had answered with advice and understanding.

"I had to come when Devin dropped into the store asking if any of us knew a Karina O'Riley. He traced you from Miss Abigail's Business School, who'd given him the lawyer Clark's address. From there, Clark said you were working for a rancher named Catlin. Devin figured ranchers would have accounts at the mercantile. I think he said we were the fifth one he tried. He's a determined man, I'll say that for him."

"And you told him I was here?"

Mary nodded. "I remember your exact words: 'Unless the man's name is Devin O'Toole, don't tell anyone where I am.' "

Kara could barely remember saying the words. Over the months, Devin had become less and less real to her. In truth, she had just dreamed he might come to get her, but never believed he would. Most of the conversations she'd had with Devin had been in her imagination.

"What did he say to you?" Kara found it hard to understand why he came all this way for her when he wouldn't take the time to come to the Pittsburgh train station to say good-bye. "How did you know it was Devin?"

"He said that he was looking for you." Mary Ann's face filled with sadness for her friend as she began to hear what Kara wasn't saying in her questioning. "I asked him his name. He told me and so I helped him."

Kara closed her eyes, knowing Mary Ann could see her unhappiness.

"I thought you'd be glad to see him," Mary Ann whispered.

Kara wanted to ask if he'd said he loved her. Was he coming after her to marry her? Had he missed her dearly?

But Kara couldn't ask. She knew the answer. Devin hadn't said any words of endearment or Mary Ann would have shared them. He'd come after her, but she wasn't sure why.

"You did the right thing," Kara made herself say to Mary Ann. "You did what I asked you to do." She couldn't bring herself to add a thank-you.

Refusing to allow even one tear to fall, Kara squared her shoulders and walked from the room. It was time to face Devin.

She opened the front door.

"Well, it's about time," Devin snapped as he passed H. B., who still stared at him with open hatred. "I thought you planned to keep me waiting all day, and me with the worst cold a man could have."

Kara led him to the office and closed the door behind them. She wasn't sure where to start to tell him how she'd changed.

"I'm here to take you home, girl. I don't appreciate

you leaving me outside while you think about speaking to me." He began even before she faced him. "I've traveled quite a way and gone to great trouble to track you down."

She'd forgotten his temper. Her father once said it would get Devin killed one day if the man didn't learn to control it.

"How is my father?" she asked.

"Fine. He asked me if you still had those papers he sent you out here with."

Kara had to think to remember what Devin was talking about. The packet her father had given her that day was still in the bottom of her suitcase, but she thought it strange he'd mention it to Devin.

"I'll have to look," she lied.

"You'd better not have lost them, Karina, or there'll be hell to pay." He rubbed his nose on his sleeve. "Now, how soon can you be ready to travel? I'm ready to be gone from this country."

"Did Papa send any word?" An uneasiness settled in the back of Kara's mind. Devin treated her like a child, as he always had. He asked nothing of how she'd been. He didn't even seem to want to talk to her more than was necessary.

"No. No message. Just that you're to come home." He said the last two words as if to end any further discussion.

Her father's last words haunted her. He told her to disappear and to be very careful who she trusted. "How did you find me?"

"Your father said he received a note from Kansas City." Devin rocked up and down on his toes as if breaking in new shoes. "I thought I'd have to ask every person in that town before I ran into anyone who knew you."

"Didn't Papa give you Mary Ann's address?"

Devin hesitated a fraction too long. "He lost it."

Something wasn't right. Kara couldn't make the pieces fit. If her father had told Devin from where her letter had been postmarked, surely he would have told the man the rest of her information. Maybe Devin only saw the envelope, nothing more. If he wanted to find her so badly, why was he so angry now? Surely, after all this time a few more days couldn't matter.

"If you'll have a seat, Devin, I'll have tea sent in." Maybe after he calmed down a bit, it would be easier to talk to him. He probably didn't feel well either. The trip must have been hard on a man not used to being out in the weather.

"Well, aren't you the high-and-mighty lady having tea sent in? You'd think you were the mistress of this grand house and not just the bookkeeper like the lawyer said." There was a cutting frost in his voice.

Kara fought down a comment as she walked away. She never remembered Devin being so furious when he spoke to her. Busy, preoccupied, teasing, but never angry. Something had changed, and she wasn't at all sure she liked the difference.

She asked Angela to take the Irishman a tray and hurried out the back door to find Jonathan. Maybe if she could talk things out, they would be more clear.

He was helping the men take care of the teams of horses. When Jonathan saw her coming he grabbed the reins of his horse and headed toward her.

When he reached her, he asked simply, "We need to walk?"

"We walk," she agreed. They headed out the back gate into open pasture.

Like a prairie dog on open ground, she knew where her spot was. Jonathan would swear she stopped within a few feet of where they had their last walk. When she faced him, he couldn't hide the smile. For once, her eyes flashed with anger, and he wasn't the cause.

She hesitated, as though not knowing where to start. "How's your head?"

"Sore." He removed his hat. The knot had turned to a bruise, most of which was covered by his unruly hair.

She reached to push his hair away so she could see the injury, but he moved out of her reach. He didn't want her to touch him. He wasn't sure what he'd do if Kara touched him. The need to hold her had become a constant ache in his gut.

"I'm sorry," she whispered.

"That makes two of us, I reckon." He carefully replaced his hat. "I didn't mean to insult you last night."

"I know."

"If it's any comfort, every man on the place volunteered to shoot me for making you cry." He stared at her and wondered if his need for her showed in his eyes. "I probably shouldn't be telling you this, but damn, Kara, if I don't want to kiss you right now."

She smiled. "You're only saying that because there are no platters present."

He grinned. "Maybe I am. But our fight last night isn't the reason you brought me out here, is it?"

She shook her head. "It's a long story, but I've got to tell someone."

Kara didn't have to add that she had no one else to talk to. Despite their fights, they trusted one another and he had no intention of ever breaking that trust. "We've got a few hours before sundown. Tell me about it."

Kara told him of the battles in the mills between groups of workers. Of how her father was always one of the leaders. Of the secret meetings and the violence against families that was never solved.

Jonathan listened without interrupting. The two groups of Irishmen sounded like warring tribes, each trying to even the pain caused by the other.

When she finally relayed all her father had said on the day he'd put her on the train, Jonathan read what she didn't say in her eyes.

"You're not sure you want to go back with Devin," he said.

Kara nodded. "I know I should trust him. He's close to my father. I grew up with him dropping by the house."

"But he came after you," Jonathan interjected, "and no one is supposed to come after you until the year is up."

"I wrote my father weeks ago. He hasn't answered. But he must have gotten the letter. Devin knew it was postmarked from Kansas City."

"Maybe it's still not safe to go back," Jonathan added. "Maybe your father doesn't know Devin came after you."

"I have no reason to mistrust Devin."

"Maybe O'Toole couldn't stand you being gone."

Jonathan already knew the truth. He'd known it the moment he'd seen Devin greet Kara without touching her. Any man who could do that was not in love or planning to marry.

"There's something else I should tell you. Though he said honest and true he would marry me one day, I'm not sure he meant it. He always had more important matters on his mind. Maybe he just said the words in passing, teasing the little girl of his friend."

"The man's a fool." Jonathan studied her closely. "Do you want to marry him, Kara?"

"I always thought I would, but now I'm not sure I even want to ride home with him. The real man I see today doesn't measure up to the young girl's daydreams I once had of him."

"Let's give him a few days. If there's something rotten about his story, it'll start to smell."

Kara agreed. "Something tells me the idea of going back with the man isn't going to grow on me."

Jonathan swung up in the saddle. "Ready to ride back?"

"If you'll go slower this time."

"I promise." Jonathan smiled as he reached down and pulled her up in front of him.

His arm rested around her as she leaned against his chest. "You're a comfortable woman to be around, Miss O'Riley."

"And so even-tempered," she added.

"Aye," he answered in a terrible Irish accent.

For a few minutes they were silent, then he added, "I'll be riding out after supper. It's a clear night, and some of the guard think it might be interesting to set a trap and see what triggers it. We're not mentioning it to any of the ranch hands, but I wanted you to know."

Kara didn't say a word, but he felt her lean a little closer into him. She knew the danger. Two men recovering in the great room were proof of it. But the past few days had been calm, and Jonathan was ready to stop reacting and start acting.

"H. B. and the others think we should run the ranch as usual, only keep extra guards posted. We plan to be ready the next time strangers step onto Catlin land."

"Maybe they'll stay away until after Christmas?"

"With the McLains coming in a few days, they'd be fools not to. Wait 'til you meet the three brothers. Adam's the kind one. Folks say he has healing hands. Wes, my brother-in-law, is meaner than a rattler, but there's no other man I'd rather have covering my back in a fight. And Daniel, he's the youngest. They kid him about being a preacher, but in truth he's a teacher."

Jonathan spread his fingers along her back as he talked of his family. "When you put the three McLains with Wolf no outlaw gang would stand against them."

"You care for them dearly, don't you?" she added.

He started to deny it, but finally admitted, "They're a hard group to hate. Believe me, I've tried." He slowed the horse and studied her face. "They wear honesty and pride and love for their women out in the open for all the world to see."

He watched her green eyes fill with tears and he could almost read her thoughts.

Encouraging the horse he crossed the courtyard, sorry that there was no more time for them to talk . . . afraid of what he might have said if there had been.

Devin waited on the long porch. His arms were crossed like those of an angry father waiting for his daughter to come home.

Jonathan swung from the horse, then lowered Kara down slowly. He could feel the tension in her body and wondered if she were afraid of Devin.

Without turning around, Jonathan said, "You're welcome to stay a few days, Mr. O'Toole. You might enjoy the holiday on Catlin Ranch. I'll have Gideon fix you up a bed in the bunkhouse."

"Karina and I will be leaving at dawn. One of the men with the wagons said he would take us as far as a town named Brady." Devin snapped the words out like orders. Then as an afterthought he added, "But thank you for your offer. If we leave soon, we'll be home well before the new year."

Jonathan tensed as if preparing for a fight, but Kara touched his arm as she moved around him.

"If you must leave at dawn, Devin, I wish you Godspeed home, but I won't be accompanying you. I was hired for a year and I plan to hold to my agreement."

"What?" Devin took a step toward her. "Your father wants you home, girl. You'll leave when I tell you it's time."

Like shadows materializing into form, several members of the guard appeared. Jonathan guessed Kara hadn't even had time to meet most of them, but they were there for her. H. B. stood at her side, his hand resting on his Colt's handle.

Jonathan closed the distance between him and Devin. "Are you any kin to Miss O'Riley?" His voice was hard with anger. "A brother, a father, a fiancé?"

Devin didn't back down. "I'm a friend of the family, and I've told her more than once that I might marry her one day—if she grows up proper. I guess that makes me about as close as kin."

"That makes you nothing of the sort, Mr. O'Toole, and in this part of the country, men who are not kin are not in the habit of bossing women around." Jonathan reconsidered. "In fact, men who *are* kin tend to hesitate. Miss O'Riley is perfectly capable of making up her own mind as to what she will and will not do."

"This is none of your concern, sir," Devin replied.

"You're wrong. Kara isn't just my employee, she's my friend. I respect her far too much to let her be bullied by the likes of you, or by anyone."

Kara moved to Jonathan's side. "Thank you all." She glanced at the guard, drawing strength from the wonderful old men. "I can speak for myself." She faced Devin. "Stay or go, as you wish, but I won't be going along."

Only Jonathan felt her hand tremble as she placed it on his arm. They walked together past a speechless Devin O'Toole.

TWENTY-TWO

KARA TUCKED HER TOES BENEATH THE HEM OF HER gown. She sat in the darkness at the bend in the stairs, hugging her knees for warmth. Garlands hung over the doorways, adding a touch of holiday spirit to the old house, but she still didn't feel like it could possibly be three days until Christmas.

She'd been told that Jonathan's grandmother established a tradition years ago. All were welcome at the Catlin Ranch on Christmas Day. A huge meal would be served. Every person who attended brought one small gift. The presents were collected and placed on the chairs around the tables. As everyone sat down, they opened a gift. No one knew who brought what. No one received more than one gift.

Kara could hardly wait. It sounded like great fun. Angela told her the swapping of gifts usually went on the rest of the day. There was even a story of how a poker game lasted until dawn with a two-dollar gift that went as the high stakes.

Memories of life before she came to Texas brought Kara little comfort. Her father allowed no decorations, seeing them as a waste of money. Gifts had to be practical, things needed. In the end, she thought, he had even sent her away because she wasn't essential.

Kara had a feeling that if she went home, it would be exactly the same. If she married Devin, she'd move to another house along the row. But nothing else would change. She'd always be useful but never be truly needed. Maybe when she left here, she should keep going. Kara hugged herself for warmth and tried to decide.

Well after midnight, she heard the kitchen door open and close. Jonathan was home. She watched him from above. As always, he stopped to remove his spurs and gun belt in the foyer.

When he pulled off his hat, he noticed her. "Morning." He sounded tired. "You're up early."

"I haven't been able to sleep." Kara viewed him through the carved staircase railing. "Any luck with your hunting?"

"None. We chased the wind all night. Maybe the trouble is over." He didn't sound convinced. "Some think the man who shot Snort and Cooper may have just been a lone rustler who panicked."

He ran his fingers through his hair but it quickly fell back in disarray. "Did your Devin try to come knocking after dark?"

Kara laughed. She hadn't missed the twin Colts he'd left for her by the door. "No, and he's not *my* Devin. I didn't really expect him after I heard H. B. tell him any man found sleepwalking around the courtyard would be buried at dawn."

Jonathan smiled. "I'm glad H. B. scared him off. I hear anger in his words when he talks to you and it grates on my patience." He raised an eyebrow as if daring her to comment. When she didn't, he continued, "For a man who traveled so far to find you, O'Toole hasn't wasted any time rejoicing."

"I've been thinking about that. Maybe he resents my father sending him."

"Maybe." Jonathan shrugged. "But I'd rather you didn't leave with him. If you really want to go home, ride back on the wagons with Mary Ann, then take the train from Kansas City."

"I agree. I'm not sure why, but I agree. I'm not returning with him."

"Are you going back?" He slowly moved up the steps. "I heard you last night after our fight and figured you were packing." He lowered beside her. "I wouldn't blame you if you didn't stay the year."

"I'm not sure," she answered honestly.

Jonathan stretched his legs down several steps. "If you're not leaving with O'Toole, does that mean you're not marrying him when, and if, he finds the time for such things?"

Kara laughed. "After seeing how he acted yesterday, I wouldn't marry him if he begged." And she could never imagine Devin O'Toole begging. "The only thing he'll be taking home is a cold."

"Then you're not engaged?" Jonathan's voice lowered.

"No," she answered. "I guess I'm not."

He shifted. "Then, would you have any objection to stepping out with me tomorrow night, Miss O'Riley?

I've been told there's a Christmas barn dance in Brady at Wilson's barn."

"Are you sure you should leave the ranch?"

"I can't hide here forever. Besides, dances don't come along in this part of the country very often. It would be a shame to miss one. I'd like to take you, if you're willing." His words were deliberate as if he'd practiced the order carefully.

Kara stood and curtsied. "I'd love to go, Mr. Catlin."

His long frame rose more slowly. "Thank you."

Before she could say anything else, H. B. stomped into the foyer with Snort close behind him. Kara glanced at her dressing gown and hurried to her room before anyone noticed her.

Jonathan thought he heard her laugh with excitement and wondered if this were the first time she'd been asked by a man to step out. For some odd reason, he hoped it was.

"Well?" H. B. met Jonathan at the bottom of the stairs. "Did you ask her?"

"I asked her."

"What'd she say?" Snort leaned in close to listen. "One day's notice to a dance don't seem like much."

"We ain't got much time," H. B. announced. "She'll be packed and on her way if he don't get to asking."

"She said yes." Jonathan watched the two men do a silent jig. Anyone would think they were the ones going out by the way they acted.

H. B. sobered. "Now there ain't but one thing to do."

"What's that?" Jonathan asked.

"I got to ride into Brady and convince Wilson he's having a dance come sundown tomorrow."

• • •

Kara spent the day working on the books. Mary Ann joined her and, surprisingly, turned out to be a great help. Mary Ann showed her ways Kara hadn't been taught in school that made the accounting make sense.

They stopped for tea at three. Devin and Newton joined them in the kitchen. Though his cold was worse, Devin seemed in a better mood, saying he'd decided to accept Catlin's offer to stay a few days.

Kara relaxed a little, not wanting to fight with Devin. They talked of news from home while Newton entertained Mary Ann.

Devin showed an interest in the house so Kara gave him a tour. To her surprise he seemed very interested in the study where she worked and was still asking her questions about bookkeeping when they came down the back stairway, crossed through what Angela called a mud room and returned to the kitchen.

H. B. and Luther had disappeared, but Snort was there, acting as guard, even with his shoulder bound. He mumbled something about Mary Ann leaving with Newton to show her children a jack rabbit they kept in the barn as a pet.

While Kara finished the tea, Devin complained about the food, the snoring in the bunkhouse, the cold and, finally, about not leaving Texas. He stated flatly that he would talk Karina into going with him as soon as his head cleared enough for him to think.

"You could leave today, Devin. If you wish." Kara tried to keep her voice calm. "I just can't go with you and whether your head is clear or muddled, my answer will not change."

"I'm not leaving without you, Karina." He huffed up and stormed toward the kitchen door. "I'll be taking you with me when I go." His words echoed along with the sound of the door slamming.

"Temper?" Snort mumbled over his mug.

Kara laughed. "My father always said it would get him into trouble."

"I wouldn't doubt that."

Angela interrupted the conversation by plopping a huge box down on the counter.

"I have these shawls," she began as if nothing of interest to her had occurred all morning. "From my mother and grandmother. They came all the way from Mexico City."

She opened the box. Rich colors covered the table. "Gideon told me women always wore these kind of things to parties. I don't have any use for them. You and Mrs. Adams are each welcome to borrow one for tonight. I understand our Newton has asked the widow to the dance."

Kara was amazed at Angela's generosity. True, she had nothing to wear, but she'd never had new clothes for dances. Now, she had a rainbow to choose from. Reds, blues, golds, greens. All with long fringe and beautiful handwork woven in intricate patterns.

When Kara hugged Angela, she thought the tall old maid might cry.

"Come with us," Kara begged. "The dance will be great fun."

"I can't," Angela answered. "I have to stay."

She said the words she must have said all her adult life, never having left the ranch after dark. But this time there was no sadness in her voice. There was someone who'd be staying with her.

An hour before sunset, Kara walked onto the porch wearing one of Angela's beautiful shawls. She felt like a queen with the bright colors flowing around her. Snort, Cooper and Angela watched from the windows as Kara waited. Everyone else, including Newton and Mary Ann, had left a few hours ago with decorations and food. But Jonathan had asked her to stay and ride in with him.

As Gideon pulled a buggy from the barn, Jonathan appeared from around the side of the house. He almost took her breath away. Unlike the cowhands, he hadn't just worn clean work clothes. His trousers, coat and vest were black, the coat cut long, the vest snug. Shiny black, square-toed boots shone from beneath his pants. He was every bit a man she might imagine coming to call on her in her dreams.

No, better than her dreams. Far better.

He offered his hand. "Shall we go?"

Kara fought down a giggle. This must be in one of her fantasies. A handsome man, a carriage, and a red shawl.

He helped her into the buggy. When they circled the courtyard, she caught a glimpse of Devin on the bunkhouse porch. He didn't look happy.

Jonathan must have read her mind, for he said, "Several of the hands invited O'Toole to ride in with them. He refused, saying he'd better stay home and nurse his cold. He swears the medicine Luther gave him makes him sleep." Jonathan laughed. "I wouldn't be surprised if it did," he mumbled to himself.

Kara guessed she should probably feel guilty about leaving poor Devin, but she didn't want anything to spoil this one night. She leaned back into the leather of the buggy and smiled, planning to enjoy every minute.

Jonathan drove without saying anything, but she could feel the warmth of his body next to hers. They watched the sun spread out along the horizon as they neared town. The wind blew low, stirring tumbleweeds across the land so that the round clumps of twigs looked like they were dancing.

Jonathan finally broke the silence. "This land grows on you, doesn't it?"

"That it does."

"When I first took over, all I could think about was getting the ranch running so I could sell it and move on. But now, I'm not so sure. Of late I worry about whether I'll have the money at the end of the year to have the ranch in the black."

"You might stay if you're in the black and the ranch becomes truly yours?"

"I don't know," he answered. "I think it would take more to make me set down roots, but the land does have a pull on a man. They say if you ever live beside the ocean, then move, you miss the sound of it the rest of your life. This land is like that."

"I'll miss the sunsets and the silence and maybe, sometimes, the wind."

"If you leave," he said as he pulled the wagon among others, "I'll miss *you*."

He stepped out and turned to offer his hand. Their eyes met. His simple statement surprised her, but his blue gaze was true and steady.

He placed her hand on his arm, and they walked into the dance.

The barn was just that, a barn. The floor had been swept, the hay freshly stacked, but the smell of manure hung faintly in the air. Garland draped the rafters and mistletoe dangled in the archways. A long table stood at one end to hold desserts, and a three-man band warmed up at the other end.

People of all ages greeted one another. Though cordial to Jonathan, Kara wouldn't go so far as to say they were friendly. Snort had already warned her that some thought the trouble between the Catlins and Wellses lay more with the Catlins than old man Wells. But tonight was a night for dancing, not feuds.

Jonathan politely introduced her to the few he knew and told her the little he'd heard of the history of the town.

A group of six soldiers, who said they were camped nearby, entered almost shyly as though asking for permission to join the party.

They were welcomed mostly by Pappy Price who, with five unmarried, but healthy-looking daughters, was always glad to see young men who earned steady paychecks.

Newton walked over with Mary Ann at his side. "Everything all right, Boss?" he asked, smiling.

Jonathan nodded. "A fine job."

Mary Ann leaned close to Kara. "I have to talk to you later," she whispered, but no urgency filled her tone.

The music began, and Newton pulled Mary Ann onto the floor. Jonathan stood rooted by Kara's side.

After a while, he asked, "Do you know how to dance?"

"I could dance before I started school. There wasn't much to do at church socials but dance."

To her surprise, he frowned.

"But you can't," she whispered. "Can you?"

His lack of response was answer enough.

"Then why did you ask me here, Jonathan?" She tugged at his arm.

"I thought you'd like to come."

Kara slid her hand down his arm to his fingers and tugged again, pulling him behind the stacks of hay framing the dance floor.

She stared directly up at him, wanting to understand his logic. "You invited me here when you didn't dance?"

"I guess I didn't think the whole thing out." Jonathan tried not to laugh at himself. "It *seemed* like a good plan. I just wanted to do something right after the mess of things I made a few nights ago."

"Something right?" She watched him closely.

"Whether you go back to your home or stay, I want you to know that you deserve to be treated far better than Devin O'Toole treats you. You're a woman who deserves to be asked proper, whether to a dance or to marry."

He hadn't moved a fraction of an inch toward her, but Kara felt as if he held her tightly with his words.

Moving her hand along his shoulder, Kara stepped closer. She lifted his hand in hers. "I'll teach you to dance," she whispered. "It's really not all that difficult."

Jonathan stepped away and removed his gun belt. He placed it on the hay well out of the way. Then, he slowly removed her shawl and tied it around her waist. "If we're going to dance, we might as well be comfortable."

For a few songs, they danced behind the hay, then she encouraged him out to the floor.

"I don't know about this." He looked like he was being tortured.

"You'll do fine. Just look around you."

They watched the others, then he smiled and pulled her into the circling couples. "Why didn't you tell me?"

"What?" She tried to follow his steps.

"That no one else knows how to dance either."

Kara moved closer and laughed. He was right. Between the cowhands and the soldiers, not one looked like they'd had more than a single lesson. But that didn't dampen their enthusiasm. If confidence counted as skill, these men were experts.

By the time someone in the band called a break, Jonathan moved comfortably to the music.

"Would you like some cider?" he asked, without turning loose her hand.

"Can we step outside?" she answered. "I'd welcome the cool air."

They walked in silence for several yards away from the barn. Kara noticed a few of the old guards from the ranch standing around. They hadn't come to dance, but to watch over Jonathan, as always. In an odd way, he had his own private guardian angels.

"Thank you for tonight," she whispered, loving the way he felt standing so close beside her. "I've had a wonderful time."

His hand tightened slightly around hers. "There are

things that need saying between us, Kara, but I don't know the words."

"Why did you truly ask me here tonight?" The thought that the dance might be one of his traps to catch troublemakers crossed her mind.

"Because I thought it was what you wanted. Though I must admit, I like seeing the anger in your eyes, I wanted to see you smiling and happy, too." He faced her. "You're a beautiful, warm woman who deserves better than O'Toole."

"You're doing pretty good with the words." A blush spread up her cheeks. She was glad it was dark. "What would make you happy?"

He didn't answer.

"Tell me, Jonathan. It's like dancing. Just step out with the truth."

He stood so near their breaths mingled in the cold air. "I want to lie with you, Kara, until the sun rises." His words were a whisper, so low they barely passed between them. "I've wanted it since I first kissed you all those weeks ago. You have a passion in your eyes that challenges me to explore and may very well drive me mad before our year together is over."

Kara was shocked into silence, not by what he said, but by the honesty in his tone. If she were just learning about the art of flirting, he was newborn in the game for he'd revealed far too much when first asked.

Only, he wasn't flirting, she realized. He was a man who might never learn such things. He was simply answering her question honestly.

She wanted to tell him that men didn't say such things to women, but she'd asked him to be truthful. They walked no closer together, for they knew others watched, but his fingers moved over her hand, slowly caressing.

She tightened her grip on his arm as she looked into his eyes. For all the world they appeared to be talking, but he was making love to her with his gaze. They both knew it.

He didn't need to woo her with words. He looked into her very soul, telling her what he wanted, asking her to accept the adventure.

He couldn't talk of love, for he didn't know of it. He couldn't talk of forever, he didn't believe it existed. All he could offer her was a touch, an embrace, a passion, but with that, he offered his heart.

When they turned and moved back to the barn, he circled his arm about her waist, lightly brushing just beneath her breast. "I want to hold you," he whispered an inch from her ear. "More than I've ever wanted anything in my life."

She didn't answer as they entered the barn, but the dancing changed. The pressure of his fingers holding hers, the way he moved close for a moment then stepped away. The slight touch of his hand at her back. All became part of something far more than dancing.

When they stood beneath the mistletoe, his kiss was brief, polite, but he left the taste of his lips on hers and a promise.

TWENTY-THREE

WHEN THE SMALL BAND PLAYED THE LAST WALTZ, Jonathan pulled Kara closer than he'd dared before, and they moved as one to the music. He wished he had the words to tell her how he felt, but he wasn't sure himself. Somehow, in the months of watching her, he'd grown accustomed to having her around. The thought that Devin might take her away upset him far more than he wanted to admit.

Much as he'd tried to avoid it, she'd become a part of his life. He looked forward to their talks, to watching her gentle movements, even to their fights. Something inside him wanted to protect her and keep her safe. He swore he'd never hold another person near, but he dearly wanted to hold Kara. She was the only woman he'd ever found who made him feel like he was completely alive. When she was near, the world tasted and smelled and bloomed with color.

How does a man say such things to a woman? he wondered.

As the dance ended, H. B. caught Jonathan's attention. The old man stood beside a post, looking like he was doing no more than watching the dancers. But Jonathan knew H. B. missed little. The guards had been near all evening, just in case they were needed.

As Kara said good-bye to the people she'd met, Jonathan stepped beside H. B. "Any trouble?" he asked, nothing casual about his tone.

"All quiet. No sign of Wells or his men. My guess is, we put this dance together so fast they didn't have time to hear about it."

"Good." Jonathan had worried about Wells all evening. Even during calm times, throwing the Catlin and Wells cowhands together wasn't a good idea. "Anything else?" He knew there was, or H. B. wouldn't have signaled.

"One of the soldiers says they captured an Apache. They're camped about a mile from town. The lieutenant said the Apache was a real troublemaker who escaped from Fort Elliot earlier this month. Said they're waiting until after Christmas to take him as far as Fort Griffin. They plan to put him on trial there instead of just sending him back to the reservation."

Jonathan studied H. B.'s face. "You think it might be my Apache brother, Quil?"

"If your friend escaped, he'd have reason to come to this part of the country. But the soldier, if he knew, didn't say any name."

Jonathan leaned closer. "Got any idea how to find out if it's Quil?"

H. B. shoved away from the post. "I'll invite them to Christmas dinner. My guess is they'll all come and bring the prisoner with them or leave him tied up somewhere safe. I never met a soldier who'd turn down a home-cooked meal. Either way, we'll have a chance to take a look at him."

Jonathan groaned. "Great plan. What's six or eight more when I already have half the state coming for Christmas dinner?"

Kara joined them as he said the last words. She glanced from one to the other, but neither man offered an explanation.

"Shall we go?" Jonathan took her hand.

Kara nodded and pulled her shawl over her hair.

He helped her into the wagon, then watched as his men saddled up. So many things needed to be said between him and Kara, but there was never time. With everyone leaving the dance at once, they'd have plenty of chaperones on the way home.

When he turned the wagon toward Catlin land, he could hear the others talking around him. Muted conversations mingled with the sounds of the wagons and horses. He wished he could think of something to say to Kara.

But what? He was no good at small talk, never had been. In fact, to most people, he'd just as soon not talk at all. Sometimes, when he was traveling, he would go for days without saying anything to anyone.

The night grew cold. The moon and stars provided just enough light to make the clouds look like watered-down milk floating above them. Kara sat closer to him than she had before. Maybe she'd stay warm. He was also glad he brought the old buggy. At least she had some protection from the wind.

Jonathan glanced back at Newton and Mary Ann in the wagon. He couldn't help but smile. From the looks of their shadows, Mary Ann would have no trouble keeping warm. Newton had her wrapped up in his arms while they talked.

Jonathan figured he had to think of something to say to Kara. If he rode all the way back without talking to her, she'd probably decide he was mad at her. He wanted this night to be perfect for her. If she went back home, this might be one of her few nights left in Texas.

Ideas rolled around in his brain. She probably wouldn't want to discuss the ranch books. This wasn't the time. If he told her of his worries about the ranch, she'd leave tomorrow. Newton and Mary Ann seemed a safe topic, but since they were within hearing distance, it might not be polite to discuss them.

About the time Jonathan gave up, he felt Kara's hand touch his leg just above his knee. He jerked slightly at her boldness, then lowered his own hand to cover hers. They didn't say a word. They no longer needed to.

When they reached home, a flurry of activity kept them apart. Men carried leftover food into the house from Newton's wagon. Kara checked on Cooper and Snort. Mary Ann's children woke up and cried, which woke Dawn's baby, leaving Jonathan to have to explain about the noise so late at night.

Finally, when all had settled, Jonathan climbed the stairs. Kara's door was closed. He stood alone in the hallway, wondering what to do. If he knocked, he'd wake everyone along the hall.

He felt restless and lost. All he'd wanted to do was kiss Kara good night, but that had become impossible.

Tomorrow was Christmas Eve, and all the McLains would be arriving. Twice as many people would be in the house. He'd be lucky to see Kara, much less get close enough to kiss her. Besides, the end of an evening is when a man kisses a woman, at least according to H. B. and Snort.

Restless, Jonathan walked back downstairs. Snort and Cooper were both asleep in the great room. They'd said that in the morning they would be moving to the bunkhouse. Both figured they'd been pampered enough.

Jonathan stared at the long velvet drapes for a minute, almost feeling Kara in his arms. He probably frightened her with his passion, but she'd been so warm and willing.

He moved on, reluctant to let the memory drown him. In the kitchen, he found the remains of the baskets of food, scattered across the counter. At the far end, Kara sat wearing her gown and robe. The one candle she'd brought cast only a small circle of light around her. On a large napkin in front of her were bits of food she must have collected from the different baskets.

"Want some?" She held up a half of a sandwich she'd just made. "I'm starving so I sneaked down the back stairway hoping there'd be food left. We were too busy dancing at the party to sample Angela's food."

Jonathan moved forward, taking in everything about her. She'd combed her hair and tied it in the long braid that curled over one shoulder. The union-blue of her robe made her eyes deep-ocean green. The candlelight sparkled in her gaze like laughter.

"I tried to go to sleep." She took a bite of cookie. "But I was too hungry."

Jonathan reached her without saying a word. When he turned her on the stool, he whispered, "So am I," a moment before his mouth closed over hers.

A need within him shook his entire body as longing collided with paradise.

She tasted of cinnamon-sugar cookie crumbs and milk and *Kara*. He felt like he could devour her completely and still have only a taste of what he longed for. The need to hold her tightly in his arms had almost driven him insane all evening, and he could wait no longer.

He kissed her wildly as his hands moved over her, pressing her against the length of him, touching her in places he'd wanted to all evening. His fingers slid over the length of her arms and down her sides, stopping near her breasts. He moved his palms inward slightly, pressing against her softness as he parted her lips and deepened the kiss.

When he realized she was kissing him back, he groaned and lifted her off the stool. He couldn't get enough of her, the taste of her mouth, the feel of her body warm and yielding against his.

In the corner of his mind, he told himself to slow down, take it easy, be gentle, but a tidal wave of need washed over him. All he could do was move with the force.

When he broke the kiss, he lifted her onto the counter and watched her face in the pale light. Her eyes were closed, her head back as she took a deep breath and smiled.

That tiny smile was almost his undoing. It wasn't a wide smile to be shared with the world, but a sparkle of a private grin that whispered of how good she felt inside.

He blew the candle out so she was bathed in pale moonlight filtering though the kitchen curtains. Leaning forward, he kissed the corners of her mouth, wanting to taste her smile. "Still hungry?" he whispered against her cheek.

"Starving," she answered with a laugh.

When he would have straightened an inch away, she plowed her fingers into his hair and pulled his mouth to hers. Again the kiss was wild. Only now, she rode a wave of passion, and he fought to keep up.

Without breaking the kiss, he hooked his fingers beneath her knees and pulled her forward so that she sat perched on the counter, her legs on either side of his waist. He tugged at her belt and pulled the robe open with fingers hungry to feel her.

As the kiss softened, he worked the buttons free and slipped his fingers inside her gown. Her skin was warm and velvet against his touch, her breasts swollen and welcoming. He caught her moans of pleasure in his mouth as his hands set her flesh afire.

When he finally broke the kiss, they were both gasping for breath. He moved his hands to either side of her and leaned his forehead against hers. For a time, they just breathed. Then, slowly, he pressed his head against hers, enjoying the feel of her hair next to his cheek.

"I've been wanting to kiss you like that all night," he whispered.

Kara didn't answer, she just stretched slightly, revealing her throat.

He buried his face in the hollow of her neck and took a deep breath, enjoying the way she smelled of roses.

He planted light, soundless kisses all the way to her ear, then whispered, "Lean back, darling."

She braced her arms behind her and did as he said, letting her head lean back, as well.

He studied her, moving his hand over her throat and down to part her gown. He pulled the last buttons free so that his fingers and his gaze could roam from her neck to her waist.

"Don't move," he whispered as his hands crossed featherlight over her skin.

She made little sounds of pleasure, but she didn't move as he reached her waist and began the journey back up, this time with slightly more pressure. Her body warmed with his touch. When he reached her throat, he moved his fingers gently into her hair, combing the braid away with ease.

Now her hair flowed free as he once more slipped his hands along her flesh. Only now, his touch was bold, stopping to explore whenever she moaned, loving the way she responded to his slightest caress.

When she would have leaned forward to hold him, he touched her shoulders. "Be still, Kara. Don't move yet."

She obeyed, mindless with pleasure now. His fingers began at her hair, once more caressing her as he circled down her body. Only this time his journey didn't end at her waist, but ventured downward.

Kara raised up with a start. Jonathan didn't move his hand away. For a long moment, they stared at one another, the fire dancing in both their eyes.

He kissed her lightly on lips that felt well caressed. "Are you all right?" he whispered as he removed his hand and pulled her gown closed. He wanted, with every ounce of his being, to make love to her on the counter and, if he pushed, he was sure she'd be willing. But suddenly, he didn't want to push her, he couldn't. Like the kiss before, when she came to him, she had to do so willingly, unafraid. He wouldn't hurry paradise until she ran full into it with him.

Kara pushed her hair back and straightened her robe. "I'm fine."

He'd always enjoyed the quietness between them. The way she didn't feel the need to crowd the air with conversation. But now, he wished she'd say more, tell him how she felt, what was on her mind.

Her hands were shaking, and he fought to keep from holding her. But he wasn't sure what she wanted. She didn't seem afraid, at least not of him.

"I'd better say good night," she said as if they'd only been talking. "It's getting very late."

He helped her down from the counter, touching her only as much as necessary.

His words stopped her before she reached the door. "Kara, are you all right?" He had to know. Had he gone too far?

"I'm fine," she whispered. "I've never felt like this before." She stepped from the room without finishing.

"Neither have I," he added. Knowing that what he felt was far more than need or passion.

TWENTY-FOUR

ON DECEMBER 24, MORNING ARRIVED AMIDST A whirlwind of activity. Jonathan felt like he was moving through the construction of a house as he made his way from the stairs to the dining room. He'd been to a few of the Catlin Christmases years ago. The great room would be turned into a dining hall with tables and chairs from the bunkhouse. A tree would be decorated in the foyer with a hundred candles and sugar cookies decorated like wreaths.

Angela and a few hired helpers cooked the meal except for the meat. The bunkhouse chuck wagon crew buried a side of beef in coals and tended it for hours. Today would be chaos, tomorrow, picture-perfect with everyone forgetting how much work had been involved.

When Jonathan made it to the dining room, he wasn't surprised to find breakfast consisted of cold biscuits and jam. He poured himself a cup of coffee. Kara came in with all the others, talking of everything that had to be done. She smiled at him, but Jonathan couldn't read her.

It seemed he'd spent the past twenty-four hours wishing they had time alone . . . or feeling that time was running out for them. Now, with everyone around, he could almost hear the minutes ticking away faster and faster like a train picking up speed.

He tried to get near enough to say something to her, but that was impossible. When he tried later that morning, he found Mary Ann in the study working over the books and Kara busy cooking with Angela. In the afternoon, she was decorating the tree with the children all around her and Snort standing close by offering advice. Before supper, most of the McLains had arrived and she was helping them get settled.

Nichole and Adam drove in first with their two children. As soon as they unpacked, Adam wanted to see Dawn and her baby. Jonathan translated as the doctor checked Dawn's child.

His sister and her husband, Wes, arrived next. Allie beamed with a newborn in her arms. Wes looked as mean as ever to Jonathan, but he'd grown to truly like the fellow over the years. The man was hard as year-old jerky, but Wes cherished Allie. When it got right down to it, that was all Jonathan required in a brother-in-law.

Wes also had a way with the children. Despite his scarred face and gruff tone, not one of them seemed the least afraid of him.

Last came Daniel McLain with his wife and two sets of twins. Daniel was a huge man with kind eyes. He'd been a preacher since he was in his teens, but of late being a professor at the university took most of his time. If ever there was a man made to be a father, it was Daniel.

When Wolf rode in with his wife, Molly, their adopted daughter and young son, Jonathan had endured enough company. He headed for the barn as soon as he could escape all the hugs.

Kara found him there at sunset. "You have a wonderful family." She climbed up the ladder and stepped off onto the loft. "I grew up an only child. I used to long for a big family. The cousins were nice, but when Papa and I went home for the night, it was always so quiet."

"They're nice, the best, for a short stay." He didn't look her direction. "When I was a wild kid, you should have seen the way they fought for me. They were like a small army, always trying to help. I owe them more than I can ever repay."

"But you're still not comfortable with so many of them around?"

He looked at her then, wondering if she'd read his mind. "You've got flour on your nose."

Kara made no effort to brush it away. "Don't change the subject. You didn't answer me."

He crossed to her and brushed the speck of flour away himself. "I've lost two families, Kara. Isn't it enough that I respect Wolf and the McLains? I can't give more than that. There is no more inside me *to* give to them."

Her beautiful green eyes filled with sorrow. "Or to me?" she whispered.

Jonathan's muscles hardened as if he'd taken a blow and knew another was coming. No matter what he said, he'd hurt her. He'd told her from the beginning that he wanted no ties. He'd told her he could never love anyone. He made no promises when he held her.

"There's nothing left inside," he repeated and stepped back, waiting for her to explode with anger. She had a right. If he had nothing to give, why had he kissed her? Not once but several times. Better that she marry the Irishman who half-loved her than him, who couldn't love her at all.

He saw the fire dancing in the green depths of her eyes. Her fingers balled into fists.

When she stepped toward him, he didn't move. He'd take the anger straight on. He deserved it. He'd hurt her feelings, her pride.

When she wrapped her arms around his neck, stood on her tiptoes and kissed him, he was too surprised to move. It took a moment for the softness of her mouth to register. And the gentle pressure of her body leaning against his almost knocked him down.

Jonathan didn't care what she was trying to tell him. All that mattered was that Kara was in his arms. The kiss turned to liquid passion as he lifted her off the ground and held her close. With her touch she was giving him a gift he had no right to expect.

He wanted her, needed her, nothing else mattered. She was matching his hunger with her own. She was asking for the one thing he thought he had to give her. Passion.

Without breaking the kiss, Jonathan carried her into the shadows of the loft. He wanted to make wild, raging love to her that would consume them both. But Kara had started this. It was her turn to set the pace.

She drew him with her as he lowered her into the hay. When his body pressed over hers, sanity left him. He would have willingly died for one more moment with her in his arms.

Her clothes did little to hide the curves of her body. When she moved, even breathed, he was aware of how wonderful she felt beneath him.

She hadn't said a word in answer to his words, but as she touched him, his body made a liar out of him and they both knew it. He needed her with a hunger he'd never known, he wanted her more than he wanted breath.

He could demand he had no love to give for hours, but one embrace proved him wrong.

A voice came from far away. Someone yelling Jonathan's name from the courtyard.

At first, Jonathan thought of ignoring it. He could be needed no greater place than here.

But the booming voice came again, closer, shattering his paradise.

"You up there, son?" Wolf's shouting echoed off the insides of the barn.

Jonathan rolled from Kara. "I'm here," he managed to say, stumbling to his feet so he could block Wolf's view of her.

Sure enough, the huge man poked his head up into the loft. "We need you, Jonathan. The soldiers are here, and you're going to want to see the prisoner."

Jonathan dusted hay from his clothes and moved toward the ladder.

"Evening, Miss Kara," Wolf said casually.

"Evening," she answered just as casually.

Jonathan stormed down the ladder. He'd just kissed a woman so passionately he thought they might set the hay on fire and she didn't seem the least bit affected.

He could hear her passing the time of day with Wolf as he helped her down the ladder.

"I'll be along in a moment," she said. "As soon as I comb the hay from my hair."

The little Jonathan thought he knew about women quickly evaporated into nothing. She didn't seem to care in the least if everyone on the place knew what they'd been doing in the loft.

Jonathan stormed out of the barn and froze. The sight before him almost rocked him to his knees.

Six soldiers stood around a wagon with scraps of wood used along the sides to build a makeshift cage. In the dying light, he saw a man spread out in the wagon's bed, his arms and legs chained to the corners. Quil!

Jonathan moved forward slowly. His friend had suffered greatly. Bruises darkened along his body, cuts had dried with blood. His wrists and ankles were raw from pulling on the chains.

"Easy now, son," Wolf's words came in warning. "I know what you're thinking, but we got to do this right, or you might get you and your friend killed."

Jonathan straightened, shutting all emotion off in his body and facial expression. "I'm well aware of the danger." He'd seen soldiers shoot prisoners with little provocation. "I'll handle this. Watch over Kara for me. Don't let her too close to Quil."

Wolf agreed and backed away.

Jonathan walked alone to the band of soldiers. Though he didn't look around, he knew the guards watched. They'd back him up no matter what he did. But if he wasn't careful, blood might run in the courtyard tonight.

"Evening, gentlemen." Jonathan's voice was strong, a

hair less than friendly. "I'm glad you could make it in for the big dinner tomorrow."

The leader of the group offered his hand. "I'm Lieutenant Travis. My men and I are mighty grateful you invited us."

"We've set up extra beds in the bunkhouse." Jonathan moved closer to the wagon without looking too interested. "I believe the chuck wagon cook is making a washtub of chili tonight. The men always play poker on Christmas Eve. You're more than welcome, as long as you're willing to keep the game friendly."

The lieutenant smiled. "That sounds mighty fine."

Jonathan's gaze met Quil's for only a fraction of a second. "What about this fellow?"

"I'll have the men pull two-hour guard shifts on him all night. This is one you wouldn't want to get free. He about killed the lot of us before we roped him in."

Jonathan tried to act like he was only mildly interested. "We've got a doctor who could take a look at him."

The lieutenant hesitated. "It's not necessary."

"I insist," Jonathan said, calmly meeting the man's gaze.

"All right." The officer backed down. "I wouldn't want him dying on us before we get him delivered for trial."

Jonathan turned his back on Quil and put his arm around the lieutenant. "You boys go have yourselves some supper. We'll take care of your prisoner for a while."

As the hungry soldiers disappeared into the bunkhouse, Jonathan issued low commands to the men around him. They moved the wagon into the barn.

Wolf walked Kara the long way around the garden and back to the house. She had the feeling something was happening in the courtyard, but Wolf was being so polite, she hated to interrupt him. When the bear of a man set his mind to it he could be almost charming.

When they entered through the kitchen door, Adam passed her carrying his medical bag. She didn't miss the look Wolf gave his Molly.

"I'll come along, Adam." Molly stepped from the counter where she'd been slicing bread. "Just let me get my bag of medicines." She winked at Kara. "Around this family, it pays to come prepared."

Wolf gave a slight nod of thanks to his wife.

Kara could wait no longer for answers. "What's going on? I think I'll find Jonathan." She took a step toward the door.

Wolf blocked her path. "I'll not stop you, but it might be best if you stay in here. Jonathan is fine. The soldiers are holding his friend, Quil, as a prisoner. Right now, all that's going on is doctoring, but if I know Jonathan, all hell's going to break loose when those soldiers try to move Quil out of here."

TWENTY-FIVE

Kara walked from room to room, waiting for the men and Molly to come back from the barn. Everything in the house was ready for tomorrow. The tables were set up and beautifully decorated. The tree glowed like a jewel in the evening shadows. Pies and cakes lined every available counter. But all Kara could think about was Jonathan in the barn with his friend, Quil.

As Kara circled the foyer one more time, she noticed Allie heading downstairs with her baby in her arms. Jonathan's sister was a gentle soul who looked as if she'd lived with only kindness each day of her life, but her childhood must have been as terrible as his. They'd both been captured but she'd been older, and her memories must be stronger. Yet, watching her with her child, Kara saw only peace surrounding Allie.

"I was coming to find you," Allie whispered as she neared. "I've just been trying to talk with Dawn." Worry filled her eyes. "My Apache is not as good as it once was. But, I understood that she's frightened with all the people in the house, and all the noise. She doesn't understand about the holidays and an hour ago, when she saw the soldiers, she panicked."

"Did you explain?" Kara asked, hoping Allie knew enough Apache to make Dawn understand that she was in no danger.

"I tried, but she's determined to leave. I think you'd better have Jonathan talk to her soon, or she'll be gone. She doesn't trust me, but she'll believe you and Jonathan."

Kara nodded, though she had no idea what to do. "I'll stay with her until Jonathan comes in."

Allie agreed. "Don't let her leave. She isn't convinced her Apache family is gone. She thinks they are camped at their winter encampment. She'll die looking for them on the frontier, and even though she has light hair, without English, no one will help her."

Climbing the stairs, Kara tried to think of what she could say, if anything, that Dawn might understand. She slowly opened the door to Dawn's room.

The beautiful young mother was dressed for travel in her leathers and fur. She'd finished the cradleboard for her child and strapped a long roll of hides, which must contain the other clothes she'd made, to her back. A pouch hung from Dawn's waist.

Kara glanced at the bowl she always kept filled with fruit near the fireplace. It was empty.

Dawn slid one of her hands slowly over the other, making a sign.

Kara knew it must mean Dawn was leaving. Somehow, she must stop her. She couldn't see herself grabbing the woman and holding her down, and she had no skills to talk her into staying.

Dawn made the sign again then lifted her child. Though she wasn't out of her teens, the young mother's eyes flickered with determination. She would not stay another night in this hostile world.

"Come with me." Kara used her hands, hoping to convey the message that her words would not. "We'll find Jonathan." Wolf had said it was best she not go to the barn, but he hadn't flat-out ordered her to stay away. With Molly there, it couldn't be too dangerous. Jonathan would be nearby to protect her, and so would Wolf, and probably all the Old Guard.

If she could get Dawn to the barn, maybe Jonathan would have time to talk to her. She had to do something. Kara couldn't just allow the young woman to leave.

Dawn let Kara lead her down the stairs and out the front door. Kara heard everyone in the kitchen and dining room having dinner, but, thankfully, no one noticed them passing.

Once outside, Dawn followed Kara across the darkened courtyard to the barn. They slipped in through the same side door Wolf had ushered Kara out of thirty minutes before.

The huge barn was dark except for a circle of lanterns in the center. Several stalls contained horses. The animals added low noises to the darkness.

As they neared, Kara heard Wolf's familiar voice ordering men to take care and stay back.

Dawn hesitated, not wanting to go further. Kara took her hand and slowly inched toward the lights.

A wagon stood in the center of the circle of men—a

strange wagon with boards placed around the sides like a picket fence. Barbed wire laced the boards so thickly it seemed unlikely anyone could get close enough to see clearly what was inside.

Kara motioned for Dawn to stay where she was, then Kara moved between the men. She spotted Jonathan kneeling in the dirt beside the back of the wagon. His rapid-fire words were Apache, but Kara recognized their angry tone.

Adam stood behind Jonathan, holding his medical bag. The doctor's kind face was drawn in concern. Molly waited a step behind him.

"We could use chloroform to put him under," Molly reasoned.

Her whisper barely reached Kara before a sudden rattle of chains filled the barn.

"It's too dangerous," Adam answered. "To get close enough, we'd all have to fight. By the time we put him out, several of us might be feeling the effects. He's not just willing to fight. He'll fight to the death."

A guard shifted, and Kara saw the man Jonathan talked to on the ground. Quil. His arms were spread wide, chained to either side of the wagon with enough slack in the chain to permit him to jerk and lunge several inches. He was battered and bruised. Hatred raged in his eyes like wildfire. For a moment he appeared more wild animal than human.

"See if he'll take water," someone instructed, passing a tin cup and a half-filled bucket forward. "The soldiers said he hasn't eaten or drank anything since they captured him."

Quil's sudden jerk sent the cup flying. Even chained, he wouldn't admit defeat.

Jonathan stood. "Let him rest. We're only making matters worse by trying to help him now. At this point, he hates all of us enough to kill us, me in particular. I just took away his one reason for staying alive. I told him I buried his son."

The men mumbled among themselves as they moved away. Adam knelt as close as he dared to Quil. "None of his wounds look life-threatening. I'd like to get some salve on his wrists before they get infected, but it can wait."

Jonathan tried one more time to talk to Quil, but his friend turned away.

As the men parted, Kara saw Dawn watching from the shadows, her eyes wide with fear and sympathy. She understood. She'd lived the same pain. Though she was the daughter of settlers, her heart was Apache. Jonathan had told Kara that Dawn had no memory of her life before she became a member of the tribe.

After a long pause, Dawn lowered her bundles to the floor and unstrapped the cradleboard. She handed her sleeping baby to Kara, then moved toward the circle of lanterns.

H. B. stepped in her way as everyone stopped talking. The beautiful, blond-haired girl dressed in leather and moccasins drew everyone's attention.

"Let her pass, H. B.," Jonathan said in a tired voice.

The old man stepped aside.

Dawn slowly walked to Quil as if there were no one else in the barn. She knelt beside him, too close to be safely out of his reach.

The silent woman who believed her blood ran the same as Quil's had tears streaking her cheeks as she spoke in Apache.

Quil watched with cautious eyes, as if he suspected a trap. But he didn't try to propel his body into her as he had when the men opened the cage and managed to wrestle him out to the ground.

Dawn kept her simple movements slow. Reaching her hand into the bucket of water behind her, she scooped as much as she could in her cupped palm. When she brought the water to Quil's lips, he drank.

Again and again, she repeated the action, giving him water a handful at a time.

"Back away," Jonathan whispered. "Give her room. She might just save his life tonight."

The guards melted into the shadows.

For an hour, Kara watched the strange couple. Dawn pulled a small knife from her belt and sliced an apple from her store in the pouch. Quil ate what Dawn gave him without saying a word or taking his eyes off her.

Kara stood behind Jonathan where he squatted, watching from the darkness. "Will he be all right?" She placed her hand gently on Jonathan's shoulder.

He covered her fingers with his own. "I don't know. If the soldiers get him as far as Fort Griffin, he'll be hanged for sure." He squeezed her hand. "I won't let them leave here with Quil in that cage. I swear it."

"How can I help?"

Jonathan glanced up at her, and for a moment, she saw the surprise in his eyes. "How far are you willing to go to help a man you hardly know?"

"As far as need be," she answered. "And I'm not helping a man I don't know. I'm helping you help your friend. I'll do whatever I can."

"You trust me that completely?"

"I do," she said, knowing that she meant it. He was a man of honor, and she'd stand with him no matter what the cause.

Without letting go of her hand, he stood and pulled her into his arms. For a long moment, he just held her, then he whispered something in Apache against her ear.

"What are you saying?"

"The words translate, 'you are of my tribe,' " he whispered. "It means forever, unbroken."

Kara turned to look at Quil and Dawn on the ground beside the wagon. "And are they the same to you?"

"Yes."

"Then we must help them. No matter the risk."

While the soldiers and the ranch hands played cards in the bunkhouse and the McLain children hung stockings in the main house, Kara and Jonathan watched Dawn tend to Quil. She wrapped his bleeding wrists and washed dried blood off him. He didn't speak to her, but his eyes showed he understood her soft words.

As the time passed, Jonathan spread his coat on the hay, and sat with his back against a stall. Kara sat next to him, leaning on his chest. The old guards moved in and out the side door, changing shifts every hour.

When Dawn's baby cried, Kara brought the child to the young mother's side. Turning away from Kara and Jonathan, Dawn nursed the child in full view of Quil.

After a moment, the Apache closed his eyes, as though he could endure the pain of watching mother and child no longer. For the first time, he stopped straining against the chains that spread his arms and legs.

Jonathan looked down at Kara. She lay fast asleep against his heart. "Kara," he whispered. "Kara."

She didn't move.

"Kara," he said louder, but she didn't wake.

If he yelled any more, he'd wake the baby Dawn had rocked to sleep. Carefully, Jonathan picked Kara up and carried her across the courtyard. As she had before, she rolled into his chest as though being in his arms was the most natural thing in the world.

He slowed his steps, enjoying the feel of her steady breathing against his throat. It would be heaven to feel her sleeping beside him all night. There was a peace about this woman, he thought. A peace he'd longed for all his life.

As he entered the house, he saw Molly and his sister talking on the stairs. Molly had considered herself an old maid by the time Wolf married her. Though she was always kind, there was a hint of propriety about her that always made Jonathan watch his manners around her.

She stood, obviously alarmed, when she saw him carrying Kara. "Is something wrong? Has something happened?"

Jonathan smiled. "She's just a sound sleeper. I'll put her to bed."

Both women followed him to Kara's room. "We'll help," Allie said in a matter-of-fact way. "I don't think it's exactly proper for a man to put a young lady to bed."

"I agree." Molly tried to sound serious but her laughter gave her away. "A sound-asleep young lady needs watching over."

Jonathan looked over Kara's hair at them and

frowned. "I can put her to bed without a committee. We've lived in the same house for months now, and this isn't the first time she's fallen asleep."

Neither woman backed away. Molly pulled the covers down. "Still, it doesn't seem right that a man tucks his bookkeeper in at night."

"Not unless he's properly chaperoned," Allie added as she tried to help.

"Be careful with her glasses. They're in her pocket. Put them on the table by her bed," he ordered. "She likes them within her reach at dawn. And Allie, hand me another quilt. It might get colder tonight."

Molly and Allie looked at one another and grinned.

"Very concerned for his employees," Allie whispered.

"Wonder if he tucks Snort and H. B. in, too?" added Molly.

"What are you two hinting at?" Jonathan mumbled, not sure he really wanted to know what they thought was so funny.

"Nothing, brother, nothing at all."

TWENTY-SIX

As always, Jonathan slept little. Having so many people around made him nervous. He longed for the peace of being alone with Kara. He'd be glad when Christmas Day was over and everything settled down.

Just before dawn, he wandered into the kitchen for a cup of coffee, still thinking of how nice it would be to sit in the study with Kara some evening and just read by the fire. She'd said she wasn't leaving with Devin, but she hadn't promised to stay. With each hour's passing, he wasn't sure he could let her leave even though he had no idea how to make her stay.

She'd become a part of his life a little at a time, like winter sometimes melts into spring. He couldn't name the hour or the moment it happened but his heart had warmed and there was color to a world he'd always thought of as gray.

As he lifted the pot, Snort hurried inside, shaking a light dusting of snow off his shoulders.

"How's Quil?" Jonathan asked, guessing the old man had just finished a shift.

"Same," Snort answered, frowning. "The girl's with him, but he hasn't said a word to her. I took them some extra blankets."

Jonathan watched Snort for a few minutes, reading him easily. "What's wrong?" If it wasn't Quil, it had to be something else. Trouble pestered Snort like fleas.

Snort poured a cup of coffee and shrugged. "Probably nothing, but . . ." He hesitated. "Cooper's missing. I figured he decided to sleep another night in the great room, but when I checked in there, it didn't look like anyone slept in the place. I walked the grounds between the bunkhouse and here twice, thinking he might have had a problem with his head and passed out somewhere in the cold. I've known folks hit in the head by a bullet that never got right."

Snort saw it as his job to keep up with everyone. It frustrated him when the count wasn't right.

"Maybe he's in the barn," Jonathan said, directing Snort back to the problem. Two or three men always watch Quil, maybe Cooper decided to take a shift. The soldiers seemed glad to give up their duty for a few days. They hadn't left the warmth of the bunkhouse since they arrived.

When Jonathan left with Kara late last night, a few of the Old Guard looked like they planned to bed down in the hay with the Apache in sight.

"No, I checked. H. B. said he hadn't seen Cooper all night."

Before Jonathan could guess again, Angela came

through the back door, smiling. "Merry Christmas." She almost sang the words.

Jonathan and Snort stared at one another in disbelief, then grinned knowingly. Angela wasn't a woman familiar with smiling, at least not until now.

Snort put down his coffee and headed for the door. "Never mind that problem, Boss. I think I found the answer."

Jonathan tried not to laugh. "Everything all right, Angela?"

"Perfect," she answered. "Everything is absolutely perfect."

Jonathan walked from the room, wishing his life were "absolutely perfect." It got more complicated every day. With all the guests and Quil there, security had become a nightmare. There were even rumors that Wells planned to make a surprise visit soon.

He walked the quiet house, realizing it didn't seem so dark and unwelcoming with all the decorations. As he stepped onto the front porch, he almost collided with Gideon.

The groundskeeper was far too old and overweight to be in his current state. For the first time since Jonathan had known him, murder shone in Gideon's eyes. The old man wielded his broom like a weapon as he stumbled away from Jonathan, huffing like a train at full throttle and mumbling in Spanish.

Jonathan didn't have long to wait for the groundskeeper to address him.

"How long have I worked here?" Gideon asked before Jonathan could even say good morning.

"I don't know. More years than I am old, I'm sure."

"And I've always been loyal to the Catlins?" Gideon asked. "Always done my job?"

"Of course."

"If I asked for one favor, you'd do it, wouldn't you?"

"Without hesitation," Jonathan promised as he watched a sleepy-looking Cooper walk from the barn.

Gideon turned and followed Jonathan's gaze. "Then I want you to shoot that man!"

Jonathan pulled his gun.

Cooper looked up as he approached. He slowly raised his hands, but kept drawing closer. He was not a man to cower, even when a Colt was pointed at his middle.

"Shoot him!" Gideon yelled.

"Whatever you say," Jonathan answered. "But would you mind giving me a reason, just in case someone asks why later?"

"I ain't saying. Just believe me, he needs to die."

"Fair enough," Jonathan replied. "All right with you, Cooper, if I shoot you? Whatever you did, Gideon says you deserve it."

"I do," the retired lawman answered. "But could you wait a day, give me time to find a preacher? If I'm going to have to leave Angela, I'd rather leave her a widow than an old maid."

"You're not leaving my granddaughter a widow!" Gideon shouted. "She deserves better than that."

"Then I guess I'll have to stay alive." Cooper lowered his hands. " 'Cause I aim to marry her."

"Well." Jonathan glanced at Gideon. "Do I shoot him or welcome him into your family?"

Gideon didn't bother to answer. He marched into the

house yelling for Daniel McLain. If Cooper wanted to marry, there was no time like the present.

Unfortunately, Angela didn't see the need to rush. She said she'd consider Cooper's proposal and let him know in a few days.

"A woman deserves the right to ponder the one and only marriage proposal she'll ever have in her life," Angela said to her grandfather when he hauled the preacher and Cooper into her kitchen.

Daniel held one of his sons on his arm and a Bible in his hand. He agreed with Angela, but Gideon swore they'd stand before Daniel before the McLains left the ranch, for no daughter of his was going to jump the broom when a real preacher was under their roof.

An hour later, Kara hugged Angela wildly when she heard the news.

"He's a good man." Angela tried not to show any excitement. "A good man. I've known it from the first."

"And he's getting a fine woman," Kara said. "He's a lucky man, our Cooper."

Angela grinned. "That's what I told him." She straightened. "I'll marry him tomorrow, but right now, we've got a meal to cook."

"How can I help?" Kara rolled up her sleeves.

"Oh, no. Not today. You go up and get ready. I've more help than I can use. If I let you in, I'll have to allow the McLain women to help and not one of them can cook well enough to get a job on a cattle drive."

Reluctantly, Kara climbed the back stairs to her room. People occupied every cranny of the house now, talking, laughing, waiting for the meal. The day would be one long party. And with snow dancing around the windows, it might last even longer.

As she opened her bedroom door, the sight of Devin O'Toole sitting in her reading chair by the window surprised her. He didn't look any happier than usual. His nose was red. A wadded handkerchief showed between his fingers. He wore the same wool suit he'd arrived in a few days before.

"Good morning." She tried to smile and remember she'd once thought of him as a friend. But lately, the more she saw him, the more she wished he'd just go away. He acted as though she'd change her mind at any moment and want to return with him.

"Do you mind closing the door, lass? I know your father wouldn't think it proper, but I've a need to have a few words with you." He sounded almost polite.

She closed the door, reasoning that she'd known Devin for years and never had any reason to be afraid of him. Also, she knew that, should she find the need to scream someone would come to her aid.

He didn't stand, but he motioned for her to take the other chair. "I've come to say I'm leaving, Karina."

"But aren't you staying for Christmas dinner?"

"No," he answered. "One of the men who came from town said there's a stage rolling out at noon for Fort Worth. It seems not everyone takes a holiday."

"I wish you a safe journey." Kara took a deep breath, glad to be rid of the man.

"Thank you, but you should wish us both a safe trip. You'll be accompanying me. I decided we can be married in Fort Worth tonight."

Kara couldn't believe what he'd just said. She almost

laughed. Once, she'd dreamed of hearing him name a date. But now ... "You can't be serious. I think I've made it plain, Devin. I don't want to go home, and I don't want to marry you."

"You've wanted to marry me all your life, girl. There's not a man or woman on the row who hasn't told me you've had your eye on me. Now your wish will come true."

"Maybe back home I thought of it, but now it's different. *I'm* different."

Devin stood and glared at her. "You haven't changed that much. You're daydreaming if you think you can marry a man who's rich, like Catlin. Well, when we get back, I'll be plenty rich." He tossed the packet her father had given her on the bed. "We'll both have more money than we ever dreamed."

Kara noticed the bindings had been cut. Paper edges peeked out. He'd opened the packet her father had told her not to open. "That belongs to my father—and me." She reached for the bundle, but he snatched it back.

"Wrong. These belong to us." He slapped the packet into his palm. "All your life, your father has been buying into the mills a few stocks at a time, in your name. I often wondered why he lived in the same poverty as the lowest paid worker. Someone of his level should have had a housekeeper, maybe even a part-time cook. But no, he used you for the work and saved every dime."

Kara couldn't believe what he told her. "Papa bought stock for me?"

"For *us*," Devin corrected. "The minute we're married, it will all transfer to me. He must have planned it that way, always telling me what a good cook you were, what a good housekeeper. He wanted me to take care of you after he was gone."

Devin's words held a truth, but it was an old truth. Something had changed. The pieces no longer fit together. "My papa didn't send you, did he?"

"He might as well have. In the middle of the fighting, I followed him home one night. He told me how he'd left you provided for just before the McWimberlys stormed in a door I'd forgotten to lock. He had only time for one glance at me before they jumped him, but in that one look, I saw that he knew the truth. But it was too late."

"What truth? To late for what?"

"That I was one of them. When I came to Pittsburgh in my teens, my cousins convinced me to act like I wasn't a McWimberly. But in the end, your father knew. I tried to get him to tell me where you were, but he chose to die."

Devin's words closed around her throat, grief choking off all air to her lungs. "You killed my father?" She was lost in a nightmare. Surely it couldn't be true.

Devin grabbed her by the arm and lowered her into the chair by her desk. He stood in front of her silently demanding she believe him. "Now don't go thinking that, girl. I wasn't the one who killed him. I swear it on all the saints. I don't want my wife ever thinking such a thing. I cared for the old man, but I had my family to think about."

He sneezed and added almost as an afterthought, "By marrying you, you'll always be safe. I'll have your money and you'll have my protection."

"No, thank you," she whispered, trying to make sense

of his words. She wouldn't believe her strong father was dead. It couldn't be true. It couldn't be. Tears slid down her cheeks.

Devin patted her hand awkwardly. "I want you to know that I am the one who saved your life." He ordered she believe him as though she were no more than a child. His fingers dug into the flesh of her arm. "The Mc-Wimberlys followed you as far as Kansas City where they said you hooked up with a man. We knew from the beginning of the trouble that your father had something of value stashed somewhere, but none of us believed he'd be dumb enough to give it to you. The man who followed you swore you didn't have anything or you'd have used it to keep from starving. But when we couldn't find something in your father's house, I knew he must have sent whatever he valued with his only child."

He sneezed a few times against his sleeve. "Get packed, Karina. We're running out of time."

"I'm not going." She couldn't think. Her father couldn't be dead. Yet Devin believed he'd left her a small fortune. It had to be true, or Devin wouldn't be here. "Jonathan won't let you take me." She refused to move from the chair. "Take the packet, if that's what you came for, and go. You don't want me."

"You're going along. The stock certificates are in your name. They're just useless papers to me until we're married and I can claim them."

He looked around her tiny room. "I've got a buggy behind the corral now. As for Jonathan and the old men he calls his guard, they won't even miss you with all

these people around. We'll be in town before they notice."

He stood in front of her and pulled a gun from his
coat pocket. "Besides, I'm prepared if anyone notices us
leaving. I'll shoot into this crowd if I have to. There's
no telling how many I'll hit. But I promise, Jonathan
will be the first. The man has treated me like trash since
the moment he saw me." Devin laughed. "And you, he
treats like a princess. You should hear the way he talks
to his men about you. As though you are to be treasured
at all cost. Well, the trash and the princess will be married before he can do anything about it."

"He won't just let me go." Somehow Jonathan would
stop this insanity. He'd told her she was "of his tribe"
like Quil and Wolf and the McLains. That had to mean
he'd help her. It had to.

"He will let you go without any trouble if you write
him a letter." Devin threw her things in her bags along
with the packet of stock. "So, get to writing."

As Devin ransacked her room, Kara wrote simply, *I've
decided to leave with Devin. I'm looking forward to seeing many happy days. I'll miss you all. Thank you . . .*

"That's enough," Devin said from over her shoulder.
"You're going on too long. No one will probably even
notice you're gone but Catlin and he'll forget you soon
enough. You're nothing but a bookkeeper around here
and no one needs a bookkeeper on Christmas Day. Just
sign your name."

Kara followed his orders and pulled off her glasses.
She placed them beside the note and stood to face Devin.

"If I leave quietly with you, promise me no one will be hurt."

Devin looked bothered. "All right. I've nothing against these people. All I want to do is leave. You'll see, Karina, as soon as you've had a few days back home you'll come to your senses and know I'm right."

He handed her one of her bags. "It's not going to be easy getting out of this house, but once we do, all will be clear. Every man on the ranch is downstairs. I'll bet there will be no guards along the wall today."

He sneezed again and nudged her with a suitcase.

A hundred thoughts flashed through her mind as he forced her into the deserted hallway. She thought of screaming. Men would storm the stairs in seconds. But one might get killed, and Kara couldn't risk that.

She'd go with him, and she'd wait for her chance. He might be a strong man, but he was out of his element and weakened by a cold. He thought she was still the girl he'd known back home, but Kara had matured over the months. She'd fight when the time was right, and when she did, she'd win.

"They'll notice I'm not at dinner." Kara moved down the back stairs to the closed-in porch. No one from the kitchen heard them leave.

"No, they won't." Devin grabbed her arm with his free hand and almost dragged her through the garden. "Your father said you were always a daydreamer. Well, you're dreaming now if you think you mean anything to these people. Catlin probably only feels sorry for you, thinking of you like he would a lost kitten he found."

Kara stared at him, trying to read his mind as he

shoved her against the adobe wall and opened the back gate behind the bunkhouse.

"I'm only doing what's best for you, girl." He pushed her out the gate toward a waiting buggy.

Kara fought to keep from getting in the buggy. Until that moment, she'd thought Jonathan would put an end to Devin's crazy plan. But how could he? Jonathan didn't even know they were leaving.

"Get in," Devin ordered with a push. "By nightfall, you'll be my wife. You'll forget all about this place."

TWENTY-SEVEN

Jonathan was listening to the toasts before dinner when he noticed Snort working his way through the crowd toward him.

"Boss." The little man twitched. The fleas of trouble jumping over him again.

"Another person missing?" Jonathan asked. He'd already noticed Devin O'Toole wasn't among the guests. The man probably still snored in the bunkhouse, sleeping off the effects of the cold remedy Luther kept spooning him.

Snort nodded. "First, I noticed O'Toole absent from his usual places on the porch or in his bunk. When I went to tell Miss Kara, I couldn't find her, either."

"Maybe she's in the kitchen," Jonathan guessed. Most of the women hadn't joined them yet.

"Tried there. No one's seen her for over an hour."

"The barn . . ."

"Looked there, too. Quil was sleeping close beside the

woman who thinks she's Indian. But no sign of Miss Kara."

Jonathan glanced around the room. "What about up . . . ?"

"Been there, too. Her door is closed, but no one answered when I knocked. I also checked the study and every other place I could think she might be."

Moving toward the front door, Jonathan whispered, "Don't alarm anyone. Let's just have a look around." Though his words were casual, his actions were not. He signaled for Wolf and Newton to follow him outside. Mary Ann also joined them, standing in the doorway just behind the men.

When Jonathan caught her gaze, he tried to smile, not wanting to alarm Kara's friend.

She stepped forward. "I noticed ten minutes ago something was wrong." Her frightened voice trembled. "I know why all of you are gathering. Kara's missing. When Snort asked me if I'd seen her, I looked around. I have a bad feeling something has happened."

Jonathan welcomed her into the small circle.

Once they were on the porch and out of view of the others, they divided the house and grounds and split up to search. Mary Ann took the bedrooms upstairs; Jonathan, the bunkhouse. Snort agreed to have another look in the barn. Newton and Wolf spread out to all other buildings within the wall.

Five minutes later, Snort was the last man to return.

"Any luck?" Jonathan asked. With Wolf and Newton at his side, it was obvious they'd placed their hopes on Snort's findings.

The old man wiped his face with a handkerchief despite the frosty air. "None, but we've got another problem. The guard on the front gate says there's a rider coming in, a man who sits tall in the saddle."

"Where's H. B.?" Jonathan nodded for Newton to summon other guards.

"That's another problem I got biting at me. I can't find H. B." Snort's count was off again. "He was the last man to take guard duty in the barn. He may be sleeping in the loft; he's not much for parties. But, ain't like him not to be here with trouble riding in. He's got a sixth sense about that kind of thing."

"We don't know the rider means trouble." Wolf grumbled. "We only know three people are missing and someone is coming. He could be just a cowhand arriving late."

Mary Ann hurried through the door. "I found a note from . . ." She stopped as a tall old man rode through the gate. He looked to be well over six feet and his hair was as white as the snow dusting around his shoulders.

Jonathan stepped forward with Snort and Newton banking him. "Wells," he said in greeting.

The old man slowly lowered off his horse. "Catlin." He nodded. "I came alone. I understand this Christmas dinner you have is open to all."

"You're right." Jonathan showed no emotion. "And you are welcome."

Wells didn't move. "Before I accept your hospitality, I want you to know that I've come because of Angela."

Twenty men stood on the porch and in the open doorway behind Jonathan, and he'd swear not one of them even breathed.

"Angela?" Jonathan questioned.

"I've known about her for years." Wells's eyes looked tired. "Knew she was born the night my son was killed. He'd asked me if he could marry Gideon's daughter weeks before, but I said no. When he died, I didn't want to think there was a child."

He removed his hat. "It was easier to hate than to admit I had a part in his dying that night. Now, I guess I'm too old and too tired to hate any longer."

Angela stepped from the crowd.

Wells stared at her, taking in her dark skin and her height.

She moved nearer. "Did you have any part in the deaths of our guards?" she asked directly. "Or the shooting of two that are still recovering?"

"I did not," he answered. "I lost a man to a rustler's bullet last week. In my blind anger I thought it was Catlin or one of his men, but we caught the shooter before he crossed my border." He turned his attention to Jonathan. "The fellow got real talkative before we turned him over to two rangers. He told of a gang of outlaws moving this direction, hitting every ranch and testing the waters before they move in for a big raid."

Wells faced Jonathan. "When I realized I was wrong about you, I figured you could be having the same problems and be guessing it was me. You were man enough to face me directly when you thought I'd caused you trouble. I can do the same. I thought next week we could talk. Maybe we can work together on fighting them."

"Maybe." Jonathan offered his hand. "Will you join us for dinner?"

Wells waited for Angela to comment. "I came because of Angela." He repeated his first statement. "The other could have waited until tomorrow, but on Christmas a man should be with whatever family he has left. If they'll have him, that is."

"There's a table set up in the kitchen. We've room for one more there." She didn't smile as she made her offer.

"I'd like that." Wells followed her inside.

Slowly, the guest moved back to the house, talking. Only those who had watched Wells ride in remained. Mary Ann stood in the center of their small circle. She still held the note.

Jonathan lifted it from her fingers and read it aloud, then crumpled it in his fist. Kara's words ripped his heart from his chest. It took every ounce of control not to allow his emotions to show. He was as hard as ever on the outside, but he was crumbling to dust inside. She'd dismissed him with the kindness of a stranger.

"I guess that answers the whereabouts of two of the missing," Snort reasoned. "There ain't no accounting for who a woman will pick to be her man."

Jonathan fought the hollowness in his gut as Snort rattled on about the time he'd lost a wife to a piano player.

She'd walked out, he told himself. Kara had walked out when she'd said she would stay. He'd thought he'd have the rest of the year to be with her. Even if she decided to leave then, he would have had the year.

Mary Ann handed Jonathan Kara's glasses. "She left these beside the note."

He stared at the wire frames for a moment before the truth slammed into him. Kara would never forget her glasses.

"That's odd." Snort leaned close. "I wouldn't think she could *see* 'many happy days' without her spectacles."

"She didn't go willingly." Jonathan carefully placed her glasses in his vest pocket. "Snort's right. These are the first things she looks for each morning. She would never leave them behind."

"Let's go bring her back," Newton shouted.

"No," Jonathan answered, "I'll bring her back. This time, I don't want any help. This is something I need to do alone."

Snort would have objected, but Newton laid a hand on the old man's shoulder. "Jonathan's right. He can deal with the Irishman by himself. He doesn't need our help."

"I'll need you here to make sure the dinner goes well." Jonathan nodded toward Mary Ann. "I know I can count on you. Will you and Newton take over as hosts?"

Mary Ann placed her hand on Newton's arm and nodded.

Jonathan grabbed his coat and gun belt then headed for the barn, knowing the Old Guard was watching and wanting to go along. But he'd face O'Toole man to man, and have that talk with Kara.

By the time he saddled up, Snort told him about a set of buggy tracks running from the back gate. Jonathan had his direction. If O'Toole was smart, he'd head straight to town. With the way the wind was blowing, the weather could turn bad within a few hours. A man with any sense wouldn't get caught out in a buggy.

Jonathan didn't know how much of a head start they

had on him. An hour, he guessed, maybe less. On horseback, he'd catch them long before they reached Brady.

Pounding hooves ate the distance. Jonathan's rage turned to worry. The buggy trail took first one wrong turn, then another. Where did O'Toole think he was going? Did the Irishman have any idea how to get to town? Why would O'Toole take Kara with him?

Unless O'Toole wanted to take all that mattered to me, Jonathan thought, admitting Kara's value. He could tell himself no one meant anything to him. He could scream it at Kara. But he could no longer convince his heart.

If she left, a part of him went with her.

The wind blew thin ice across his face. He didn't slow down. He wanted to kill Devin for taking Kara away, for driving her out into this weather. But, what if the man loved her? What if he thought he was doing the right thing? Kara had told Jonathan often enough that O'Toole planned to marry her. Could he kill another man for loving her?

His hand crossed over the glasses in his pocket. Kara hadn't wanted to go. He knew it. She would never leave her glasses . . . she would never leave him. She had to have known he'd understand the clue she'd left him. And she had to know he'd come after her.

If Devin took her by force, he'd be burying the man by dawn.

Jonathan used senses beyond sight to stay on the road as snow drifted across the land. He slowed when a black speck appeared in front of him. He neared. The buggy came into view.

He was within twenty feet before he realized the small carriage leaned dangerously to one side. Jonathan swung from his mount and walked the rest of the way.

He saw Kara trying to get the horse to pull the buggy from a deep rut. "Come on, give me some help, and I'll see you have oats soon," she coached, with little skill as to how to guide the animal.

Reluctantly, Jonathan pulled his gaze from her and looked around for Devin. The man lay flat on the ground beside the buggy. At first, Jonathan thought he might have been thrown when the buggy hit the rut, but Kara's travel bag beside his head suggested otherwise.

Jonathan stepped over the Irishman's body. "Good afternoon," he said to Kara as if it were a bright, sunny day and all was right with the world.

She jumped, then faced him. "I didn't want to come along." She held her chin high. "He made me write that note."

"I figured that." Jonathan took another step toward her and handed her the glasses.

She put them on. "Devin said he'd shoot you if I didn't leave with him."

Jonathan poked the Irishman's body with the toe of his boot. "Speaking of O'Toole, unusual place to take a nap."

"When he got out to check the wheel, I clubbed him." Kara smiled. "I had no intention of going with him or of marrying him tonight."

Jonathan nodded, as if only mildly interested, and took another step toward her.

"Would you club me if I asked you to marry me?"

Kara grinned. "I might. You want no ties, remember?

So you'd best be prepared to duck if you ask."

"I've been trying to ask you something for days," He slipped his hands around her waist and tugged her against him. "When you left, you confirmed what I'd been thinking might be true." He leaned forward touching his forehead to hers. "My heart doesn't beat without you near. Whether I want ties or not, I don't seem to be alive without you."

She moved into his arms.

He closed his eyes and took a deep breath. Kara was in his embrace. Back where she belonged.

"Very nice!" O'Toole's voice shattered the moment. "It looks like true love."

Jonathan stared at the gun in O'Toole's hand and nudged Kara slowly behind him.

The Irishman stood rubbing the side of his head. "I didn't want to kill you, Karina. Honest, I didn't. But now I have no choice. You're making me do things just like your father did."

He moved closer, his voice now a whine. "I'm sure, for a few dollars, I can find someone in Fort Worth to forge a marriage license. Then I'll tell everyone you died in a carriage accident on the way home. Which won't be far from the truth."

"You're not going to kill her." Jonathan stood his ground, watching O'Toole closely. "You haven't got the guts, because you will have to shoot me first."

"No problem with that." O'Toole fought down a sneeze. "I'll be out of the state before anyone finds either of your bodies. And to think I killed you with one of your own guns."

He waved the weapon, pleased with his own wit. "I

found it in your study. Who knows? With luck, they'll think you killed her and then yourself."

Jonathan glanced down at the small Navy Colt in Devin's hand. "That's not the gun from my desk drawer, is it?"

Devin nodded. "I noticed it when I helped myself to a little traveling money. I figured you'd think Karina took it and probably not even report the loss."

Jonathan moved nearer. "That gun hasn't been used since the war. I meant to get it fixed. Now, I'm glad I didn't."

Devin looked worried.

"You didn't find any bullets with it, did you?" Jonathan took a step closer to Devin.

"I borrowed some from a gun belt in the bunkhouse. Why?"

"That gun has a bent barrel. It's as likely to go off in the shooter's hand as to fire. And the aim is far from true if it does fire."

Devin moved backward a few inches. "I don't believe you."

Jonathan shrugged. "That's why I kept it unloaded in my study."

"You're lying. And I'm through talking."

O'Toole raised the weapon to Jonathan's chest. As he hesitated, he sneezed, suddenly giving Jonathan the moment he'd been waiting for.

Like an animal springing on his prey, Jonathan flung himself at O'Toole.

The weapon fired.

TWENTY-EIGHT

❦

KARA WATCHED AS JONATHAN'S BODY SLAMMED into O'Toole, knocking both men to the ground. The sound of the shot shook her senses like liquid thunder rattling through her veins. Fear robbed her breath and panic chained all reason.

She waited for Jonathan to move, afraid to even hope that the bullet had missed him. He'd plowed into O'Toole, flattening the man in the snow-covered dirt. He'd risked his life for her without hesitation. And in the risking, he may have lost.

For a long moment, the men were both silent, both still. The wind's low howl whirled around them, erasing the echoes from the gun.

Until now, Kara had never realized how much she loved Jonathan. Until she may have lost him. Her already grieving heart pounded out each beat as she stared at the men.

The Irishman remained on the ground, but slowly, Jonathan rose to his feet.

Kara closed her eyes, thanking the saints for watching over him.

With a deliberate jerk, Jonathan ripped the weapon from O'Toole's fingers. The Irishman moaned and rolled to his side in the dirt.

Kara still tasted panic in her throat. "Are you hurt?" she whispered between sobs. "I thought when you charged the gun, he'd surely kill you, even with a damaged weapon."

"I'm all right." Jonathan hugged her close, proving he was sound. "I had no other choice, for I would have been mortally wounded if I lost you, Kara. He wasn't taking you off Catlin land while I was still alive."

She cupped the side of his face, guessing that he must have felt her leaving as dearly as she feared his loss.

"I'm all right," he whispered against her hair.

She couldn't stop the tears. "Lucky the gun was damaged." She buried her face against the leather of his coat.

"A Catlin wouldn't have a weapon that wasn't true on the ranch," H. B.'s low voice came from a whirlwind of snow several feet away.

Jonathan laughed. "I knew you were there, old man. Smelled you when I walked up. Why didn't you say something?"

"I figured you could handle it." He knelt to make sure the Irishman was still breathing. "Knocked the wind out of the poor man." H. B. lifted O'Toole's body and tossed it in the buggy with no more effort than if it had been made of straw. "No sense in a guardian angel working overtime. I've been following the buggy since it left headquarters. Didn't plan on letting any harm come to Miss Kara."

Jonathan bundled her in his arms. "You took your time helping out. Can you get the Irishman back to the barn? I'd like Kara to ride double with me, if she's not too cold."

"I'll be warm enough," she answered. She pulled a blanket from the buggy as Jonathan and H. B. uprighted it from the ditch.

"Have any idea where we are?" H. B. asked.

"A little. The way O'Toole kept turning, he never would have gotten off Catlin land."

H. B. agreed, then added, "Up ahead a few hundred yards is the strangest sight. I saw it through the snow."

"What?" Jonathan had had enough surprises for one day.

"A pine growing out of a boulder." He said the words slowly as if they held a secret meaning.

"We might just have to check that out before we head back." Jonathan swung onto his horse, and offered his hand to Kara.

"Stay warm," H. B. warned as he tied his horse to the buggy and climbed in beside O'Toole. "If the Irishman wakes up on the way home, I may have to put him to sleep again."

The old man looked like he was truly enjoying the thought.

Jonathan turned his horse toward the pine and held Kara close as she wrapped the blanket around them both. "We'll be plenty warm," he whispered against her hair. "For once, I plan to have a little time alone with you if you have no objections, Miss O'Riley."

"None at all," she whispered.

He held her tightly as they climbed the trail toward

the lone pine at the top. Jonathan didn't want to go back to the party, and H. B. had offered him the excuse he needed.

"Russell told Gideon once that he found the flowers he sent into headquarters at a place where a huge pine grows from a rock." Jonathan told the story in Kara's ear as he held her. "No one really believed it, but all the guards have been watching for the spot. No one dreamed it would be along this stretch of dry, rocky land."

But, there it was, Jonathan thought, as they neared. A tall pine stood square atop a boulder as if its roots sank deeply into the stone.

When they were within twenty feet of the top, Jonathan found a sheltered place big enough to leave the horse. He slid from the saddle, then helped Kara to the ground. He secured his rope to one of the elm trees that circled the boulder. In summer, when the elms bear leaves, the pine would be impossible to see. But in the dead of winter, it stood forever green among the bare-branched skeletons.

Snow dusted the surface of the rock, but not so deep Jonathan couldn't walk on it. He had no idea where the flowers grew, but he figured if he could make it to the top of the rock, he'd see them.

Kara followed. When they reached the pine and stood atop the outcropping, they could see nothing but a sheer cliff of stone in front of them and the way they came behind them.

Kara moved closer to the tree. "The flowers have to be here somewhere." As she bent a low branch of the pine aside, she studied the tree's base. "Look, it grows from a hole in the boulder."

Jonathan turned in time to see her disappear, vanishing into the tree as if the branches had swallowed her up.

"Kara!" he yelled.

As he reached the spot where she'd been, his foot gave way to the incline of the rock. He slipped, falling down into the crevice where the tree was rooted.

Kara laughed as he landed next to her atop years of pine needles. They both looked up, five feet above, where they'd stood only a moment before. "I hope we can get out of here." Kara laughed as she crawled deeper into the cave and out from beneath the branches.

Jonathan lifted the end of rope he'd managed to hold onto. "We can climb the tree, or the rope. Getting out is no problem, but still no flowers. At least part of the story was true."

His eyes adjusted to the light. Glancing around, he realized the opening they'd fallen through widened into a cavelike crevice that appeared open on one side.

Kara followed the light to the opening, carefully testing each step as she moved across the cave. Jonathan was a step behind. Ten feet into the cave, one wall widened to the light.

The sight before them shocked them both into silence. The opening, like a ten-foot canvas, spread in front of them in brilliant color. Nature had painted a tiny valley hidden between two cliffs with bright, beautiful wildflowers.

"I've never seen anything like it," Kara whispered. "It's magical. Flowers everywhere, and the snow has disappeared."

Jonathan guessed there was little magic involved. The

overhanging cliffs sheltered the valley and somehow reflected sunlight, making a natural greenhouse.

They walked out into the meadow. Flowers as high
as his knee grew for a hundred feet around. Indian paintbrush, bright scarlet sage, bluebonnets and dozens of
others that he didn't know the names for.

"Oh, Jonathan, it's beautiful." Kara's fingertips lightly
brushed the petals. "It's like a paradise hidden from the
world. The loveliest thing I've ever seen."

"Yes, it is," he whispered without taking his eyes off
of her.

They walked to the far edge of the clearing where the
field stopped. Ten feet past the meadow, the air cooled
once more to near freezing and the land dropped off
suddenly, again becoming rocky.

Jonathan looked down at the wide box canyon below.
A river ran through the only entrance of the canyon. To
his amazement, he saw cattle. His cattle.

"How did those get in here? They'd have to swim the
river upstream to reach this canyon."

"How long do you think they've been here?" Kara
asked as she moved back to the warmth of the natural
green house.

"Since the storm a month ago when it snowed and
everything froze up." He studied the river. "Everything
froze."

Kara followed his thoughts. "You think they came up
the river when the water froze?"

Jonathan nodded. "And when it thawed, they had no
way out."

"Then you were right. The flowers were the answer.

Only they weren't in a ravine, and the cattle never left your land."

Jonathan smiled. "I can hardly wait to get back and tell the guard. No one will believe this until they see it. Except for a few times a year when the river freezes, the only way in or out of this canyon is through the small opening we dropped through at the pine."

"But first, before we tell anyone," Kara took his hand. "we stay awhile. This is the first time we've been alone, truly alone, for weeks."

They strolled across the field. "There's so much I have to say," Jonathan admitted. "I'm not sure where to begin." He took a deep breath "It feels so good to be able to talk to you without others listening, and suddenly I can't think of what to say."

"I know," she answered, removing her glasses and placing them in her pocket. "In my mind, I've had hours of conversation with you. Sometimes when I'm alone in the study I try to figure out the books by imagining myself explaining them to you."

"And did we only talk ranch business during those times?"

Kara looked away. "Not always."

He tugged at her hand. She stopped walking and faced him. Staring at him with eyes that had the depth of forever. "You don't have to imagine now. I'm right here. Talk to me, Kara.

"Until I met you . . ." He brushed a strand of her hair away from her face. "I was traveling from place to place, all different views of hell. Nothing mattered to me. I felt like I died years ago, but my body was still walking around on earth." Somehow he had to make her understand how he felt. He never wanted to worry about her leaving again without knowing.

She removed her jacket as he talked and laid it among the flowers.

"I know I rushed you when I kissed you," he stammered as he watched her remove her belt. "And I want you to know I didn't mean to frighten you the last time we were alone." He tried to think of the proper order he needed to say everything. "I sometimes have trouble being what others think I should be. Part of me wants to run wild like I did when I was young."

She slipped off her shoes and smiled up at him.

"There's just something restless inside of me." He tried to concentrate on what he was saying as she slid her skirt to the ground and stepped out of it. "I'll try to keep myself in check and be the kind of gentleman you deserve."

She added her stockings to the growing pile of clothes and faced him as she unbuttoned her blouse. He saw the rise of her breasts just beneath her undergarments.

He closed his eyes, trying to remember what else he needed to tell her. When he opened them again, she was unbuttoning the rest of her blouse. He could endure the torture no longer. "Kara, what are you doing?"

She smiled that little smile that drove him wild. "I'm waiting for you to finish talking so we can make love. I've dreamed of it for days, but before the sun goes down this day, I won't have to dream. By tonight, I'll be remembering."

All he thought so important to say to her, all he'd planned to tell her, all he swore he'd tell her . . . vanished.

He pulled her into his arms and kissed her, loving the feel of her next to him. With hundreds of wonderful fragrances around him, it was the smell of roses against her skin that drove him mad. He'd been holding back, afraid his need for her would frighten her and now she was running full speed into his arms.

Breaking the kiss, he knelt in the flowers, pulling her gently with him. When she leaned back, he leaned above her and let his fingers slide over the opening in her blouse. The warmth of her body radiated through the material of her camisole.

"Don't you have anything to say to me?" he asked as he tugged the last few buttons free.

"Yes," she whispered, "I want to lie beside you until dawn."

He laughed as she repeated the words he'd whispered to her the night of the dance.

"Are you sure?"

"Jonathan, take off your clothes," she answered with no doubt or hesitation in her voice.

For the first time in his life, he gladly followed orders.

If he lived to be a thousand, he'd see no more beautiful sight than Kara lying among the flowers. Her dark hair fanned out over the green leaves. Her eyes full of longing. Her arms pulling him closer.

He watched the rise and fall of her breasts beneath the thin layer of her camisole. His hands hesitantly lowered the straps from her shoulders. He couldn't hurry for she took his mind and body hostage, intoxicating him completely.

Her beauty had slipped up on him slowly and now he wanted to treasure her a little at a time. He played with the ribbon between her breasts, brushing lightly over the material.

When he tugged the garment lower, she closed her eyes and smiled, enjoying the game as much as he did.

Slowly, an inch at a time he moved his fingers over her body, exploring, worshiping, savoring the feel of her. For a long while, he watched her sway gently to the movement of his hands along her flesh. Her face blushed with pleasure when his hands finally covered her breasts and molded them against his palms.

He bent over her and kissed her full and long, then moved away to caress her once more. Her body rocked gently with his touch and with a longing that grew with each breath. When his mouth returned to hers, she was hungry and ready. He tasted deep and long, then pulled her up to her knees so that their bodies brushed one another as the kiss continued.

Slowly, she grew bolder, touching him, letting her hands roam over his skin, laying claim to his flesh as completely as she'd claimed his heart.

When he finally moved over her, her entire body welcomed him. The feel of her moving beneath him sent a bolt of pleasure through him so great Jonathan wouldn't have been surprised if it shattered his brain.

This was it, he sighed with the weariness of a lonely traveler. This was home.

Wrapping his arms around her, he rolled, pulling her atop him. When she braced her hands on his shoulders and rose above him, he would have stopped her from pulling so far away, but the sight before him drowned his senses. She was perfection.

She leaned down slowly, letting her breasts brush his

chest before her mouth covered his lips. The kiss was deep and demanding. He raised his hands and moved lightly over her body in contrast to the fiery kiss. His feather touch drove her hunger, and he wondered if he could satisfy this woman of few words.

He laughed against her mouth, knowing he'd die trying if need be. Rolling her onto her back, he entered her suddenly and caught her cry of pain in his mouth.

For a moment, she was still, and he almost pulled back. But, instead, he kissed her with more tenderness than he'd ever known he possessed. He caressed her gently until slowly, she responded.

When he rocked inside her, she tensed once more and he began again, kissing, loving, worshiping. Until finally, he moved and she moved with him.

He silently ordered himself to take it slow, but the need for her pounded through his body at full gallop. Be gentle, he thought, yet when she shifted beneath him, she drove him wild.

Finally, he could wait no longer. He pushed one last time and felt his very soul flow into her. For a while, he drifted from heaven, mindless. Nothing ever would, ever could, feel so good. Nothing mattered but Kara in his arms.

Slowly, he became aware of her beneath him and shifted his weight. She moved away as silently as a breeze.

For several minutes he lay still trying not to die of pure happiness. No words could ever explain how she made him feel. Whole, he thought. She makes me feel whole.

He could hear her dressing and forced his eyes open.

"Kara, that was wonderful." He watched her pull on her undergarments.

"Yes," she answered. "It was nice."

"Nice?" he shouted as she slipped into her skirt. "My brain and heart were competing to see which would explode first, and you say it was *nice*?" The woman had lost her mind.

She pulled on her blouse. "I've really nothing to compare it to, Jonathan."

"There *is* nothing to compare it to, Kara." He grabbed his trousers, angry that she'd be so calm. If she'd felt one tenth, one hundredth of what he'd felt, she never could have called it *nice*.

She picked up her shoes and jacket and walked toward the cave without a word.

Jonathan scrambled with his clothes and followed her, suddenly angry. When he reached the cool darkness of the cave, she stood beside the rope trying to decide how to climb out.

All reason left Jonathan in a flood of emotion. Here was the perfect woman, who'd made perfect love to him, and all she'd said was "it was nice."

Grabbing her by the arm, he whirled her to face him. "Maybe we should give you something to compare it to." He cupped the back of her head and drew her mouth to his.

He'd half-expected her to shove him away, to say once of *nice* was enough, then tell him good-bye. But, to his surprise, she wrapped her arms around him and kissed him back.

He wasn't sure how their clothes got off again, or how they ended up on the soft bed of garments and pine needles. All he remembered was running full speed into paradise and this time she was with him. Their love-making was wild and tender. He was starved for Kara, as though it had been years since he'd touched her.

In the shadows their every move seemed magical, full of mystery. Her body was still warm from his lovemaking in the pasture, her skin still blushing. She tasted of passion. This time when he caressed her body, she reacted to his touch and to the promise she knew would come. Her lips were swollen and sensitive to his kiss, her breasts full as she strained for his touch. He spread his hand across her abdomen and moved lower, loving the way her legs moved apart in welcome. She was his, totally, without restrictions, as surely as he was hers.

When he moved within her, she whispered his name and, this time, he took her to heaven with him. Passion drove them higher and higher until her body was fiery hot against him and his hands moved in bold strokes branding her forever with his touch. He tasted her kiss hungrily as he moved within, loving the way her breasts arched to brush his chest.

And somewhere in the madness, he realized they were doing exactly what she'd planned when she'd first whispered "nice." He was giving her more. All he had. Body and soul.

As they held one another and drifted back to earth, Jonathan decided he must surely be dead. He no longer had the energy left to move.

Kara curled against him and whispered, "Now *that*, darling, was wonderful."

Jonathan found the energy to smile.

TWENTY-NINE

Snow hung like thick frost in the air as Jonathan and Kara rode into headquarters. It was almost midnight. The main house was quiet with only single candles showing from a few windows. He could hear card games still going on in the bunkhouse.

His grandmother had set up rules long ago. No drinking or gambling on the ranch except on holidays, and then only after sunset. The ranch hands took advantage by drinking and gambling all night despite knowing they'd have to be up and in the saddle come daybreak.

Gideon held his horse as Jonathan climbed down, then helped Kara to the ground. Unlike before, he boldly kissed her. Jonathan didn't care if the world knew how he felt about her.

"Boss." Snort materialized from the shadows as though he didn't notice them kissing. "H. B. got the Irishman back, and I put Miss Kara's bags back in her room." The old man looked nervous even in the dark. "O'Toole had a headache so Luther gave him a double dose of that snake oil he uses. The Irishman passed out in the buggy inside the barn."

Jonathan wasn't really interested. He'd just had the most wonderful evening of his life and he didn't want the problems of the ranch to filter into his thoughts. "Put a blanket over O'Toole and leave him there 'til morning."

He took Kara's hand and started up the steps, enjoying the way she walked close enough to him to brush lightly against his side.

"Well," Snort interrupted as he followed. "That's only part of the problem."

Jonathan faced the old lawman and waited. He'd never be alone with Kara if he didn't give the old man time to say whatever it was Snort thought couldn't wait until morning.

"Somehow Quil got loose." Snort fidgeted. "We closed off every exit, but he's in the barn with the passed out Irishman and the girl who thinks she's an Indian. There weren't enough of us to go in after him, and we sure didn't see any need to let the soldiers know. They're all drunk. They'd shoot him for sure and probably half the horses in there."

Frustration twisted Snort's brow into deep furrows. "Since you weren't here, we didn't see anything to do but wake up Wolf and Adam. Quil's not likely to hurt the girl or her baby, but if he finds O'Toole, the Irishman may never wake up. We hoped Wolf could think of something, and we figured we might need Adam if things turned bloody."

Jonathan ordered Kara to go inside and turned toward the barn. "Who else knows, Snort?"

Snort fell into step on his right. "Wolf woke Daniel and Wes."

"Great!" Jonathan frowned deeper when he noticed Kara on his left side marching along with him as if she'd been called to war.

"Go back to the house," he snapped. Then realizing she'd probably think him harsh, he added, "Please."

"Not a chance," she answered with her chin high. "If you fight, I fight."

Jonathan looked toward heaven. Quil would snap her in half if she got close to him. Her only chance might be that the Apache people disliked killing the crazy. If Kara walked in the barn with Quil untied, she was definitely insane.

The three McLain brothers and Wolf stood near the barn door. As always, the strong men were like an army. Their silent presence reminded Jonathan again of how many times in his life they'd proved there was nothing they wouldn't do for him. To them, he was family, whether he wanted to be or not.

Jonathan looked at Wolf. "Is he still in there?"

The hairy ranger nodded. "But he'll find a way out soon. I heard him and Dawn arguing. From the few words I could catch it was obvious she wants him to take her and that baby with him."

Wes leaned into the conversation, absently brushing the scar he'd earned in battle years ago. "We thought of storming the place, but we don't want to take a chance of hurting Dawn and the child."

"How do you want to handle this, son?" Wolf asked.

Jonathan smiled. The powerful man might still call him son, but he was letting Jonathan know that he was there to follow his lead. They all were. Jonathan was no longer the kid they had to keep out of trouble; he would be leading now.

"I go in alone." Jonathan stripped off his coat. "If we rush him, Quil will fight to the death. And if he's found a weapon of some kind, several of us could be hurt. But I know him—if I face him unarmed, he'll stand the same way."

"We'll back you up. All you have to do is call." Wolf said the words as though swearing an oath.

"Thanks." Jonathan unbuttoned his shirt as he stepped through the barn door. The others followed, but only a few feet.

Jonathan glanced back at Daniel, then cut his eyes to Kara and back, silently telling the preacher to watch over her.

Daniel smiled his kind smile and nodded slightly. "Keep an angel on your shoulder," he whispered as he caught Jonathan's shirt.

"And your fist drawn." Wes stood at full attention. "For this time, we're all here to cover your back."

Jonathan glanced from one to the other. Four men. His brothers in spirit. For the first time in his life he realized his luck. He'd traveled around the world looking for a home and it had been right here waiting for him all along.

He squeezed Kara's hand to let her know everything would be all right and faced the circle of light from a single lantern in the center of the barn.

"Quil!" he challenged as he stepped away from the others.

The Apache moved from the shadows as Jonathan

guessed he would. They'd both been taught that when an opponent comes straight into battle, he earns the right to be met in kind. The years may have separated them into two worlds, but the teaching of their childhood remained strong.

Jonathan spoke to Quil in Apache as he removed his gun belt.

Quil nodded then glanced behind him to say something to Dawn.

Kara pulled at Wolf's sleeve. "What's going on?"

"Jonathan's challenging him as leader of the tribe." Wolf's whisper traveled several feet. "The fight is to be without weapons."

"But Jonathan said they were the only two left of their tribe."

"That doesn't matter. Quil has to fight. If he wins, he's determined to leave and knows he'll be killed by the soldiers. If Quil loses, he has to listen to Jonathan's advice. But he doesn't consider Jonathan a friend anymore. He'll not listen unless Jonathan wins."

"How long do they fight?" Kara whispered as the two men circled, drawing closer and closer to one another.

The first blows shattered the silence of the barn echoing off the rafters. Both fighters backed away and began the dance once more.

"The times I've seen this challenge, it was to the death." Wolf answered Kara's question without looking at her.

Kara bit into her knuckle and turned to watch. The two were like strong young bucks, ramming against one another, then pulling apart to circle. Again and again, she heard the pounding of fist against flesh. They moved in and out of the lantern's light, dancers caught up in a deadly waltz.

The blows she heard when they were hidden in the darkness were worse. The sounds drifted from the shadows to strike fiercely against her heart. While Jonathan fought for Quil's life, the Apache fought just as hard for the right to die.

"Can't you stop it?" She stared at the four men beside her. Adam, Wes, Daniel, Wolf. They were all intelligent men, most seasoned in battle, but they did nothing to stop the challenge.

Both fighters were bloody now, gasping for air in the moments between blows.

"We'd all take his place if we could." Adam's caring eyes finally focused on her. "But Jonathan is the only one who can save Quil. If he wins, he proves he's a brother—a member of the tribe."

Kara stared as Jonathan wiped blood from his cheek, smearing crimson across his face like war paint. For a moment she saw the boy running wild across the plains. Then the fighters moved once more out of the light.

One shattering blow rang out. Kara tried to peer through the darkness. Suddenly, from the far side of the barn, Dawn screamed. Quil staggered into the light and tumbled to the ground.

Jonathan stood above him, his legs wide apart, his chest heaving for air. He spoke first in Apache, then in English. "Come no nearer, it will shame Quil."

Dawn spoke to Jonathan from the shadows in a frightened voice but came only close enough to offer a blanket. Jonathan's gaze never left Quil's body as he pulled on his shirt.

Jonathan wrapped his friend in the blanket, then lifted Quil and carried him to a horse. "Kara, bring Dawn. She says she must come along. I'd probably have to fight her to get her to stay."

"Where are we going?" Kara was almost afraid to ask.

"To bury Quil forever," he answered in an angry shout.

She fought back tears as she let the men help her onto a horse. When her eyes met Dawn's, all words choked in her throat. The young mother's stare filled with pain. Kara had to look away.

Kara took the reins of Dawn's horse and followed Jonathan while Dawn wrapped an extra blanket around her and her baby.

Wolf mumbled something to Jonathan. All Kara heard was that he and H. B. would follow as fast as they could get everything together. Wes and Adam were already moving among the horses, saddling several mounts.

Jonathan rode silently out into the night, leading a horse with Quil folded over the saddle.

It took several minutes before Kara realized they were headed in the same direction as the pine growing from the rock. They were almost there when H. B., Wolf and the McLains caught up to them. H. B. and Wolf pulled pack mules loaded with supplies.

Jonathan spoke to Dawn as Adam and Daniel carried Quil atop the boulder. Dawn stepped into the darkness beside the tree as Wes pulled lanterns from the supplies. Jonathan lowered her baby then followed with a glowing lantern.

A light shone from below, making the pine glow. Kara followed next, allowing Adam and Wes to lower her. She took the baby from Dawn and moved out of the way as the men slowly handed Quil's body through the opening.

He moaned, making Kara jump.

"He isn't dead!"

"Yes, he is." Jonathan faced her. "Quil has to be dead. No one, not even the ranch hands, can know that he's still alive or he'll be hunted. He'll know no peace until he's dead, so he's dead to the world as of now."

The men dropped down supplies. Blankets, weapons, tools. Quil tried to sit up.

Jonathan moved close to Kara as Adam joined the group. He didn't speak to her, but pulled her close as if having her near was enough. No words were needed

They watched as Adam treated Quil's wounds while Jonathan knelt and talked to his Apache brother.

Kara sat beside Jonathan, brushing her hand along his leg, sensing somehow that he needed her to stay close.

Quil made no move to push Adam away, but he frowned at the bandages Adam wrapped around his ribs.

"I need to take a look at your eye," Adam said as he turned from Quil to Jonathan. "And that cut on your cheek may need a few stitches when we get back home."

"I'm fine. Kara's damaged me worse."

Adam knelt beside them and ignored Jonathan's protests.

"This is the only place I can think of where Quil might be able to live," Jonathan explained. "If he stays within this canyon, no one will find him. There's food and water, and I'll check on him from time to time."

Jonathan stared at Dawn and Quil. "It's not an answer for them forever, but maybe for a few years. When the

Indian Wars are over, they can leave and maybe find someplace to live in peace. I've promised them more supplies in the months to come."

"Are you sure Dawn wants to stay?"

Jonathan nodded. "I explained. Here she can keep her child and not have people think she's crazy. But it's more than that, she wants to stay with Quil. She says he's her man now, he just doesn't know it yet. I'll make sure they are not bothered."

Wolf stood. "Does that mean you're keeping the ranch?"

Jonathan looked at Kara. "My heart is here. My family is here. If we can meet the terms of the will before next summer, the ranch will be ours. And once it's mine, I'll never let it go."

Without another word, all but Quil and Dawn climbed out into the cold night. Kara glanced back and saw Dawn kneeling beside Quil, who lay bandaged atop a blanket. In a thin sliver of moonlight Kara saw the Apache's hand cover Dawn's fingers, and Kara knew they would be all right.

Without a word, Jonathan clasped her hand and gently pulled her toward the horses. They covered the distance back to the ranch in record time. The men took care of the mounts while Kara walked into the house alone.

Allie was in the study, nursing her new son when Kara tiptoed in. The rest of the house was in shambles. It reminded Kara of how a turkey looks a few hours after Thanksgiving. The basic skeleton of the Christmas party was still there, but rearranged. Wrapping littered the floor in the dining room and great room. Several of the cookies that had been decorations a day ago now had bite marks out of them. There was nothing but crumbs left of the cakes and pies that had lined one wall this morning.

"We missed you at dinner," Allie said as Kara passed the study.

"I'm sorry," Kara lied as she tried to think of some reason she could give other than explaining the entire story. She could hardly tell Allie that she'd been kidnapped, rescued, and made love to in the few hours she'd been missing.

"There will be other Christmases." Allie winked as though she'd guessed a small part of what might have happened.

"I hope so." Kara tried to remember if Jonathan had spoken of marriage, or forever, or love. He had come after her, that was something, but Kara was tired of trying to make fabric from the threads in her life. She believed her father loved her. She pinned her hope on Devin marrying her from one statement he'd made. Was she making a lifetime from one wild, wonderful afternoon?

Kara said good night to Allie and slowly climbed the stairs. She'd given herself completely to a man who'd told her more than once that he had nothing to give her. Oh, he'd said she was one of his tribe, but that hardly counted as a proposal.

She closed the door to her room and sat on the bed next to her bag. Christmas was over. The parties, the company, the excitement would all pass. Would she go back to being the bookkeeper?

Suddenly, the old house with its shadows and whispers was too much for her to endure. She ran down the stairs and out the front door, needing more than anything to be alone.

THIRTY

JONATHAN WAS WALKING TO THE HOUSE WHEN HE saw Kara storming across the courtyard toward the back gate. He knew where she was going. Her spot on the plains. It might be dark with snow whirling around making everything blurry, but he figured she'd find her place.

He grabbed the one horse still saddled, a huge bay owned by H. B., and headed out behind her.

Sure enough, when she stopped she was no more than a few feet away from where they'd had their previous talks.

"Evenin'." Jonathan swung down from the mount and dropped the reins, knowing any horse trained by H. B. would stay ground tied and not wander off. "Nice night for a walk," he lied as he fought the need to pull Kara close against him.

She didn't answer.

"If you're worried about Devin O'Toole, I checked on him. The man is sleeping soundly in the barn." Jonathan said the words, but all his mind could think about was how he could still feel her skin against his.

Fighting the need to touch her, he shoved his hands in his pockets.

"I wasn't worried," she answered without raising her gaze to him. "I never want to see the man again. He can disappear from the earth, for all I care."

Jonathan grinned. "A little hard on a man who just wanted to marry you." He knew she had more reason to hate the man than a proposal. Kara had told him Devin was responsible for her father's death. Jonathan only hoped the teasing would cheer her.

She began pacing once more, wearing down the frozen buffalo grass.

He tried again. "Quil and Dawn will be fine in the valley of flowers. There's plenty of lumber to build a shelter, and I'll check on them—"

"I know they'll be fine." She cut him off before he could continue.

"Then what's bothering you, darling?" Jonathan tried to keep the frustration from his voice. "Don't tell me you just came out here in the middle of the night for a walk."

"Nothing's wrong," she answered under her breath. "Everything is just fine."

Jonathan fought the urge to grab her and shake her until the truth fell out. He'd had more meaningful conversations with his horse. All he could think about was making love to her whenever she was near but, somehow, he didn't think that was the right thing to do at the moment. She wanted something. Needed something. But he had no idea what.

He climbed on his horse and was halfway back to the barn when he turned around. All his life he'd been a fighter, and he would fight for her now.

When he reached her again, she didn't look like she'd moved an inch. He climbed down, pulled her awkwardly into his arms and kissed her soundly.

Kara made no protest or response of any kind.

When he broke the kiss, he whispered, "I don't know what you want, or need, but I'm not going anywhere until I find out."

She watched him as if she thought he was the one who'd gone mad.

"Are you sorry?" he whispered, unable to form more into words. If she regretted the only perfect time in his life, he wasn't sure he wanted to know. "Do you wish this afternoon hadn't happened?"

"No," she finally answered.

"Good." He cupped his warm hands around her face. "If you had, I'm not sure what I would do. You're all the beauty and wonder I've ever known, Kara. Saying I love you or I need you would just hint at how I feel."

He brushed her lips with his thumb and felt her smile. He'd finally said something right. "If there is no lifetime for us to spend together, I'd still take the pain of years alone just to have you by my side for one sunrise."

"And if I live by your side until we're old?"

"Then I'll be the luckiest man ever to have breathed." He kissed her lightly. "I've figured out something, darling. If we part, I'll always have the way I feel for you inside me. I'll never be completely alone as long as I have one memory of how I feel."

"And how do you feel?"

"Like a man in love." He leaned closer and whispered, "Like a man needing desperately to marry. Would you consider such an arrangement, Miss O'Riley?"

Kara smiled. "I would, Mr. Catlin, provided I don't have to keep any books."

He laughed and swung her up into his arms. "Agreed."

As he lifted her into the saddle she added, "I come with a dowry."

He was barely listening as he moved up behind her on the saddle and pulled her against him. "I would hope so," he teased, not caring how little money she had. The feel of her against him was priceless. "We'll make it, Kara. I promise. This ranch will belong to our grandchildren's grandchildren."

She pulled an inch away. "You wouldn't be sorry if I bring nothing into the marriage?"

"No, as long as you stay with me."

"And if I bring a great deal of money? Enough to put the ranch in the black for years? Enough to build a new house with wide windows and doors that close solid?"

Jonathan kissed her nose. "I guess I'd still marry you, darling. How else will we have grandchildren?"

The next morning, just after sunrise, Kara and Jonathan were married in the little unfinished chapel with a dusting of snow as thin as lace all around. All the guard were there as well as the McLains and Wolf with his family. A few of the ranch hands attended, as did the six soldiers dressed for travel.

Mary Ann acted as Kara's matron-of-honor. Jason Newton was Jonathan's best man. They tried to do their part but, in truth, Mary Ann and Jason spent most of the wedding staring at one another. Just before they'd walked to the chapel, she'd told him Jonathan had asked her to stay on as bookkeeper. She hadn't told Jason what she'd answered. But most could see the answer in her eyes.

As the wedding party crossed the courtyard, the soldiers prepared to leave.

Kara heard the lieutenant thank Snort for wrapping the Apache in blankets for the trip. With the wind from the north, they'd be sure to hit bad weather before nightfall.

"No problem. I wouldn't want him to be uncomfortable." Snort patted the man on the back, shoving him along as he added, "You've got a hard day's ride ahead of you, Lieutenant. Best be traveling."

Kara could barely make out the silhouette inside the boarded wagon, and she wondered how long Snort thought he could fool the soldiers into believing there was a man beneath the blankets.

The soldiers mounted. As their wagon passed Kara, she swore she heard the prisoner sneeze.

She stared at Snort.

He looked as innocent as a guilty man can look. "All accounted for," he mumbled and moved away before she could ask any questions.

Kara leaned close to her husband and asked, "Are you sure one day you won't wish you were heading out, running with the wind across open country?"

He laughed as he pulled her against his side. "You make home a nice place to be."

She smiled that little smile she knew tamed him. "I'll work on making it wonderful."

"Kara." His words were low against her ear.

"Yes, husband," she answered.

"You make me believe in forever."